LINN B. HALTON

I live in a small village in Gloucestershire with the man I fell in love with, virtually at first sight. We were at a party and our eyes met across a crowded room! My days are spent with characters who become friends and Mr Tiggs, a feline with catitude. I always knew that one day I would write romantic novels, but I never dreamed they would have a psychic twist! I've experienced many 'unexplainable' things, but it took a long time for me to accept the reality of what that means. Love, life and beyond…but it's ALWAYS about the romance!

http://linnbhalton.co.uk/

@LinnBHalton

A Cottage in the Country

LINN B. HALTON

Harper*Impulse* an imprint of
HarperCollins*Publishers* Ltd
1 London Bridge Street
London SE1 9GF

www.harpercollins.co.uk

A Paperback Original 2015

First published in Great Britain in ebook format by Harper*Impulse* 2015

A catalogue record for this book is
available from the British Library

ISBN: 9780008146924

Automatically produced by Atomik ePublisher from Easypress

Printed and bound in Great Britain

MADDIE

CHAPTER 1

The queue of traffic inches forward slowly as I glance at the clock on the dashboard for what seems like the millionth time. Ahead of me someone honks their horn in sheer exasperation. The farmer seems completely oblivious as he slowly rounds up the stragglers to rejoin his large flock of sheep. If I wasn't so stressed, I'd probably enjoy this quaint little scene that's a million miles away from the bustle of city life. However, I'm nearly fifteen minutes late for an appointment to view my dream cottage, which has literally just come on the market. Life without a love interest is going to be simpler, I've decided; no more having to pander to the whims of a man, and at least bricks and mortar can't break your heart.

I'm the first to view and if I don't get there before the next couple arrive, well, I simply can't let that happen. The truth is that cottages in my price range are few and far between. I glance at the property details lying on the passenger seat and grit my teeth. Ramming the gear stick into reverse I edge back a little, sending the driver behind me into panic mode. He's safe enough – I'm sure there are inches to spare. It's not exactly a three-point turn, but after a series of manoeuvres I finally manage to turn the car around and leave the queue of traffic behind. My satnav goddess kindly informs me that in two hundred yards I should turn around, even when I explain to her, very politely, that I have to find another route.

"Drive two hundred yards and turn around," she reiterates for the third time.

"But I need you to recalculate and find me another route," I plead. She ignores my request, so I stab my finger at the screen while trying to negotiate the narrow country lane.

"Take a left and turn around," her perfect and calm voice fills the car.

"Please, just recalculate and find me another route before I have a total meltdown!" I'm mortified to hear my own voice sounding worryingly unhinged, but it does the trick.

"Recalculating. Drive fifty yards and take a right turn."

I adjust the air-conditioning and reposition the vents until a waft of deliciously cold air sweeps over my flushed and perspiring face. The lane becomes even narrower and steeper, branches flicking against the sides of the car as I speed along as fast as I dare. If I meet someone coming towards me now there is nowhere to go. I have to drop down into second gear as the gradient increases rather suddenly. I wonder if I'm being punished by my satnav goddess for ignoring her instructions. Is this the alternative route from hell and this is how she exacts revenge when someone chooses to ignore her instructions? I had no idea that there were lanes as narrow as this, the hedges either side are barely clearing my wing mirrors. It's bordering on claustrophobic and hard to believe this is going to lead anywhere, other than into a field. I must be lost.

"In one hundred yards turn left into Forge Hill and your destination is on the left."

Unexpectedly, the lane begins to open out again as I approach the top of the hill and take the turning.

"In seventy-five yards your destination is located on the left."

"I find that hard to ..." The words die on my lips as I round the corner and am surprised to see a small collection of farm buildings and cottages. As I continue on past a rather sharp bend, the view suddenly opens up as the hillside falls away. There, in front of me, is my chocolate-box cottage.

"Your destination is on the left," my satnav goddess confirms and I respond politely.

"Thank you, thank you and thank you!" A wave of excitement grips me as I pull onto the short drive in front of a rather quirky-looking garage.

Stepping out of the car, I immediately spot an older woman walking towards me. Well, I say older, she's about my age.

"I'm very sorry I'm late," I extend my hand. "I'm Madeleine Brooks." We shake and exchange smiles.

"Sarah Manning. Lovely to meet you. Glad you were able to find it. We have back-to-back viewings this afternoon, but the next couple has phoned in to say they're lost and are running late, so it's not a problem. Have you come far?"

"Only thirty miles, but I've been in the car for well over an hour. I managed to get held up by a flock of sheep," I laugh.

"Ah, country living. It's a different pace of life the minute you get away from the city. If you're looking for peace and tranquility this is it."

As I follow Sarah along the winding footpath that takes us from the road down to the cottage, I can't take my eyes off the view. The valley unfolds gently in front of us, belying any true sense of height or distance. The lower level of the cottage nestles back against an outcrop of rust-coloured rock, with a canopy of leafy-green forest high above it, creating a perfect backdrop. Every window in this property faces out onto the panoramic view. It sweeps down to what looks like a stream in the distance and then across to the other side of the valley. It is, quite simply, breathtaking.

The entrance is via a glazed door into a large conservatory, which runs the entire length of the cottage. As we step inside a mixture of joy, apprehension and knowing, hit me. I've found my new home and it's going to be the perfect place to begin my new life.

"Of course, it's a bit unloved at the moment and requires some work. It's a probate case; the owner, Aggie, died about a year ago." Sarah casts her eyes over my face to see whether I register any concern. "The bank is handling the estate as there are eight beneficiaries. All are distant relatives and tracking them down hasn't been easy. I'm afraid there's no room for negotiation on the price. We've been instructed to market it at five thousand pounds below the current valuation in order to achieve a quick sale. It's sold as seen."

I have no idea what that means, but her words fall on deaf ears. I'm too caught up in the moment to process what I'm being told.

"I'll take it." The words echo around the large conservatory, which looks like the only room in the cottage that can be even loosely described as anything other than bijou.

"The kitchen is small, but very quaint," Sarah throws in, as if reading my mind. My eyes are everywhere, imagining how it will look once it's renovated. Much of the conversation is one-sided. Sarah's voice continues to float over my head, as if I'm surrounded by a force field.

I'm picturing myself at a Belfast sink, gazing out of the window at the sweeping vista below as I wash the dishes. I notice a dove-cote on the other side of the valley in the garden of a rather large farmhouse. A flight of doves circle and swoop, diving in formation and landing elegantly on a nearby roof, as if they've been lovingly choreographed. After a few minutes they take to the air again, the stark contrast of their white feathers against the cornflower-blue sky creating a magical moment.

"You don't mind the main bathroom being off the kitchen?" Sarah asks, bringing me back into the moment.

"Sorry? Oh, no. I like quirky. There is a shower room upstairs, isn't there?" I'm sure I saw that on the details.

"Yes, but the only bath is in here." She pushes open a rather narrow door and I'm delighted to see a surprisingly spacious room beyond. The suite is tired and needs replacing, but the proportions of the room are totally unexpected. In the centre of the vaulted ceiling is a large Velux window. It's a window that has nothing to obscure it, filled only with clouds and blue sky, as if it were a framed picture.

"Imagine lying in the bath and looking up at the stars," I murmur, thinking out loud.

Sarah laughs. "Well, that's one way of looking at it, I suppose. You really have fallen in love with Ash Cottage, haven't you?"

"I'm serious about the offer. I'm a cash buyer and I'd like to move things along as quickly as possible. I'm desperately in need of a home."

I see a slight frown cross her brow as her business head kicks in.

"Nothing dodgy," I quickly add. "It's a cash settlement from my ex-husband following our divorce. Ironically, we'd spent many years turning a rundown Victorian house into the perfect family home. I always dreamt of owning a little cottage like this some day, but I thought it would be somewhere to spend leisurely weekends together."

"Oh, I'm so sorry to hear that." Her voice softens and I kick myself, thinking that this was too much information. My emotions are still raw. I find myself constantly struggling to avoid bursting into tears or letting slip details people simply don't want to hear, particularly strangers. When you're hurtling towards fifty and your whole life is suddenly hanging around you in shreds, it's as if you don't know who you are any more. Sometimes I'm not even aware I'm saying my thoughts out aloud.

"Sorry, and it's fine, really. I just wanted to reassure you that I'm in a good position. I'm in rented accommodation and the cash is sitting in the bank. Please don't sell Ash Cottage to anyone else."

I'm mortified when my eyes begin to fill with tears and Sarah is clearly embarrassed. Damn it! I have to stop making a fool of myself and I utter a silent prayer of thanks that I've finally found a place that feels right. Now, at last, the first step towards the rest of my life is within reach.

We exchange glances that soften into polite smiles and Sarah holds up her mobile.

"Right, I ... um, well, I'll ring in your full asking-price offer while you take a look at the bedrooms. If you're sure, that is?"

"I'm sure. Every box on my list is already ticked, it couldn't be more perfect. I have one condition – that they take it off the market immediately. I'm not sure I could face another disappointment at this point in my life."

Something akin to an awkward grimace flashes over her face as she turns to exit; her finger is already on the dial button.

I know it's not perfect at the moment, but the point is, it will be. Our second house was a wreck, literally. So, I know what can be achieved if you are prepared to roll up your sleeves, get a little dirty and make endless cups of coffee for plumbers, electricians and carpenters.

The bank is happy to recommend my offer to the beneficiaries, together with my proviso.

"You won't sell it to anyone else in the meantime, Sarah, will you? I mean, I've heard about gazumping and I can't really afford to increase my offer."

"Don't worry, there's no reason at all why the beneficiaries would say no. The sale price is fair and it's just a formality. Ash Cottage is yours."

True to her word, Sarah rang to confirm just that the very next day and it was a major boost to my confidence. This middle-aged, recently divorced woman felt as if she had finally taken back control of her life.

CHAPTER 2

I had assumed I'd be moving in within a few weeks. Perfect timing, as that would give me a couple of months before winter set in. After all, this was the shortest chain you could possibly have for a house purchase. It felt as though the storm clouds were retreating and the sun had finally decided to come out and shine once more. Life had a master plan for me and I hadn't been simply cast adrift and left to flounder, unloved and forgotten.

Pull yourself together, Maddie, you're made of strong stuff and you can do this, really you can. I feared there was an implied strength of resolve and determination in my thoughts that didn't quite match my actions at the moment. But pride alone wouldn't allow me to sink into depression. Even when your heart is smashed to pieces, you still wake up each morning to face another day. Crawling into a hole and hiding away might sound comforting, but it's never a real option, is it?

The radio flashes, indicating an incoming call and I turn up the volume.

"Guess who is back from his vacation sporting a tan and looking good?"

Ryan's velvety tones seem to fill the car. Bluetooth loves him, for some inexplicable reason. I can't ever recall losing signal whenever he's on the line, which is rather weird because it breaks up all the time when I'm running around town. Is charisma like some sort of invisible power source that coerces everything in life to work more smoothly? If that's true, then I need to get me some!

Ryan could be a radio-show presenter. He has that smooth quality to his voice that oozes charm and sophistication. But then he could be a heart-breaker, too. He just chooses not to be. He is the definitive bachelor and I've known him for what feels like forever. My husband, Jeff, was always wary of him. Oh, I mean my ex-husband, Jeff ...

"Men don't have women friends unless there's an element of attraction, or something funny going on," he'd once informed me. With hindsight I can see exactly why my scheming ex would think that. At the time we moved past his comments and he never alluded to it again, knowing full well I thought he was talking utter rubbish. I do remember feeling just the teeniest bit proud that he cared enough to be jealous, but I'd worked with Ryan long enough to feel completely safe with him.

Ryan maintains that he still isn't ready to settle down, despite having recently celebrated his forty-ninth birthday. What he means, I think, is that he still hasn't found that special someone. He would be a dead ringer for Michael Fassbender, if you add a few years, a sprinkling of grey hair and shave off the designer stubble. He's ageing gracefully, I keep telling him, and he has that suave, dependable, look. He went through a phase of pulling out each grey hair he found, until I informed him that they don't always grow back. I was joking, of course, who knows? But he's a man who spends more time looking in the mirror than most women. That's because he hasn't had to pander to children or a partner, or experience the delights of bathroom wars. That's a bit like Star Wars without the light sabers, but involving all the tricks you can employ to jump the queue for that leisurely soak in the tub.

He's used to the luxury of being home alone, other than accommodating the occasional overnight guest. I sigh. It's not that I regret all those years of marriage; I simply thought it was going to last forever. I willingly gave up my freedom for my husband and the two sons who left home as soon as they became young men. It was a future I'd invested in wholeheartedly, because it defined who I was – a wife and mother. It was my raison d'être.

"Are you still there?"

"Sorry Ryan, I'm wallowing a bit today. I'm so glad you're back, I've missed you. I'm guessing you had a good time?"

Of course, I didn't just lose my husband; I also lost my life-long friend, Eve. Mistress Rat, as I now refer to her. A sob catches in my throat as I try to wind down my wayward thoughts and concentrate on Ryan's dialogue about his fabulous trip to Dubai.

"... and I'm going to plan another visit, meet up with a few of the group again next year. First time ever I didn't want to board the plane and fly home. You know me, I usually get bored after two weeks and pine for my home comforts, but it was amazing. Anyway, enough about me, how are you doing?"

I'm back in the moment, mind clear as a bell, but the motorway traffic is heavy and I'm following the satnav on a route I don't know. It's bumper to bumper and I'm trying to change lanes, indicating and easing forward gently. The driver in the car parallel to me is doing everything he can to keep me out.

"Ryan, I hate to cut you short, but it's really bad timing. I'm in a huge snarl-up on the M4/M5 interchange and the satnav is telling me I'm in the wrong lane. A bit stressed at the moment – can I call you when I get home? A lot has happened since you left and I'd appreciate your input. I'm off to measure up my new home for blinds."

"You found somewhere! Awesome! Well done, Maddie. Has there been any communication from Mistress Rat or Cheating Ex?"

"No, and yes ... eek! Sorry, have to go, promise I'll ring you later."

As I bring our call to a premature halt, the guy to my right edges forward another few inches. Now I'm in an impossible situation, half-slewed across two lanes. The traffic ahead of me is starting to move off and the car behind me honks impatiently, but there's nowhere I can go. There isn't enough room to reverse and continue in this lane and Mr Nasty looks as if he'd rather cause an accident than let me in.

"In one hundred yards keep to the right," the satnav goddess reminds me for the fourth time. If I can't get into the right-hand lane now then it will be too late and I'll end up travelling to London instead of Wales.

"I know, I know! Tell Mr Nasty," I mutter. I glance across at his stony face in the hope that he'll graciously give way, but he's obviously seen my lips moving and thinks I'm talking at him. He gives me a hand gesture that is less than gentlemanly, probably assuming a lot of the dialogue consists of swear words.

"In one hundred yards, keep to the right."

"Oh, shut up!" I wail, as someone else starts honking repeatedly. There's a gap that could fit a dozen cars ahead of me and the front of my car is directly in line with the mid-section of Mr Nasty's BMW. Now he's ignoring me and my face starts to flame. The idiot is refusing to move, even though there's a big enough gap for him to pull forward and for me to tuck in nicely. I glance apologetically at the very patient man in the car behind him, who is holding back ready for me to filter in when the BMW finally decides to pull away. I nod my head in grateful appreciation. Chivalry isn't completely dead.

Honk, honk, honk.

"In one hundred yards keep right."

Mr Nasty glances my way and he actually has a smirk on his face. Right! That's it. My nearside front wing is still a few feet away from his car and I slip into first gear and edge forward another foot. I hold my breath, wondering how close I'm prepared to go. If I hit him, how much damage can you do at, oh, all of two miles per hour?

His jaw drops and he looks at me with fear in his eyes, as it dawns on him that he's decided to tango with the wrong woman. Instead of slowly rolling forward he stops completely, allowing the growing gap in front of him to widen even further. I veer the steering wheel to the left and cruise past the front of his car, slipping neatly into the gap, but ensuring I clear the front of his car by a mere whisper.

"Now who's smirking?" I throw the words at him over my shoulder. Well, he deserved that. Suddenly, he puts his foot down and swerves across behind me, and our positions are reversed. He's now alongside me in the inside lane. He winds down his window for a few seconds, shouts out, "Scary lady, are you insane?" and then floors the accelerator. He speeds off, taking advantage of the huge gap that has opened up while we've been dancing around on the motorway.

I'm speechless. He was in the wrong lane all along! As our respective traffic lines peel off in opposite directions, a big smile crosses my face. I pick up speed thinking, hey, I'm a scary lady and maybe it's about time I started asserting myself... it might be rather fun!

When I pull up in the driveway leading down to Ash Cottage, the estate agent who comes to greet me isn't Sarah but a colleague. He's very smartly dressed, but looks almost too young to be anyone's employee. He extends his hand as he introduces himself and I reach out to clasp it and shake, only to feel mortified as my firm grip meets no resistance at all. Goodness gracious, young man, you need to work on that. I keep my thoughts to myself and give him a bright smile.

"I only need to take a few measurements, Connor," I explain, fearful he might burst into tears after the assault on his hand.

"I'll ... um ... sort out the key, then," he mumbles, digging deep into his jacket pocket. I follow him down the winding path as we head towards the front of the cottage, when suddenly a loud, "Hello" makes us both stop in our tracks. Spinning around, I see a guy in his late fifties, sporting a mass of unruly grey hair, ambling towards us with a big grin on his face.

"So glad to have caught you," he remarks, jovially. "I'm Terence

Darby. My wife, Joanna, and I live in Bay Tree Barn – the one at the end of the track," he points his finger along the overgrown lane that runs high up behind Ash Cottage.

"Great to meet you, Terence, I'm Maddie Brooks. This is Connor from Cooper and Tate Estate Agents. I've come to measure up."

Terence steps forward and we shake hands, his firm grip reassuring me that I wasn't being over-zealous earlier. I notice that Connor stands well back, no doubt still nursing a sore hand.

"It's going to be lovely having a neighbour again," Terence replies. He's obviously a seasoned walker, his boots have that lived-in look and his stout walking stick has probably fended off many a bramble.

"I had hoped to be in by now, but there have been several delays." I shoot a glance at Connor, who is engrossed in scraping his shoe against a small mound of long grass. He swipes it several times to remove the dust from the lane. Even if he was listening, I think it's unlikely he'd know what was happening anyway, but it was worth a try.

"Ah," Terence shakes his head. "I can only imagine what it's like today with all the paperwork. We've been here for nearly thirty years and the house before that was our first. We do miss Aggie, she was a lovely lady."

I realise that Connor is waiting impatiently, his shoe-scuffing has stopped and he's now sorting through a handful of keys, with purpose. Terence and I exchange glances, his eyes twinkling and a little smirk lifts his lip as he tries his best not to laugh.

"Well, lovely to meet you, Terence, and fingers crossed that Ash Cottage won't remain empty for much longer."

Terence gives a little salute, a brief nod to Connor, who is still head-down and totally oblivious and he walks off down the lane whistling.

"Nice chap," I say out aloud, as I crane my neck to see if I can spot the barn. The track has a turn in it and already Terence is out of sight.

"Is this the only entrance to Bay Tree Barn?" I enquire, assuming Connor will at least have some knowledge of this property.

He shrugs his shoulders, "I don't know". With that, he turns on his heels and heads off back down the path, still sorting through his handful of keys.

"Are they all for Ash Cottage?" I ask, rather surprised there are so many. When Sarah showed me around I'm sure she only had a small ring of keys in her hand.

"Well, I thought they were." He begins trying each one in turn, picking out a few that obviously won't fit and putting them back into his jacket pocket. Several look as if they belong to outbuildings and one is quite primitive, made out of cast iron. He's becoming rather frustrated and the colour is rising in his cheeks, so I wander off to give him space and begin looking around the garden. However, it's hard not to simply stand and admire the view, though I'm also excited to explore. I remember the wooden shed that stands halfway down the sloping garden, raised on a semicircular patio area and with an old wooden bench running alongside it. The view from the bench is at a different angle to the view you get from the house and on a bright, warm, autumnal day like today it's a little sun trap.

The colour of the trees now has an orangey hue, the breeze carrying a few leaves here and there as it teases them from the branches. In a week or two they will be falling by the sackful and it dawns on me that this garden is going to be quite labour-intensive. But the stunning vista is mesmerising, and I'm actually looking forward to the hours I'll be spending taming this garden and getting it back into some semblance of order.

"It's no good," Connor calls over his shoulder. "None of these keys fit. Seems I might have picked up the wrong ones from the cabinet. The problem is," he looks at me with unease, "I'm due at my next viewing in twenty-five minutes. I don't have time to drive back to the office to pick them up."

While I do feel sorry for him, I also feel exasperated. "It's taken me over an hour to get here. Can you ring the office and see if someone else could pop out with them? I don't mind waiting – now that I'm here."

He seems annoyed, as if I created the problem and am being unreasonable expecting him to sort it out.

"It might be better if you make an appointment for another day," he replies, drily, fixing me with a stare. A flash of anger finds me struggling to hold back the first retort that pops into my head. Instead, I take a deep breath and speak slowly, but distinctly.

"I think it might be even better if you ring the office now and have the conversation, so that you aren't late getting off to your next viewing."

Connor looks at me, surprised by the forcefulness of my words and heads off back to his car, mumbling something totally incoherent as he brushes past me.

I wander down to the bench by the shed, fighting my way through one of the overgrown pathways that traverse the garden. A large fuchsia bush is covered in deep, double pink heads, the branches hanging low overhead causing me to duck. On the other side a climbing rose has suckers extending three feet and making it almost impossible to squeeze through without getting snagged. However, I persevere and take the final steps down to the bench. I was right, the view from here is completely different and it feels protected, despite being very open. With the terraced garden rising high above it to the rear, the sloping grassy bank falling away below it and a high hedge to the side, it sits in a hollow.

The sun is warm on my face and I close my eyes for a second, taking in the peacefulness of the setting. All you can hear are the birds and the odd ripple of leaves caught in the breeze. A crack in the overhanging branches of a hazelnut tree, about five feet away, announces the appearance of a young, grey squirrel. He jumps with ease across to a large branch on a neighbouring ash tree. It isn't until this moment that I scan around and really take note of the trees. The variety is amazing; however ash seems to grow particularly well here and is a fitting winner for the aptly named cottage.

"Mrs Brooks!" Connor's agitated voice calls out – a few seconds later he emerges from one of the overgrown pathways.

"I'm here and it's Miss Brooks," I reply, trying hard not to over-react to his faux pas.

He approaches the bench, inspecting the arm of his jacket as he walks.

"I think that rose has pulled a thread," he utters, sounding really fed up and choosing to ignore my comment.

"Poor you," I reply, dourly. "What did the office say?"

"There's no one available. You'll have to ring in to arrange another appointment and I'm going to have to shoot off now." He looks at his watch impatiently and that makes me really cross. I make no attempt to move, despite the meaningful glance he throws my way.

"So, I've driven all this way and I can't get access to the cottage today?"

He at least has the good grace to look a touch embarrassed, but I realise there's absolutely no point in making a fuss.

"Well, just so my journey isn't a *complete* waste of my time, is it okay if I take ten minutes to look around the garden?"

My request clearly presents him with a new dilemma. He's torn between having to think through the implications of leaving me here to my own devices and, after yet another flick of his wrist to check the time, being late for his next appointment.

"Well ... I suppose it will be all right." He looks at me as if appraising whether or not I can be trusted.

"I am in the process of buying the property and contracts have already been exchanged." I throw this in, not to reassure him, but to remind him I'm not some total stranger who is here merely to nose around.

He nods and without another word begins his retreat back through the undergrowth.

"An apology would have been nice," I pipe up, "or a goodbye ..." hoping my words will carry and perhaps remind him of common courtesy, let alone good manners.

I wait until I hear his car pull away and then venture down to locate the boundary at the bottom of the garden. The grass is on such a steep slope that it's not easy to walk down without slipping. Thankfully, I manage it without mishap and discover two crowns of rhubarb hidden among a border that also holds a beautiful mock orange blossom shrub. Everything is leggy and overgrown, sadly neglected over the past few years by the looks of it. Behind this is a hedge that runs along the bottom. The other side abuts a large grassy area, belonging to a cottage that is almost completely obscured by trees. Well, it's private, that's for sure.

Making my way slowly back up the grassy bank, I notice that the two large apple trees are badly in need of pruning. Hidden in the branches is a telegraph wire that is almost low enough to touch. Aside from that, the garden needs a lot of weeding and a tidy to take away the debris that has built up over a number of years. However, it is packed full of a whole variety of plants, trees and shrubs. It's enchanting, and a little thrill courses through me. This is going to be my garden very, very soon.

I discover a different pathway to take me back up to the top level that isn't quite so overgrown. Thankfully, it doesn't have any thorny branches to contend with. As I emerge, directly in front of me is the garden room. It's still full of old furniture, although I'm sure it will be emptied before I take possession. It was used as a piano room and that, too, is built into the slope of the hill. Either side of it are storage rooms hewn into the rock face. Both are rather dank and full of cobwebs, but they will be useful. To the left stands the oil tank for the central heating and I'm dismayed to spot a small pool of oil on the floor. A little investigation is enough to confirm that the pipe going into the tank appears to have been vandalised. Well, maybe today hasn't been a total waste after all. If I hadn't spotted this it would have been a nightmare moving in to discover the tank was empty. I make my way back to the car to ring Cooper and Tate, thankful that this is one problem I'm not going to have to sort out on moving day.

LEWIS

CHAPTER 3

"Can I speak to Sarah Manning, please, it's urgent?"

"Who's calling?"

"Lewis Hart."

"Hold the line, I'm putting you through."

Clearly, Sarah isn't there. It switches straight to her answerphone and I'm in no mood to leave a message. I'm so angry, my hands are shaking. As if the long drive home wasn't bad enough, when I passed Ash Cottage there wasn't just a *For Sale* sign outside, but it was almost obliterated by a *Sold* banner. Now I know what they mean when they say a red mist can descend out of nowhere.

I slam down the phone, desperately trying to regain control of my anger. I can't remember the last time I lost it – the feeling isn't a welcome one and reminds me of my youth. I simply can't believe that Sarah has sold Ash Cottage to someone else.

I try to straighten out my thoughts. The last couple of weeks have been a nightmare; planning a funeral messes with your head and I thought I'd made it clear I had every intention of buying Ash Cottage once it was on the market. Heck, I rang Sarah and left a message!

It dawns on me that I haven't checked my own messages for a while and, sure enough, the flashing icon tells me that was a mistake. There are two messages and they are both from Sarah. I let out a sigh, unable to stop myself from shaking my head at my own stupidity.

"Hello, Lewis, I'm ringing to let you know that Ash Cottage is officially on the market. I have no idea if your situation has changed and whether you are still interested, given recent events. I was sorry to hear the news about your mother, such an awful time for you. I'll await your call."

Damn! That must have crossed with the message I left her. What did I say? My mind tries to replay the phone call, but there was so much going on at the time. Maybe I only asked her to call me back. I meant to give her permission to match the asking price once the bank pressed the 'go' button. I listen to the second message.

"Lewis, I'm returning your call as requested. I don't know what you were going to say to me … um … oh, I hope this isn't going to be bad news for you. Ash Cottage is sold. If it makes you feel any better, an offer was made on it before I received the message to ring you. When we finally received the instruction to market it, there wasn't anything I could do without confirmation that the sale price was acceptable to you. I'm honour-bound to forward every offer that is made in a timely fashion, once a property is officially up for sale. This purchaser happened to be in the right place at the right time. Let me know when you are back and I'm sorry if your plans haven't changed, but there was nothing I could do."

It's not Sarah's fault, it's mine. I understand her situation. For me nothing has changed, but she wasn't to know that. This is a bitter blow I'm going to find very hard to accept. In my head Ash Cottage was already mine and I can't believe some stranger has stepped in to snatch it away from me.

MADDIE

CHAPTER 4

Popping back to the cottage the following Saturday to finally measure up and have a really good look around, Ryan offers to drive me. He knows how much I hate being behind the wheel and it's a thoughtful gesture. This time Sarah is the one to greet us and, after unlocking the cottage, she very kindly allows us to walk around unaccompanied. Ryan seems mesmerised by her. She's an attractive woman; blonde, quite curvy and a smart dresser.

"Take your time," she smiles, encouragingly. "I booked out a forty-minute slot. I have a few phone calls to make if that's okay with you, but if you need anything, just let me know. Here are the keys for the shed, garden room and store rooms. Enjoy!"

"Lovely woman," Ryan comments as he watches Sarah walking back up to her car.

"Yes. And extremely polite. You should have met her colleague, Connor. Well, what do you think – first impressions?" I'm buzzing and holding my breath to find out what his reaction is to Ash Cottage.

"Well, there's only one word to describe it, really, and that's wow!" Our eyes are, of course, focused only on the view. The valley is now sporting a full coat of autumnal colours; deep reds, oranges and browns, reflecting the drop in temperature early in the morning and late at night. The chill has begun and autumn is making its mark.

"You'll never get any work done. How will you be able to drag yourself away from this?"

That now-familiar little thrill courses through my body. It's a sense of excitement at the prospect of actually living here and waking up each morning to this beautiful picture of tranquility.

"I haven't heard a single car since I've been here. It's so peaceful and so very *you*." Ryan turns to face me, placing his hand on my arm. He gives it a friendly squeeze, his grey eyes warming as he takes in my expression. "I can see that you love it. I'm excited for you, Maddie – your new start."

In fairness, the conservatory is probably the only part of this property that doesn't need extensive work, but I can see he is caught up in the ambience. As we walk around I talk him through some of my ideas for the renovation and he throws in a few suggestions of his own.

"Who is going to do the work?"

"Well, that's the big question. Christmas is looming and, obviously, I'm unlikely to find anyone prepared to work over the period between Christmas and New Year. But the kitchen is small and even if it isn't finished in time, I hope to have the essentials installed ready for the holidays."

Ryan nods, then his jaw drops when I throw open the door to the bathroom.

"Another *wow*. That's what I like about old cottages, you never know what to expect. Rather bizarre having the bathroom off the kitchen, but this is going to be amazing."

I'm delighted Ryan can see beyond the current sorry state as I glance around at the very tired, and slightly musty-smelling, room.

"Think slipper bath, white accessories and shaker-style panelling on the walls."

Ryan peers up at the Velux window, watching the clouds floating by as if it's the first time he's ever seen the sky.

"Imagine this at night," he exclaims.

"Soft candles, aromatherapy bubble bath and a glass of wine

in one hand – I'm already stretched out in the tub and enjoying the view!" I laugh.

"Well, it's going to be a lengthy project, but this is a diamond in the rough. What did the home survey report say? Any nasty surprises?"

"Um ... not exactly. I didn't want to hold things up in case the bank changed its mind and kept it on the market until contracts were exchanged. Ironically, with all the silly questions my solicitor has raised, there would have been plenty of time to ..."

"You've buying a house without having a survey? I know that technically you don't need one because you are a cash buyer, but please tell me you're joking, Maddie. Financially, you're putting everything you have into this property and that represents a *big* risk."

One look at my face confirms I'm telling the truth and he shakes his head in dismay. A little quiver of fleeting doubt enters my head and I shake it off.

"The cottage has been here for more than a hundred and fifty years, I doubt it will suddenly decide to slide down the hill."

Ryan shrugs his shoulders. His expression is enough to make me feel more than a little uncomfortable.

"Let's continue the tour," I say jauntily, pushing back my shoulders in an attempt to reassure myself I know what I'm doing.

We retrace our steps back through the cottage. Climbing the stairs, we walk around the two small bedrooms and poke our heads into the rather dank shower room. Descending back into the sitting room, Ryan remarks on the beautiful old cast-iron fireplace, which is in remarkably good condition for its age.

"An open fire – imagine those winter evenings ..."

"There's a dining room through here, too, but I'm thinking I should turn that into a media room. I'm not sure a TV would look right in the sitting room, what do you think?"

The dining room is perfectly square and lends itself to a variety of uses, including a home office. When space is at a premium you have to make the most of every square foot. My eyes sweep the room, imagining the computer in the corner, two comfy chairs facing the TV and an elegant sideboard to house all my paperwork.

"Great idea. Why would you want to eat in here when you only have the one window looking out onto the valley? If this was mine I'd live, eat and probably spend all of my time in the conservatory."

I let out a huge sigh of relief.

"What?" Ryan looks at me with concern reflected in those telling eyes of his.

"I wondered if you'd think I was completely mad taking this on ... you know – at my time of life."

He looks at me rather sharply. "Your marriage might be over, but Maddie Brooks' life part two is about to begin. I know you are still devastated and it's dented what little confidence you had, but I think you need this project. Yes, if I'm honest, it is a lot to take on for anyone and it's a pity you don't have the summer stretching out ahead of you. But life, as we know, is never perfect. There are worse things than being on your own." He shoots me a reassuring smile.

"Yes, like living with a love rat."

He cringes, wincing at my words.

"Come here! You need a hug."

I step forward and he throws his arms around me quite casually, as only long-standing friends can. We've known each other for longer than I knew my ex-husband, initially working alongside one another for nearly five years as project managers. Mostly designing re-fits for shops and stores, but occasionally working on the high-end domestic market. I gave up work about a year after I married Jeff to have our eldest son, Matt. Ryan and I lost touch for a while, but following a big promotion he contacted me to see if I was interested in working part time from home as a consultant. By then Matt was three and youngest son, Nick, was four months old. His timing was perfect, as work on our house was eating up every spare penny we had. From there on our friendship continued to grow. When he started his own business, it seemed only natural to take the job I was offered, particularly as it meant I could continue to work from home. Our friendship was something Jeff could never really accept, but I guess the money was an adequate pacifier.

"Do you know what I miss?" I ask, turning to look up at him as he shakes his head. "That struggle to keep everyone happy. I'm not used to making all the decisions without having to accommodate other people's needs and wishes. It feels lonely at times, and scary." A sudden hitch catches in my throat and seems to coincide with a distinctly watery view of Ryan's face.

"It's called freedom, Maddie. You'll get used to it. Heck, it's kind of like a drug once you grow accustomed to it and it's the reason why I'm still single. Being with someone permanently means life is a constant compromise. Sometimes it works out okay, but often it's one-sided and ..." He hesitates, obviously in two minds about how honest he can be with me when it's clear I'm still very emotional.

"You can't stop there. You might as well finish off your sentence and get it over and done with."

His frown deepens. "Sometimes one person becomes a doormat."

My chest constricts, forcing me to draw in one long, deep breath. The ache in my heart is becoming less about losing Jeff's love as the days roll on, and more about a bigger loss. I feel betrayed and unloved. I gave everything because I cared, and my reward? People looking in on my relationship could see with a clarity I didn't have. I'd been fooling myself I was loved in return, but the truth was that I was being walked over and used.

"Hey," Ryan moves closer and places a hand on each of my shoulders. "Look at me! Come on, raise that chin! You're a good person, Maddie and you've brought up your sons well. Don't let anything rob you of that fact, because there aren't too many selfless people around these days. You're a nurturer; you simply forgot that there was a person inside there who deserved to have her voice heard. That's what threatens to hold you back now, if you let it.

31

"Now me, I'm selfish through and through. I'm in total control of my life; it runs smoothly because I don't let other people mess it up emotionally, or otherwise. Am I missing out? In some respects, yes: I'll never have a son, or daughter, of my own. But I'd make a terrible husband and an even worse father. To me it's simple. Understanding *who* and *what* you are is fundamental to attaining a life that has the right balance for you. Think of the future as a blank sheet. You get to start all over again, but this time it's all about *you*."

He draws back, letting his hands slip down to catch mine and give them a reassuring squeeze.

"I know you mean well, Ryan, but you've missed the point." I raise my tear-filled eyes to meet his enquiring gaze. His expression is pained and I know it's hard for him to offer the advice he's so convinced will make me see sense. "What if I don't want my life to be all about *me*?"

"Then you run the risk of putting yourself through this all over again. If nothing changes, then you'll be like so many others going around and around in the same flawed circle. I don't want that for you, my friend. You deserve more than to let people simply use you."

He walks away from me and out of the cottage, leaving me standing there with my mouth hanging open. In all the years I've known him he has never opened up his deepest feelings to me; never offered advice or judged me. To find out now that that wasn't the case and he held back because he didn't want to risk destroying our friendship is a surprise. But his words were so raw. That little speech wasn't just about me – it was also about something buried deep within Ryan. What exactly the root cause is I have absolutely no idea and clearly it's something he isn't about to share.

CHAPTER 5

Project managing is what I do, so now contracts have been exchanged and I have a completion date of the nineteen of December, there's a lot to do in a short time. My solicitor is still concerned about a potential boundary issue, ironically to do with the path that runs along behind Ash Cottage; the one leading to Bay Tree Barn. It began when I asked her to check it out after meeting Terence that day, and I now wish I hadn't raised it at all. She's like a dog with a bone and she won't give up. It's hard to believe that the bank don't have something in Miss Agatha Brown's paperwork that will show who owns and maintains the track. Prior to the existence of Land Registry, most of the paperwork was by way of notarised letters people kept with their deeds.

"What's the worst-case scenario?" I ask, trying not to let my voice reflect the frustration I'm feeling.

"Well, Miss Brooks, without clear ownership there is the issue of maintenance – which could raise its head if the owners of Bay Tree Barn feel the track is becoming neglected. If a third party owns that strip of land, then that is another unknown ..."

She continues in the same vein, listing a whole host of problems that might crawl out of the woodwork – *might* being the operative word. I ask her to leave it with me to make a decision about what I want to do next. Her preferred option is to insist the bank get to the bottom of it or, failing that, take out an indemnity insurance policy. The problem is that this is something I should have alerted her to much earlier. Now we've exchanged, we're locked into the deal and she has no real leverage. I was hoping to mention the vandalised oil tank, which is something I feel is much more important to me, but I don't feel I can raise that now. I hadn't realised that 'sold as seen' had such an impact. It's a simple statement and, it seems, a licence to wriggle out of answering virtually any question raised. There's one thing I need to do before I instruct my solicitor to drop her enquiries and hopefully it will give me some peace of mind.

"Sarah, it's Maddie Brooks – Ash Cottage?"

"Hi, Maddie, how can I help?"

"I want to ask your opinion about something. Have you ever met the owner of Bay Tree Barn?"

"Terence? Yes, lovely man. I had a long chat with him the day I was there taking photos, before we put Ash Cottage on the market. He's lived there for nearly thirty years. Why? Is there another problem?" Her voice reflects a weariness we both feel. This has turned out to be the purchase from hell, considering it's the shortest chain possible.

"To be frank, my solicitor isn't giving up on the issue over the track at the rear of the cottage. I've been online and found a telephone number for Bay Tree Barn. I wondered whether you thought it was a good idea, or not, to contact Terence to have a chat about it? Is it too cheeky? I wouldn't like my new neighbour to think I was being pushy or anything."

"To be honest, if I was in your position it's what I would do. He's a genuinely helpful man and if he has any issues with the track then you are better off knowing about that now."

"Thanks, glad you agree. My solicitor is annoyed I left it so late to query it, but the lease on my rental property runs out at the end of December, so it was crucial to ensure everything was tied up before then. At one point I thought I'd actually find myself homeless. So I am relieved, to be honest, but this issue is a little worrying." I can't even contemplate what Ryan would say if he knew.

"Make that call and if there's anything I can do from this end, just let me know."

"Mr Darby? I'm sorry to bother you, but it's Madeleine Brooks, the purchaser of Ash Cottage."

"Hello, Madeleine, lovely to hear from you! Please, call me Terence. Do you have a moving-in date yet?" His voice booms out, causing me to yank the mobile away from my ear. I press speaker phone and set it down on the desk in front of me.

"Yes, I'll be in on the nineteenth. There's one outstanding issue about the track that runs along behind Ash Cottage. I wondered if you knew who the owner was."

"Ah, that's just the sort of issue that solicitors love. We went through this when we were buying Bay Tree Barn and in the end we talked to Aggie. It seems there is no documentation to confirm ownership and the assumption made was that it was a strip of land that was never claimed by anyone. Aggie was perfectly happy for us to use it as a back entrance to the barn, to save us walking all the way around to our front access. That's the other side of the hill. It's not wide enough for vehicular access, which was Aggie's only concern, as obviously the track is level with the first floor of Ash Cottage."

"So it's definitely not mentioned in your deeds, either? What about maintenance?"

"Well, I usually hack back the brambles every summer. It doesn't lead anywhere other than to the barn, so ramblers don't use it. Aside from Joanna and me, Aggie's handyman, Lewis Hart, uses it once a year to clear the leaves out of the gutters to the rear of the cottage."

That is just what I was hoping to hear.

"From your point of view it's not an issue, then? No one is likely to suddenly step in and put a road through there?" I can't hide a chuckle, voicing one of the worst-case scenarios my solicitor had thrown up, and which had sent me into a panic.

"Goodness gracious – no! It would run straight through the barn. You know, it's turning into a world where common sense seems to have become a dirty word. It's a pathway leading to the barn and an access point to the rear of Ash Cottage. It's probably a throwback to the days when it wasn't necessary to tie up every little thing tighter than a drum; jobsworth, I call it."

We both laugh and I'm delighted my new neighbour is as laid-back about this as I am.

"Thank you, Terence, your reassurance means a lot. I'm just relieved to know I'm going to be in before Christmas. As we're chatting, could I trouble you for the details of any local tradesmen you could recommend? I'm going to need to get the work started as quickly as possible."

"Give me your email address and I'll send you a list. It's a busy time for the plumbers of course. Plus most of them take off an extended holiday period, as the icy mornings make parts of the Forest treacherous to drive through at times. If we get snow then everything grinds to a halt, so you'll have to make sure you stock up on provisions. If there's anything Joanna and I can do, just call."

His words aren't exactly what I want to hear right now, but I guess forewarned is forearmed.

"Thank you, that's very kind. If you can also give me the details of your local oil delivery company, that would be great. My email is mbrookspropman@sl1dotcom. Hope to see you very soon!"

With my last real worry put to bed, I am a woman on a mission. First I ring my solicitor and tell her to drop her enquiries, then I do the bit that I'm trained to do: manage this project to within an inch of its life.

CHAPTER 6

Terence's email has a long list of contact names and addresses, which immediately perks me up. I know it isn't going to be easy to get everything sorted, but I'm pretty confident I can at least make a solid start.

I walked away from my marriage with barely enough to fill my car and most of it consisted of the contents of my wardrobe. I felt that everything in that house had been tainted when I learnt that my unbelievably callous husband had entertained Eve there. I was away on a two-day course that Ryan had talked me into, oblivious to what was happening at home. Jeff paid in other ways, of course, and I know he wasn't happy with the size of the cash settlement. But now there's only my income and no safety net I'm going to have to stretch my budget as far as I can.

It's time to make some big decisions about what I can, and can't, afford. I drool over some fabulous kitchens and bathrooms, dreaming of how it could look and then seek out more modest alternatives. The thing I've learnt over the years is that a high price tag doesn't always guarantee you the best, or most practical, design. By the end of day three I have 3D visuals of the new kitchen, bathroom and the shower room. The bottom-line figure is just within my budget, albeit I had to reduce the contingency line to virtually zero. I have lists of the items that can now be ordered, so that's the next task.

The one teeny little problem is that I still can't find anyone to do the work, unless I'm prepared to wait until the spring! Terence's list was comprehensive and what I have found is that people in the Forest are not only friendly, but helpful. My list of tradesmen has now doubled with recommendations, but each call has had the same response. A sharp intake of breath is the first reaction when I say that work must begin in four weeks' time. There were two numbers I called where I had to leave a message, so I'm living on nerves and hope at the moment. Perhaps blind faith will get me through, or do I mean a stubborn refusal to give up until all avenues have been exhausted?

What doesn't help is that I'm working from Ryan's suite of offices while I'm in the rented house. The daily commute into central Bristol from my rental in Bath is a grind. It's stop/start all the way and the traffic congestion seems to have extended well beyond any sort of recognisable rush hour. Whether I leave earlier or later it's bumper to bumper, sharing the road with a lot of angry and stressed commuters. I find myself day-dreaming about my desk in the corner of the media room at Ash Cottage. Traipsing into my sparkling new country kitchen in off-white shaker style and flicking the switch on my new espresso maker ... toot, toot. What is it with horns these days? Aren't they supposed to be used for emergencies only? Like warning people they are about to get run over?

"What do you think?"

Ryan continues to flick through the screens, scrutinising each page with a professional eye.

"Hmm ... it seems pretty comprehensive." He sits back in his leather swivel chair and chews on the end of his pen. "Only two issues, as far as I can tell."

"Fire away." That sounded a little more confident than I feel. Two issues? Really?

"The first is in relation to the labour costs. I assume you will be doing some of the basic redecoration yourself, but even so, that figure is highly optimistic. The other thing is the contingency line. You really are leaving yourself wide open there, Maddie. With a cottage, you never know what problems you will encounter until you begin pulling it apart. With the conservative figure you've put in for labour costs, reducing the contingency to a mere thousand pounds is a huge risk."

I shrug, indicating that I don't really have a choice. I can't pluck money out of thin air. He sits forward, resting his elbows on the desk and flicks through the small pile of papers I put in front of him.

"I've used worst-case figures for the larger items of expenditure. I'm pretty sure I can come in at least two thousand under budget when I place the order for the kitchen. I figure I can add that into the labour costs. As I get a handle on the actual costs I'll be clawing whatever savings I manage to make on purchases into that contingency pot. This is something I do all the time." I feel uncomfortable under his gaze. He isn't smiling and I'm not sure if that's because it's been a hard day or my figures really are concerning him.

"There's a big difference, Maddie. This is your money, not some wealthy client who can afford to over-spend or cut costs at a stroke because of the size of the budgets. You're going to have to make sure you don't order with your heart instead of your head. No falling in love with the perfect bathroom suite that will blow your budget or the solid-wood flooring that costs the earth. You might be lucky and find there are no hidden problems, although I'll be amazed if that's the case. Plus you might manage to employ a guy who spends more time working than he does texting on his phone. But *might* is one of those words that make me very, very nervous. If this was a client's proposal I'd continue to poke holes in it until they agreed to up the budget."

I can't decide whether I'm grateful Ryan is being so honest, or I'm disappointed that he doesn't have more faith in my abilities.

I'm not sulking: I simply don't feel like justifying myself. He's looking a little exasperated now.

"You're being creative with the budget because you need it to work. That hampers you in terms of being objective. Can I make a suggestion?" He holds my gaze and then suddenly winks at me. I burst out laughing.

"I think you're going to say what's on your mind, even if I say *no*."

"The main bathroom is a big chunk of the budget because of all of the re-plastering and plumbing work that will be required before the refit can be carried out. Don't place an order for any of the materials, or the bathroom suite, until after the kitchen is finished. By then you'll have a much better idea of how the costs are stacking up and if you have to find emergency funds, that's the budget to raid."

"So I'll have to wait for my leisurely soak in that fabulous slipper bath? No glass of wine and staring up at that inky, star-lit sky after a hard day's work ..."

Now it's Ryan's turn to laugh, although it comes out as more of a snort.

"I'm trying to keep you grounded; it's the smart decision."

I nod, grudgingly, having to admit it does make sense. But order times vary and a ten, or twelve, week delivery time is quite typical. If I wait until the kitchen is finished, it could be four months before I have a bathroom I can relax in. The shower room is going to be convenient, but even something as simple as storage is going to be an issue in there.

"Okay, common sense will prevail. Aside from that, is there anything else there that bothers you?"

"One thing ..."

Now I'm beginning to feel a little concerned; I think I did an amazing job considering the restrictions of time and cost.

"How long will you be taking off work, exactly? I'm not sure we'll be able to cope if you disappear for more than a few weeks."

He's serious and I feel myself blushing. I don't want him to think I'm being unreasonable and ignoring the fact that he has a business to run.

"I'll be there on call if anything goes wrong. The Anderson's project will be completed at least a week before moving-in day. That's plenty of time for me to tie up any loose ends. I was thinking of taking at least a month. After that I'll have to juggle work and the renovation for a while. It won't be forever, things will eventually get back to normal. I've already talked to the internet people and that will be connected the day I move in. The modem is due to arrive in about ten days' time."

It's the first item on the utilities checklist. Ryan nods.

"Well, now all you have to do is find yourself a man who will actually turn up on time and is capable of keeping up with your programme. Good luck with that," he adds. My stomach does a backflip as it occurs to me that time is fast running out.

CHAPTER 7

When the voicemail icon pops up on my phone I silently pray it's either Mr Chappell, the small building company who are based a stone's throw away from the cottage, or Aggie's 'man who can', a Mr Hart. I'm delighted to find two voicemails and immediately I perk up.

"Ms Brooks, this is Lewis Hart. Thanks for your call, but I'm not sure I can help. I'll be in the area on Saturday and will swing by to take a look if I have time."

In the area? I thought he was a local guy? The next voicemail is Mr Chappell.

"Hello Miss Brooks, this is Frank Chappell. We close for two weeks over the holiday period and in the New Year all of my men will be tied up on the new community hall project. It's unlikely I will have anyone free until the middle of April at the earliest. However, you mentioned some plastering work and there's a chance I could free up one of our guys for the odd half day here and there to help out, if that's convenient. Call me back and we can discuss it. Thank you for ringing Chappell and Hicks."

A sense of relief begins to roll over me like a wave. It's only a pinprick of hope, but it's better than two outright rejections. Mr Hart sounded rather lukewarm, but he wasn't totally dismissive. On the other hand, Frank Chappell sounds like a man with many years' experience; a consummate professional. Although he's only offering a plasterer, maybe I can convince him to divert a little more labour to Ash Cottage. I immediately re-dial, crossing my fingers as I wait for him to pick up.

"Mr Chappell, its Madeleine Brooks. Thank you so much for returning my call."

"Oh yes, Ash Cottage wasn't it? Lovely location, Miss Brooks. I hope you are going to enjoy living in the Forest."

He sounds sweet. His voice is deep and very friendly.

"Look, I'll be very honest with you, Mr Chappell. I'm desperate here. The cottage has been empty for over a year. It's cold and a little damp because the bank handling the probate case won't allow any of the services to be turned on. It's in case of a leak, or fire, apparently. I'm moving in on the nineteenth of December and I need a working kitchen installed before the twenty-fifth. Is there any way at all you can help?"

Again, that distinctly sharp intake of breath.

"I would love to be able to say *yes*, but the truth is that all our guys will be working flat out right up to the shutdown. I'll ask around to see if any of them are interested in doing a few days' work during the holiday, but please don't get your hopes up. However, I'm confident I can get a plasterer for you, if you are prepared to be flexible. I'll send him across as and when I can. Simon Griggs is a quick worker and he'll do an excellent job."

Darn, I was hoping for a bit of a miracle here. I can hear the sympathy in his voice, I only wish there was more he could do.

"Mr Chappell, if you have any delays whatsoever and can spare anyone, will you think of Ash Cottage first? I'm a prompt payer and you would be doing me a huge favour."

"I'll pin your telephone number up on the board, Miss Brooks. You'll be my first thought if I catch anyone standing around without something to do," his voice reflects the smile I know he has on his face.

"Thank you so much! And, please, call me Maddie."

"I'm Frank. I might not be able to part the waters, but I'll do the best I can."

The wave of relief doesn't exactly dissolve the knot in my stomach, but this is a life-line. Now to see what Mr Hart has to say.

"Hi, it's Madeleine Brooks from Ash Cottage. Thanks for returning my call."

"I wasn't expecting you to get back to me. Didn't I say I'd call in on Saturday, or something?"

Or something? I'm rather taken aback by his tone, which is distinctly dismissive.

"I ... um ... thought it might be polite to let you know that I don't yet have my own key. I don't move in until the nineteenth. However, I'm sure I can talk the estate agent into letting me have access for a couple of hours."

Heavy breathing down the line seems to indicate the phone is nestled between his chin and his shoulder. The short blast of a drill confirms as much.

"Sorry, are you on a job?"

"I'm always on a job. It's what I do."

Well, that was downright rude, if not sarcastic. I'm not sure how to answer that, but Mr Hart quickly jumps in to fill the silence.

"I'll drop by at eleven. I won't be able to hang around for long."

Right.

"Oh, thank you. Um, am I assuming you have some time in your schedule to begin work quite quickly?"

"I said I'd take a look, lady, not that I'd bring my toolkit and make a start. See you at eleven."

The phone clicks and the line is dead.

Guess it's going to be a case of working with Frank Chappell, then. I can only hope that he can talk one of his men into installing my kitchen instead of kicking back for the holidays. It's a tall order, but what choice do I have? What I'd really like to know is why there don't seem to be any women out there in the building trade. I refuse to believe it's a one hundred per cent male-dominated workforce. Maybe I need a woman who can ...

My phone kicks into life and I wonder if it's Mr Hart calling back to apologise for his rudeness.

"Mum, how're you doing?" The sound of Matt's voice makes my eyes tear up. In the midst of all this madness, it's a reminder of the life I had and how much I miss it.

"Good – really good. How is Dublin?"

"It's pouring with rain here. I wanted to check up on you; sorry it's been a while. I also have some news. Do you want the good news first, or the bad?"

My knees quiver, I'm not sure I can survive any more negativity at the moment. My voice wavers as I try to sound as if I can cope with anything.

"What's the bad news? Do you need me to fly over?"

He clears his throat. "We won't be able to get over for Christmas after all, I'm afraid. There's a lot going on as Sadie is working flat out at the moment and I'm only able to take a couple of days' holiday. I'm really sorry. I know you'll be disappointed."

The motherly bit of me instantly goes into guilt-mode, as I acknowledge that I'd assumed everyone would give me a wide berth this Christmas. I keep forgetting that the boys haven't seen Ash Cottage and have no idea what I'm taking on. They probably imagine a cosy, warm little place in the country.

"Oh, darling, don't worry. To be honest, the facilities on offer here aren't going to make for the most relaxing Christmas. I suspect the cottage will be little more than a building site. What's the good news?"

"We're having a baby."

My hand goes straight to my heart, my head repeating his words over and over again. He's twenty-two years old and he's only been living with Sadie for eighteen months – a baby?

"Congratulations, I'm ... well, I'm ... thrilled. It's great news, Matt. Have you told Dad?"

He doesn't sound excited, he sounds ... accepting. I guess this is a surprise he wasn't expecting; maybe neither of them was expecting it.

"I'll ring him next. I wanted to tell you first. Sadie has just phoned her mum; she says 'hi', by the way. It's a bit sooner than we'd planned, you know, we thought the wedding would come first and all that. You're not, um ... you don't feel awkward about a baby coming before we tie the knot, do you, Mum?"

"No, darling; it's only a piece of paper. It's what's in your heart that counts."

"I told Sadie you'd be fine with it. We just feel awful that we're going to miss your birthday, especially as it's a big one and the first since ..."

My heart constricts.

"Matt, darling, I'll be spending it covered in paint and looking like a builder's apprentice. Next year will be very different and maybe you will be able to come over with the baby. A summer birth, how lovely! Oh, I wish you were both here so I could hug you. Wonderful, wonderful, news."

Matt explains that Sadie is suffering from morning sickness and he's trying to make sure she doesn't over-tire herself. She works in marketing and it's a busy environment, especially when the first part of each day is spent feeling so awful. I'm so proud of my son being empathetic: caring enough to help out as best he can. Maybe Ryan was right, and I did do a good enough job. It seems that selfish streak running through Jeff hasn't been passed on, after all. If it were, maybe my example was enough to show the boys that love is about putting the other person first. Whatever – my heart is singing. Then it hits me. I'm going to be fifty very soon and I'm going to be a grandmother. I'm getting old, how did that happen? Inside I still feel like a thirty-year-old.

CHAPTER 8

Saturday arrives and I find myself sitting in the car outside Ash Cottage for two hours on a very chilly winter's day. It's freezing and I have to keep kicking the engine into life to put a blast of heat on my poor, frozen toes. I'm afraid to leave it running for too long in case I run out of fuel. Fortunately, the estate agents let me have a front-door key on condition that I return it as soon as I've shown Mr Hart around. Of course, Sarah knows him and I think that connection had more to do with being entrusted with a key than the fact that I'm the soon-to-be owner. As the end of the first hour of waiting comes and goes, I feel I ought to at least explain why the keys aren't going to arrive back at their offices imminently.

"Sarah, this is Maddie Brooks. I'm really sorry, but Mr Hart hasn't turned up yet. I'm not sure what to do ... whether to wait or head back to you. The trouble is that he might be my only option. Is he known as a reliable tradesman?" I don't know whether to cross my fingers and hope she says *yes*, or face up to the reality that he is the 'man who can't' on this particular occasion.

"I suspect he's been held up. He's a hard worker, but he does tend to ... well, I suppose I want to say 'get pulled into helping people out'. He always dropped everything whenever Aggie had a problem and he tends to be the first choice for many of the elderly people in the community. He probably won't tell you that, though. He's a bit of a mystery to most people, very private. Maybe his van has broken down; he doesn't have any family locally and that's a real disadvantage in the Forest. I'd say hang on for a bit. If he's not going to turn up I'm sure he'd call to let you know."

She sounds positive, which is reassuring.

When he eventually turns up, he's driving a beaten-up old van. And a white van, at that. On the side there's a huge decal, 'The Man Who Can', and written underneath in smaller letters it says, 'renovations and maintenance'. The moment I spot him, I have to stop myself from rolling my eyes. I don't know quite what I was expecting after our rather abrupt conversation, but he looks a darned sight more cheerful in the flesh than he sounded on the other end of a phone.

His clothes, though, are even more surprising. He's wearing an old tee-shirt advertising a 1987 Metallica tour. It's been washed to within an inch of its life and would be perfect for cleaning windows. You know, when the cotton is so limp it flies over the glass like a dream. His jeans have the knees hanging out and he probably considers them to be a walking advertisement. I can see virtually every colour of paint, what looks like traces of white filler and a splattering of something the colour of concrete. Maybe he doesn't fold the jeans up at night; they just stand to attention at the foot of his bed. I realise I'm staring at him and he's walking past my car without acknowledgement, already heading down the path leading to Ash Cottage.

"Mr Hart?" I call after him, quickening my pace to catch up with him.

He barely takes the time to glance around, shrugging his shoulders and continuing to stride out. Each movement is purposeful and powerful; the man is all muscle. His head is shaven; from this vantage point I can see that's because he's lost most of the hair on the top. That tell-tale clean stripe down the centre is bordered by a fuzz of new growth. His face isn't clean-shaven either, but it also couldn't be described as a beard, more designer stubble. I don't think that's intentional, I just think he probably spends more time in the gym than he does looking in the mirror. His age is hard to determine. He has the physique of a man used to lifting heavy things – huge, muscular arms; lean, and a neck I probably couldn't get my hands around at full stretch. The question in my mind is will I feel comfortable having this man in my home? He looks more like a bouncer than a kitchen-fitter, but there's a magnetism about him that just made something inside me turn to jelly. What on earth? I take a very deep breath and assume it's merely hunger. Clearly, I'm in need of a quick sugar-fix. He isn't my type – too rough around the edges and very little in the way of manners, it would appear.

"I'm late," he throws the words over his shoulder with no hint of an apology whatsoever.

"Well, erm ... thank you for coming. Let me just open the door ..."

He doesn't move aside, but stands directly in my way, so I have to scoot around him. He's about my height, five foot eight, and as I swing open the door and spin back around, we're standing eye to eye. He raises his eyebrows at me and my knees start to cave. How ridiculous! I'm a grown woman, not some love-sick teenager!

"You're older than I expected." His voice is casual, but I'm rendered speechless and now I'm fuming. Suddenly those wobbly legs stand firm. How rude! Keep calm, keep calm – you need this guy more than he needs you. Ooh, that didn't help ... the thought of *needing* a man like him inspires a totally different chain of thought.

"I was thinking the same thing." I throw the words back with a casual air, to indicate that he's going to have to do better than that to offend me.

"I can see why you were sounding so stressed out. On your own, are you?"

If this is his normal mode of conversation, I'm not sure I can put up with it. He's here to look at the kitchen, not make small talk.

"I'm in need of someone to rip out the old kitchen and put in the new one. All the goods and materials are on order, but the kitchen units won't be arriving until the twenty-third of December. If work starts on the day after I move in, that would give you three days to strip it out and lay the new floor, first. I have a plasterer coming in to make good the walls. I'm assuming you could at least get the basics in by Christmas Eve? Can you handle that?"

It strikes me that I'm being unnecessarily abrupt, but he's beginning to unnerve me. Mr Hart follows me into the kitchen and stands with his arms folded, muscles rather ridiculously popping out of the arms of his seen-better-days tee-shirt.

"I've already put you in my little book." His face doesn't give me a clue what that means and I wait, assuming he will explain. As the seconds stretch out I realise that's it.

"Which means?"

He looks directly at me and his forehead wrinkles up into a puzzled frown.

"I'll be here on the twentieth, early."

Another silence begins to stretch out rather awkwardly and I find myself being out-stared.

"Don't you want to write anything down or look at the kitchen plan? Can you cope with re-plumbing the sink, or do I need to get someone in to do that? I'm not sure what your skills are exactly, Mr Hart."

Another frown and I get the distinct impression that I'm bothering him.

"I can re-fit a kitchen, Miss Brooks. In fact, I can do just about everything. And I don't need to write anything down. I know this place inside and out. I was Aggie's maintenance man."

I'm not sure that gives me a lot of confidence, considering the state of the cottage. I have to make a quick decision here. I'm in his *book*, which means I have a contractor, but can I put up with his rather bizarre and surly attitude?

"Right ... um, good. Um ... so what is the purpose of today's visit?"

"I thought I'd check you out first. I like to be left alone to get on with a job and not have someone peering over my shoulder every two minutes, changing their mind about what they want. It happens."

That makes my eyebrows shoot up into my fringe. Is he purposely trying to wind me up?

"I know exactly what I want, Mr Hart. Here is the new layout and on the second page you will find a breakdown of all of the items that are on order. I'm assuming you will provide things like plumbing fittings, filler, caulk and any additional timber you might need. If there's anything not on that list that you want me to purchase, just let me know. If I can have a price for the entire job, including connecting the cooker and the plumbing work, that would be very helpful. I have rather a tight budget."

We both know price isn't really relevant. There's no one else available at such short notice, as Mr Chappell didn't have any luck finding me someone. It does worry me slightly as to why Mr Hart is free when everyone else is rushed off their feet. I figure that that's information I'm probably better off not knowing. If Aggie used him and Terence is prepared to recommend him, too, then I have to trust that he will do a good job. Even Sarah, at the estate agents, seemed to think highly of him.

"Your budget is your business, Miss Brooks. The price is the price. I'll text it to you later today. See you on the twentieth. I'll be here by seven. I'm also Gas Safe registered, which means I can fit cookers. This one is dual fuel; Calor gas hob and electric oven. If you're replacing it, make sure you order a conversion kit. But I expect you knew that." There's a hint of sarcasm in his voice and I feel myself reddening. Of course I realised it was dual fuel, but no one mentioned a conversion kit when I placed the order.

We've been inside for less than five minutes and he's out of the door before I have a chance to ask any more questions. I spin around, taking in the tired kitchen and the ancient cooker.

"Aggie," I mutter in desperation, "I hope I can trust your judgement. He sounds like he knows what he's doing, but he's so damned arrogant. He'd better not let me down."

I zip up my padded jacket as the damp chill in the air sends a shiver through me. I hope the plumber turns up to fix that vandalised pipe and the oil delivery arrives before my first sleep here.

"I'm sure it will all be fine, Aggie, and the cottage is going to look lovely. It's in safe hands; promise." Sharing my problems with her might gain me some good karma, but it's sad to think there's no one else to listen to me.

As I place the key in the lock I almost have to pinch myself. Very soon this will all be mine and even if I have to put up with people like Mr Hart, it will be worth it in the end. I stop for a minute to take in the view and revel in a sense of something akin to renewal. The stresses of modern-day living seem far removed from this scene of peaceful tranquility. As I watch, grey squirrels leap from tree to tree in search of any last remnants of bounty. Even in winter the scene is magnificent.

On the drive back the rain begins to fall once more.

My phone pings and it's a text.

> *Ryan: You've been on my mind. How's it going?*
> *Me: Good. I have a kitchen-fitter.*
> *Ryan: Go you! We should celebrate.*
> *Me: Rain check on that one. Too much to sort out. Sorry. How r u?*
> *Ryan: Disappointed. I'm here if u need me.*

Now I feel bad.

> *Me: Thanks, really. It means a lot. See you soon, promise!*

Besides, I'm not sure I'd be good company at the moment, but it's too difficult to explain. It strikes me that Ryan has always been there for me no matter what else is happening in his life. I suppose he filled the void that Jeff created as we drifted apart. I don't know why that comes as such a surprise, really.

The subject of the vandalised oil tank seems to dominate my thoughts. I decided it's madness not to address the problem, as the rain continues to pour relentlessly. There seems to be no let-up whatsoever and it isn't just drizzling rain, but the stuff that soaks you in seconds and makes you feel distinctly miserable. Time for an update.

"It's not good news," Sharon Greene's very professional tone conveys no emotion, despite her words, and I wonder if that's something a solicitor has to learn. "The bank is insisting that the cottage is sold as seen. They are not prepared to have the vandalised oil tank fixed, and they've rejected my request for you to be allowed access prior to completion to sort out the problem."

"Can they do that?" I'm rather shocked at what feels like a callous reaction.

"Their policy with probate cases is that everything in the property is switched off at the mains. The estate agents do not have the authority to switch anything back on in case of a potential leak or the risk of fire. An empty property is at risk, simply because if something happens it could be a while before it's discovered. If the plumber did any damage while carrying out the repair, the bank would be held liable in the first instance. I know it seems harsh, but it's pretty standard practice, it just doesn't come up very often."

"Well, thank you for trying. It seems I'll have to get a plumber lined up to start work the moment I have the keys and book the oil delivery for later in the day. At least the heating should be on by the evening, so that's some comfort."

There's absolutely no reaction from Sharon.

"Is there anything else I can do for you?" It's not a question aimed at evoking a response and I have the distinct feeling she's signing off on this case.

"No, I think that's it, Sharon. Thank you for your help and I'm only sorry I bothered you with this matter." I feel slightly embarrassed, as if I should have known that dealing with an institution isn't like dealing with a normal person. They don't care if I freeze, or whether the oil tank ever gets filled.

By some miracle, in less than twenty-four hours I have a plumber who specialises in emergency call-outs. He says he can make himself available from eleven o'clock on moving day.

The universe must have been sending out good karma and taking pity on me as things begin to fall into place. So the order of play will be keys, plumber, oil delivery – what can go wrong? As if by magic I seem to have everything covered.

Tick-tock, tick-tock – moving-in day can't come fast enough! Now if I could just do something about that incessant rain ...

LEWIS

CHAPTER 9

I don't know who this Miss Brooks thinks she is, but she can't just expect me to jump because she has a problem. Some people are all *me, me, me*. Does she think I just sit around waiting for the phone to ring and jobs to come in? I've never had any downtime between jobs and if I accommodate her, then someone else will have to wait. Well, I suppose I am lashing out a bit and the truth is that I had built a little slack into my work timetable. But working for *her* wasn't in the plan.

I can't refuse, because it's Ash Cottage and I know every inch of it as well as I know the back of my hand. Little Miss I'm-Having-A-Crisis thinks she's smart, but if you ask me she's taken on way too much. Even if this woman does lighten up at some point, I seriously doubt she'll lose that *I'm better than you* attitude. I'm a tradesman, not a servant. Well, you need me more than I need your money, Missy, so you'd better be careful.

The mobile kicks into life and it's Sarah from the estate agents. I wonder what she wants? I don't suppose Miss Brooks has changed her mind and realises it's not quite the little project she thought it was going to be!

"Hi, Lewis. You said to let you know if anything new comes on the market. We've just taken on a little two-bed cottage in Lybrook. It has a lovely garden extending over a quarter of an acre and it's in your price range. Have you started looking again?"

I can't get my head around looking at properties at the moment. I know Sarah feels awkward and would love to find me the perfect place to put down roots.

"I've decided to wait a while before I start looking again. My plans have changed slightly and I'm up to my eyes in work."

"Does that mean you are going to take on the renovation work at Ash Cottage? Miss Brooks did mention your name. I just thought it might be … awkward for you."

I bet she did.

"Well, she isn't going to be easy to work with, but at least I'll know it's been done properly."

"Oh, I didn't mean …"

I know exactly what Sarah meant, but it doesn't hurt to let it be known that I'm doing this for my own reasons. It might even get back to Miss Brooks and make her realise she's lucky I didn't refuse her point blank.

MADDIE

CHAPTER 10

Even the grey sky can't dampen my excitement today. I'm awake for quite a while before the alarm finally kicks into life at six am and I don't need to pull back the curtains to check on the weather. I can hear the rain driving hard, as the wind rattles at the window. Switching on the bedside light and sitting up, I pull out my project notebook. Running down the action list for today is more for reassurance than a final check. I've been running over and over it in my head since one o'clock this morning. I could repeat it parrot fashion from memory. Everyone on it is probably already completely fed up with hearing from me, as I have checked and double-checked with them all several times over during the past week, to ensure everything goes smoothly.

I feel I've organised this down to the last detail and, in theory, the actual move itself is going to be straightforward – even if everything is going to get very, very wet in the process. Both Ryan and my younger son, Nick, offered to help out, but it's not as if I'm moving the contents of an entire house. Aside from my clothes and personal effects, I do have a stack of things I've recently purchased for the new cottage, but the removal guy assured me it's only half a load. One trip, four hours in total with travel, he said.

There's no point in unpacking everything at the other end until most of the really dirty work has been carried out. The mess and dust from stripping out the kitchen and hacking off the plaster on the two damp walls is going to be a nightmare, but hopefully the worst of the mess will be out of the way in the first couple of days. Ash Cottage, here I come.

By the time the removal van arrives, the rain is driving hard at a forty-five-degree angle. The wind makes it impossible to use an umbrella and I end up settling for an old woollen hat, pulled down tightly over my ears. Gareth, the van driver, seems oblivious to the rain.

"Can I help carry a few boxes?" I offer, as he passes me in the hallway and I notice rain drops dripping off the end of his nose.

"It's not a problem, Miss Brooks. I'm used to it. Nothing gets through this jacket or these boots," he gazes over the box he's carrying and down at his feet. "Best boots I've ever had," he adds.

"Oh. Good. Well, I'll get back to cleaning, then ..."

The pile of boxes is quickly diminishing and I'm only thankful I decided to move them all into the hallway yesterday. With the dust sheet covering the carpet, at least I won't have a soggy mess to deal with. Those boots must be at least size tens and the number of times they've been in and out – well, I've lost count.

He's finished loading by ten past nine. A quick flash around with the vacuum cleaner, then two phone calls to confirm the final gas and electricity meter readings, and I find myself locking up the front door for the very last time. Goodbye house, thank you, but no apologies for saying that it hasn't been the best period in my life. Things can only get better from here on in.

"What do you mean, the funds still haven't arrived?" It's almost noon and I'm sitting in the car, which is parked two streets away from the estate agent's office. The windows keep misting up. I think of the plumber, who has been sitting in his van outside Ash Cottage for well over an hour now. The removal guy, poor chap, has been there for nearly two hours and has already phoned me four times to remind me of that fact. "So what's holding it up?"

I'm conscious that in about an hour's time there will be several lorries arriving at the cottage and expecting to gain access to drop off their goods. The plumber says the oil tanker hasn't turned up yet, so fingers crossed that's not a complication I'm going to have to face.

"The funds have been sent, Miss Brooks, I can assure you. The transfer is in the system and it's a matter of waiting for confirmation from the bank's solicitor."

"Can't you at least let me have a front-door key? If the funds are on their way, then surely it's as good as mine now?"

"Ooh, we can't do that," his tone infers complete disapproval. "Anything could happen, even at this stage."

"Really?" Now I'm seething. "Really? You think I might change my mind, even when all my belongings are in a van outside Ash Cottage as we speak? If this purchase doesn't go through today, I have nowhere to sleep tonight. I hardly think the bank will change its mind and decide they aren't going to sell it to me after all. The money is practically in their account. Don't you think you are being just a tad unreasonable here?"

I'm afraid the sarcasm in my voice is disappointing; I should know better and the response it invokes is deserved.

"Hassling me, Miss Brooks, is not going to get you access to Ash Cottage until I've received the call from the bank's representative. I require their authority to release the key. I will ring you when that happens." The click cutting off the call is instantaneous and my heart sinks into my boots.

Okay, keep calm Maddie and think of a plan. My fingers dial quickly.

"Mr Trent, do you need access to the cottage in order to replace the vandalised oil pipe?"

The plumber sounds hesitant.

"Well, no, but if you don't have the keys ... I don't want to end up being prosecuted for trespassing."

It's just my luck that I've picked probably the only plumber in the world who would ask that question. I push back my shoulders, not that he can see, but it has the desired effect.

"They're fine with it, but we can't have access to the house just yet. The funds are in the system, so they've assured me it will be any moment. As soon as I have the keys I'll be on my way. Can you ... erm ... do me another favour?"

He doesn't respond. Funnily enough, I don't seem to have any pangs of guilt about lying to him, which I presume will absolve him of any blame if anything goes wrong. That still doesn't prevent me from feeling awkward imposing like this.

"There are several deliveries on their way. They've all been told not to deliver before one o'clock, but key release by then is looking doubtful now. If they turn up, could you see if the garage is unlocked and ask them to leave the parcels inside? I'm not expecting you to check the boxes or anything, but if they won't leave them without a signature, could you sign for them? I accept the risk is mine if they mess up, but I simply don't have any other options."

On my last two visits the garage has been unlocked. After all, it's empty and I mentioned to Sarah that I would be grateful if she could make sure no one locked it, just in case we had problems today.

Heavy breathing accompanies the silence as Mr Trent rather reluctantly hurries off to check the garage.

"It's pouring with rain here, you do know that?" he mutters. "They have the sandbags out down on the lower road again, so it doesn't look promising."

Promising?

"In what way?"

"A repeat of the big flood they had last winter. The road through the village was closed for the best part of three weeks."

Flood? What flood? A feeling of utter panic hits me square in the gut and then starts to spread outwards. No one mentioned anything about flooding. What if the deliveries can't get through?

What if I can't get back to the cottage even when I have the keys in my hand? Pull yourself together, Maddie, panicking isn't going to change anything. You can only deal with one thing at a time and it's too late to back out now.

"Nope, it's not locked. You're in luck."

Luck has nothing to do with it. I thought ahead and anticipated this scenario, although in my head it was worst-case. How can it take over three hours to move money from one account to another? I thought it was instantaneous these days. They type in the details, press the enter key and there you go!

"Thank you for checking. I really hope that I'll be there before any of the deliveries arrive. The oil tanker isn't due until later this afternoon. How long will it take you to replace the pipe?"

Heavy breathing and rustling indicates that he's walking back to his van.

"Maybe an hour. It depends. Once the new pipe is in I'm going to have to flush through the system, so I'll need to turn on the central-heating boiler."

"Oh, right. Well, I'm glad it's outside. You could possibly have it all done by the time I arrive, then! That's brilliant news."

He makes a sound that doesn't sound very encouraging.

"Nope. You'll need to turn on the heating first to fire it up. The thermostat is inside the cottage and I assume the electricity is off at the moment?"

This is one of those awful 'doh' moments. He must think I'm a total idiot.

"Yes, yes, of course. Sorry, too many things going around inside my head at the moment. If you can start on that pipe, I'd be very grateful."

"It's still raining," he mutters, before the line goes dead.

"Why me?" The pitiful half-sob that comes out of my mouth is unbidden and I look around to check that it wasn't so loud that pedestrians around me heard it. Fortunately, no one seems to be looking directly at me, but I'm going to have to pull myself together. You can get through this, Maddie, I whisper from behind gritted teeth.

CHAPTER 11

"Mum, it's me. How's the move going?"

It's lovely to hear Matt's voice, but I thought it was the estate agent and my stomach does a backwards flip. Tick-tock. It's nearly two o'clock and my back is beginning to ache from sitting in the same position for the longest few hours of my life. Even my damp clothes are now almost dry, but I've had to keep the window open a little because of the condensation.

"Fine. Lovely to hear your voice, darling, but it's rather difficult to talk right now as I'm expecting a call to pick up the keys at any moment. I'll ring you in a day or two when I'm sorted. Promise! Love to you both."

I feel awful cutting him off like that, but if I stay on the line I'm likely to burst into tears. As I put the mobile phone down on the passenger seat, it immediately kicks into life again.

"Ms Brooks?" It's a voice I don't know. "We have key release on Ash Cottage. If you'd like to call in whenever it's convenient ..."

"I'll be there in three minutes."

Jubilant is an understatement. Ecstatic doesn't really do it justice, either. As I hurtle back through the windy lanes to Ash Cottage, the windscreen wipers are barely coping with the downpour. Until the car begins the downhill cruise into Bybrooke, any mention of flooding is still the very last thing on my mind. And then I hit it. As I round the last bend before the first of the cottages on the outskirts of Bybrooke come into view, I see the sandbags. Water is literally spewing out of what looks like a hole in the ground and as it runs down the side of the road it doesn't have to travel very far to be consumed by a lake of grey, muddy water. Part of the grassy bank to the right-hand side of me has been washed away and traces of the rich, red soil run in swathes, mixing with the general pool of murky water. I slam on the brakes, the car slewing to a halt just in time. In front of me are at least a dozen vehicles blocking the road. I pull the woolly hat down over my ears and step out of the car with determination.

"How deep's the water? Is it possible to get through?" I level the question at a group of guys with shovels, all busily filling sandbags from a trailer.

"It's passable at the moment and you'll be fine, as your four-by-four isn't too low to the ground. It's only about two feet deep in the middle, but it's rising fast. The culvert is blocked again, but this time we think it might have totally collapsed."

A couple of heads turn in my direction, giving curt nods and I feel sorry for them. Despite wearing heavy waterproofs, this sort of rain seems to find ways in and I seriously doubt they are cosy and dry beneath their gear.

"Best get through while you can." One of them chips in.

"Is there another way into the village? I live up there – Forge Hill. I'm moving in today, actually, and I have deliveries booked."

Several of them stop shovelling and give me a look of pity that starts alarm bells ringing in my head.

"There is access from the top road, but the lanes are quite narrow and I'm not sure a twenty-six-tonne delivery lorry would be prepared to use that route. The smaller ones could get through. This is the main road and, unless we can keep that water level down, the possibility of another closure seems inevitable. You chose the wrong day to move in, Miss, that's really bad luck."

He gives me a grimace, shaking his head to disperse the rivulets of water running off his cap and down his face.

"Thanks, and sorry to have held you up. Are you local?"

He indicates with a nod in the direction of the first cottage on the slope down into the village.

"Lived here nearly ten years. We thought last year's flood was a one-off. Seems we were wrong."

Glancing across, I can see that the sandbags were too late to save the water flooding into the ground floor of the property. It's a quaint cottage, quite modest and obviously his pride and joy. My heart goes out to him.

"I'm so sorry. I really hope the rain lets up soon."

He gives me a smile and a nod, appreciating my acknowledgement of his dire situation.

"It's in the hands of the gods." His response is sobering. "Take it steady driving through, use a low gear and you'll be fine."

It seems wrong to wave as I drive past the men. All eyes are on my vehicle, checking the water level doesn't come up above the door line. I put up my hand in a stiff acknowledgement and they all raise theirs in return.

As I continue to drive very slowly through the worst of the flooding, I lose count of the number of properties I see that have been affected. The waters rose too quickly for many of them to get the sandbags in place before the inevitable happened. As the road begins to level out, a couple of fire tenders are parked on the verges and a dozen firemen are unreeling hoses to start pumping the water away. Turning off just before them to climb up Church View, for the first time I feel thankful for the hill and the hairpin bends. Just as you swing the car around one of them, the next one looms up. On the few occasions I've driven up here to date, I've nervously done the climb in second gear, ignoring anyone behind who might be feeling frustrated that I won't speed up. If it's not grappling with the steering wheel to keep the turns tight, it's avoiding cars coming down the hill at speed. There are a couple of places where the two lanes are very narrow and, with a brick wall on one side and a drop on the other, there's no room for mistakes.

Pulling up outside Ash Cottage I'm conscious it's nearly three o'clock and there are two very fed-up guys sitting in their vans. They might be relieved to see me, but I doubt either of them really wants to jump back out into the rain. Neither responds to my wave, so I hurry on down to the cottage. This time there's no thrill – instead my eyes are everywhere checking to see whether the water running down from the top of the hill is likely to cause a problem. Whether it's because the garden is terraced, I'm not sure, but I'm relieved to see that there doesn't appear to be any sign of water building up. The plumber is now two paces behind me, eager to get inside as I fumble with the keys.

"You're lucky," he shouts over my shoulder. "All the water from Forge Hill seems to be directed down a large pipe that runs alongside the road and down through the hedge bordering your garden. If it wasn't for that, part of your garden would have been washed away by now."

I swing open the door and stand back.

"I'm Martin," he says. "We have a problem."

Great! I hope *we* can fix it!

"The new pipe is in and the oil tank is full. The driver left this for you," he hands me a soggy envelope. "But I'm not convinced we're going to be able to fire up the boiler. I need to access the central heating thermostat to confirm that's the case."

As we stand dripping, Gareth appears with the first box in his hands. The cardboard already dark as the rain soaks in. We move out of his way and I point to the sitting room.

"You can stack everything in there, thank you. And I'm so sorry for the delay."

He gives me a half-hearted smile on his way past.

"Martin, I'll turn on the electricity and the controls are in the dining room. I'm keeping my fingers crossed for some heat. It feels even colder in here today, if that's at all possible." The temperature outside seems mild by comparison. Who in their right mind would leave a cottage without heating for over a year? Presumably, only someone who had no intention of moving into it!

He doesn't reply, but heads off to find the controls, as I reach up and pull down the cover to expose the meter. Pulling a pen and some rather soggy paper from my pocket, I note the meter reading and flick the switch.

"The thermostat seems to be working, that's a good sign," Martin says, as he heads off out into the rain again.

I pop back to my car to get the supplies box, taking a moment on the way back to peer in through the garage window. Yes! I can see a large stack of boxes heaped in the middle of the floor.

"I'll have coffee and biscuits ready in just a few minutes, guys," I call out as both men pass me, going in opposite directions.

Then, that little thrill hits me. It might be one of the worst days ever to move into a new property and each task might feel like pushing jelly uphill, but the plan is beginning to come together. Even in the rain that view simply takes your breath away. Nature is glorious, no matter what it decides to do.

I throw off my sopping-wet hat and coat, then walk through into the kitchen with the box. I can't stop myself from peering into the bathroom just in case of leaks. Thankfully, everything looks fine. It smells distinctly musty, but there's no visible sign of water ingress. I'm beginning to relax a little, glancing at my watch and wondering about the modem and the telephone line. But, first things first.

Martin appears in the doorway just as I'm stirring the coffees. "Problems."

That must be the most annoying word in the dictionary. I plaster a fake smile on my face, silently praying he isn't going to say I don't have any heating.

"You don't have any heating. The boiler has seized up, tight. No one in their right mind would leave a heating system turned off for a whole year without firing it up every now and again to keep the parts moving. Ridiculous!" He scowls, although I don't think it's

69

actually directed at me. He can see the shock on my face as I pull my scarf tighter around my neck against the damp and chilly air.

"Is there a solution?" I'm not even sure I understand what he's saying. Surely if something is stuck there are ways to *un-stick* it?

"I have a mate who has worked on this model before. He's coming over in a bit to see if there's anything he can do. He has a few spare parts in his van that might help, but he says if it's more than seven years old then it might be worth considering replacing it."

"How much would that cost?"

"Well, if you're going for that option then I'd suggest upgrading it to a combination boiler, so it supplies you with hot water as well. I had a quick look at your emersion tank upstairs and it's not even full size. I have no idea how you would fill a bath tub – it would take forever. In total I'd say you were looking at around three thousand pounds."

My mouth suddenly goes dry and I think of my one-thousand-pound contingency budget.

"How long would it take?"

"Well, by the time we ordered everything and with installation, best part of three weeks, but with the holiday that would affect delivery, so you'd be looking towards the end of January."

Tears well up as I can't even contemplate living here and feeling as cold, damp and miserable as I do at this precise moment. Already the chill has seeped into the core of me and all I can think of is diving in to find the box in which I've packed the warm clothes.

"I don't know what to say. I simply can't be without heat ... it's not even an option."

"Look, let's see what happens when my mate arrives. We'll replace the fuel jet, as it's probably blocked with muck from the damaged fuel line. If we can get a steady, clean flow of oil going through, then who knows, we might be in luck. There is another alternative. We could just replace the motor and hope that does the trick."

My watery smile is one of hope, as I can see how hard he's trying to come up with a quick and easy solution.

"Thank you, really. Here, at least the coffee is warm and help yourself to biscuits."

He reaches across, giving me a look of appreciation.

"If my mate thinks it's worth replacing the motor, it might take a few days to get hold of one. In the meantime, I have several electric fan heaters in the van that I can let you use. You won't freeze, but it will ramp up your electricity bill, I'm afraid."

Gareth joins us, relieving himself of his soggy outer coat. With three bodies squeezed into the small kitchen, I fancy it's beginning to warm up a little. Suddenly another voice floats through from the conservatory.

"I seem to have arrived at the right time. One delivery of garden chairs for you, madam." Ryan's head pops around the door and he looks like a lonesome cowboy. Sporting a wax jacket and what appears to be a Stetson, big blobs of water continue to drop down onto his shoulders.

"Perfect timing," I laugh, glad to hear his voice. "I'll make you a cup. And now I have chairs, my goodness, this is about to feel less like roughing it and more like a home."

It is meant as a joke, but none of the men laugh.

What have I gotten myself into?

CHAPTER 12

Ryan was only popping in, but ended up staying until after the plumbers left at four-thirty. I felt sorry for them, working outside with no shelter from the rain, but suddenly there was a plume of smoke and a humming sound.

"It's working," Martin's smile was more one of relief, I think, that they could finally pack up and go home. "There's no guarantee it won't suddenly stop, but I suggest you keep the heating on continuously for the time being. I'll show you how to fire it up in case it trips out again, as there might still be a little muck in the pipes. You only have to take off the outer cover and there's a button to press. If it doesn't fire within three presses, then it's seized and you'll need to call us out to see if we can manipulate it again. I'll get those heaters for you just in case. My mate has managed to track down a replacement motor and it's going to cost around five hundred and fifty pounds. The problem is that I seriously doubt it will be delivered this side of Christmas. If we can keep this one ticking over and it lasts that long without breaking down, it might not even be worth considering replacing it. With the new parts we've put in, and once the fuel coming through is completely free of muck, you might be lucky."

I settled up with him, adding a big tip and thanking him profusely for putting himself out under such awful conditions. Ironically, the rain began to ease a little as I waved off the two vans.

Ryan was on his mobile, trying to find out why the phone line was still dead. No engineer has appeared and the modem was still sitting in a box on the shelf.

"This is a business line," his voice was firm and purposeful. "The letter I'm looking at clearly states that the service will be connected today. If there's a fault on the line, then surely a new connection has priority? I think I need to speak to a supervisor or the complaints department. Please put me through to someone who can escalate this matter."

Well, I wouldn't argue with him and I guess from the ensuing silence he's been put on hold.

"Dammit ..." he pulls the phone away from his ear and moves his mobile around, checking his signal status.

"Has it dropped out again? It never occurred to me that the trees would be such a problem when it comes to using the mobile. Thanks for getting onto the phone company. I'm just off to the garage to start carrying down the parcels. I'm going to start assembling the bed frame." He looks frustrated, pulling on his coat and heading out to walk up the hill and see if he can get a better signal.

"I'll be there to help out as soon as I've spoken to someone."

I feel really bad; I bet this isn't how Ryan envisaged spending his usual Friday-night happy hour.

Walking up the path in the gloom, I realise there's only one outside light and it's not very effective. At least the rain has eased off and it's merely a cold, dank drizzle now. Throwing open the garage door I fumble around for the light switch and then look at the pile of boxes, doing a double-take. The pile looked bigger when I peered in through the window earlier on. A mattress takes up a lot of space and the bed ends will be in quite a sizeable box. All of the parcels in the pile are either small, or medium-sized. As it sinks in that the bed isn't here, I let out a loud moan. Groceries, microwave, blinds, what looks like a vacuum and painting supplies ... things that I can manage without tonight, but a bed? Why didn't I engage my brain and take a moment to check it was there earlier in the day?

Pulling the mobile from my pocket I see that it has no signal at all and is showing the red emergency status. Walking up the hill I'm surprised that Ryan is nowhere in sight, then I spot him quite a distance away. Already the climb is beginning to bite at my calf muscles, tiredness suddenly kicking in as the effort of the climb brings on a cold sweat.

As the bars begin to register I continue walking, scrolling through the contacts as I go. International Bed Land. Click. I'm in luck – a friendly voice answers almost instantly. A glance at my watch shows I've probably caught them just in time.

"Hi, I'm waiting for a bed frame and mattress to be delivered. I'm afraid I don't have the reference number with me, will the postcode suffice?"

"What's the name?"

She seems to call up the details with no problem at all and I await confirmation that it's on the way, delayed probably due to the flooding.

"Your delivery has been returned to the warehouse. They were unable to find you, I'm afraid. Two voice mails were left around four o'clock this afternoon. I assume you're calling to rearrange delivery?"

I'm speechless. Don't they have a satnav? I pull the phone away from my ear and see that the voicemail icon is flashing. Obviously now the signal is stronger they've just come through.

"I didn't get the messages; my mobile doesn't appear to work inside the property. Ash Cottage has been here for well over a hundred and fifty years, and you're telling me they couldn't find it?"

There's a couple of seconds silence on the other end of the phone.

"It wasn't a local carrier and they might not have been familiar with the area, or have a satnav in the cab. Let me check the notes." There's some keyboard tapping and then silence. "It seems the road into Bybrooke was flooded and they couldn't find an alternate route. However, this has now been resolved. Shall I re-book it for tomorrow morning?"

Resolved? You mean someone actually looked at a map? I'm so annoyed that I decide it's best just to make grunting noises, accept her apology because it really isn't her fault, and the reassurances that it will be here tomorrow. I end the call as quickly as I can, the depressing reality sinking in. Ryan walks back to me, the grim look on his face mirroring my own.

"Don't tell me, I can guess. There's a fault on the line and they don't know when they can fix it. No phone line, no internet and a dodgy mobile signal. Add to that, no bed, but the upside is that I can vacuum through, so the floor will be spotless."

Clearly, he doesn't know whether or not my words were meant to raise a laugh, but he can't control his reaction. He links arms with me and we walk back down to Ash Cottage, at least content that the rain has finally stopped.

"How about coming back to mine for tonight?" Ryan offers, as we walk past the boiler, which is emitting a wonderful plume of white clouds.

"I can't, as much as I'd like to. I need to keep an eye on the heating and, besides, Mr Hart is arriving early tomorrow morning."

"Then I'll stay."

"Really? It means sleeping on the floor ..."

"That's what friends are for," he shoots me a wicked grin. "If this continues, though, I might have to re-think our friendship. I'm a guy who enjoys his creature comforts and am someone who always assumed a little cottage in the country was the epitome of peace and relaxation."

We burst out laughing in unison as I go in search of wine glasses and a bottle of something that will help take the edge off a day that seems to have gone on forever.

The heating died at eleven-fifteen. One moment the comforting drone was there and then next thing there was this awful silence.

It was so quiet you could hear a pin drop. Even the rain seemed to fall noiselessly, belying the fact that it was heavy and relentless. Ryan gallantly braved the wet to go outside and take off the boiler cover. At one point he managed to get it to kick into life, but over the next hour it kept tripping out and eventually he admitted defeat. I think that was as much down to the rain as pure frustration.

We unpack the electric fan heaters, placing two in the largest bedroom and one in the conservatory to try to warm that up a little. It feels rather awkward laying our bedding on the floor and knowing we're going be sleeping in the same room. Even with the heaters blasting, there is still a distinct chill in the air and a general feeling of dampness. Ryan lies with his head up against one wall and I lie with my head up against the other wall, facing him. There is a gap of about eighteen inches between our feet. Even lying on folded duvets and blankets, the floor is hard and there are only just enough covers to ensure we have a good layer over the top as well.

"Are you warming up a little?" Ryan's voice is soft in the darkness.

"My toes haven't thawed out yet, but I'm getting there. How about you? I could unpack some of the cushions if one pillow is too low for you."

"I'll be honest. I can't be bothered to move. You must be shattered, though, considering I only came in at the tail end of this day. Was the flooding a surprise?"

I wriggle around a bit, unused to going to bed fully clothed. While I appreciate the warmth, it's so alien a feeling that it's hard to relax.

"It was a shock. I had no idea the village was flooded last winter. And, yes, before you say anything, I didn't have a survey, but I did have all of the searches done. I can't understand why that didn't show up, though."

"Clearly flooding isn't an annual problem or it would have been

76

on the flood risk report, so I doubt you need to worry about it. If it's all down to a collapsed culvert, though, obviously that's going to take a while to fix. The main worry is that I'm not sure all of your deliveries will get through. If the flood water rises and the main road is closed, it's only the smaller delivery vans that can use the top road because some of those lanes are more like tracks. I can't believe the timing of this, Maddie, talk about bad luck!"

It's a surreal night, neither of us is able to sleep for more than the odd half an hour here and there. At one point my back is so stiff, my groan awakens Ryan. As I roll over onto my side to ease the pain, my hand plops down onto the outside of the duvet.

"Goodness, this bedding feels damp to the touch."

"Well, I didn't like to say, but I think that back wall is soaking up the rain. I know this floor is above ground level at the rear, but most of the plaster is hollow if you tap it. I think that's why it smells so musty in here. In the spring, a coat of external damp-proofer should sort that problem out."

"Hey," I reply, brightening up. "That's one of the problems on the list. Fingers crossed the plasterer will be popping in to hack off the plaster, seal the wall inside for the time being and make it good again. Fingers crossed that will be within the next day or two. A local company are going to look at the water-proofing solution when they re-point the chimney, but that has to wait until the weather clears up."

As I begin to drift off again, I find that thought comforting. At least ending the day on a problem that is on the spread sheet and does have a budget is a plus. Isn't it?

CHAPTER 13

We're both awake before five o'clock and there's little point in lying there in the gloom. Ryan and I spend an hour sitting in the conservatory and drinking coffee, watching the sun rise behind the clouds. At last the heavens seem to have run out of water. I wonder what sort of night it was for the poor people down in the village, as there seems to be no movement at all on the road. I know it's Saturday, but lots of people still have to get up and go to work.

I have to coax Ryan to leave, knowing that what he needs is a full cooked breakfast and not the toast or cereals my scant larder can offer. We hug and this time it's a bit different; I feel myself blushing as it runs through my mind that I actually spent the night with my boss. Innuendo aside, I'm extremely grateful to him, as I have no idea how I would have felt being here all alone under such difficult circumstances.

His parting words are to leave the phone company to him, he'll chase them today. He suggests that I take *the walk* to check my mobile every couple of hours for messages. It's something that hadn't occurred to me and my stiff back is a constant reminder that I can't spend another night on the floor.

I busy myself assembling the portable hanging rails, which I decide might as well stay in the sitting room. I begin foraging around in the boxes for some comfortable old clothes and hang them up. I also hang up all the garment bags that are laid out on the floor. Well, it might not be a wardrobe, but at least I feel just a teeny little bit more in control of the situation. I decide it's unfair to ring the plumbers until eight o'clock at least. They probably work Saturdays anyway, but having been through the various options I'm not sure there's anything they can do. If I had the internet I could re-work the figures and see if I could pare anything back enough to afford a replacement heating system. I then spend an hour doing a few calculations in my notebook. I don't want to take all of the budget for the bathroom, but maybe I can find a reasonably priced slipper bath rather than the funky, modern one I'd set my heart on. Most of the larger areas of expenditure I can recall off the top of my head, so I write down the original budget figure and then a revised one. I can only claw back eighteen hundred pounds before I run out of options. The plumbers' costs for yesterday are already double the estimate and racking up an overspend on day one doesn't bode well. Frustration sets in and I close up my notebook, accepting that until I'm online I can't commit to purchasing a new system. I'm going to have to plump for a replacement motor. Once the decision is made, I stare out of the window at the view, watching the low cloud rolling across the valley like little puffs of smoke. A hammering on the glass door breaks my chain of thought and I look up to see Mr Hart standing there. It's six forty-five.

"Good morning," I offer, cheerfully, as I open the door to him. In truth I don't know how pleased I feel to see him here, except that obviously it means the work will begin.

"Yep." He utters that rather odd word begrudgingly. It's a form of dismissal, I think. Does he think a simple greeting is wasting his time?

"Can I make you a cup of tea, or coffee?"

"Nope. It's cold in here."

He deposits two large tool boxes in the middle of the floor and walks back out to his van.

I have a dilemma. Do I just leave him to his own devices, given that obviously he prefers not to engage in conversation? But that assumes he knows what to do. We've not discussed any detail, although I did give him a copy of the plans and the list of items being delivered by the kitchen company.

He enters, carrying a large cardboard box that seems to contain everything from filler to plumbing bits and pieces. Without uttering a word, he walks past me, deposits it next to the tool-boxes and heads out once more.

I'm not in the mood to stand here being ignored, so I think, 'What the heck,' and after his next trip I sidle out to bring in my painting supplies from the garage. He walks fast and the last thing I want to do is have to pass him on the ramp leading up to the parking area. Fortunately, it seems he's finished unloading. I manage to walk back through, carrying my decorating materials, with no sign of him at all. Only the sounds coming from the kitchen confirm he's started work.

After last night I've had a change of plan. It's just too cold to sleep upstairs until the heating is working properly. There's little point in trying to heat the whole cottage with just three small fan heaters, so I'm going to paint through the old dining room and when the bed arrives that will be my temporary bedroom. If I keep two of the fan heaters on in the conservatory and one in the sitting room, the warm air should circulate into the dining room, which seems to be one of the warmest parts of the cottage.

Within an hour the dust sheet is down, the walls have been washed with sugar soap and I begin painting. The ceiling is hard work as I have to stand on a small, if sturdy, side table I purchased to use as a coffee table. The first coat goes on like a dream with the large roller and I turn my attention to the walls. Suddenly a sharp voice booms out from behind me.

"You're not doing that right." I turn around to see Mr Hart watching me from the doorway, arms crossed over in front of his chest in confrontational mode.

A strand of hair escapes from the scrunchy holding my ponytail and as I whip it back behind my ear I can feel a streak of wet paint on the side of my hand transferring onto my face. I ignore it and give him a less-than-friendly look.

"I know. I think my method achieves a better result, though."

"What? Doing the ceiling and walls first and leaving the skirting boards to last? Some crazy system you have going on there." His voice has now toned down, but his words are full of mockery.

"Is there something in particular you wanted?" My clean hand surreptitiously checks out the side of my face, hoping I can wipe away any vestiges of white emulsion. I'm trying to keep calm and look as dignified as one can with a roller in one hand and, no doubt, paint-splattered hair.

"Fridge."

He turns and I follow him through to the kitchen.

He's already taken down most of the wall units and the tiny kitchen looks twice the size. He notes the look of surprise on my face. It's only half-past eight – this guy might be the rudest person I've ever met, but he works fast.

"I've taken the units apart and stacked them in the garage. They're only good for firewood. I need to move the fridge out, where do you want it? Did you know there's food in it?"

I stare at him. He can see that I'm managing with the bare essentials. He has the delivery list and it clearly shows all the new white goods are not being delivered until the twenty-second of December.

"Yes, I knew. I'm happy to empty it, if that makes it easier to move. It can go into the sitting room for the time being. Do you need a hand?"

He has his back to me the whole time I'm talking, but suddenly he spins around and the look on his face makes me feel I've offended him somehow.

"From whom?"

With that he places his vast arms around the body of the fridge and lifts it off the floor with ease. I have to back away quickly to

81

get out of his way and within seconds he's placing it in the corner of the sitting room.

He stalks back into the kitchen without uttering another word and I slope back into the dining room, wondering why that ridiculous display of macho overkill made my stomach do a somersault. Anyway, how dare he criticise the way I work! I don't care if the professionals do it a different way, I was instrumental in renovating a sprawling Victorian house and every single inch of wall, ceiling and woodwork was painted with these hands. Admittedly, if I'm wallpapering I do the skirting boards first, but you get a much better finish when it comes to painting bare walls if you do them first and the woodwork second. Maybe it's a left-handed thing. Um ... what am I doing? Who gives a damn what Mr Hart thinks? As for me looking over *his* shoulder, I can't believe he has the audacity to be looking over mine as if he's in charge.

Before I can pull myself together enough to pick up the roller again, there's a sharp tap on the door. Walking back into the conservatory I don't recognise the guy standing there, a polite grin on his face. Maybe it's the bed ...

"Hi, I'm from Chappell and Hicks. The boss said you had a couple of plastering jobs?"

I utter a silent prayer of thanks and quickly whisk him around the cottage, apologising for the lack of heat. We end up in the kitchen, where Mr Hart is lying on the floor, his top half obscured by the sink unit. He immediately pops his head to the side to look at us and mutters, "Griggs," in some sort of Neanderthal grunt.

"Nice to see you, Lewis. Sorry to hear about your mother," my visitor offers, with real sympathy in his voice. His mother?

Mr Hart's face doesn't register any visible response; he simply swings his head back and continues to disconnect the pipes under the sink unit.

"In the kitchen it's just making good the wall after Mr Hart has chipped off the ceramic tiles. The real problems are through here."

After an inspection, Simon Griggs follows me back into the

sitting room, where it's easier to chat. Clearly, he, too, feels a sense of unease around the surly Man Who Can.

"Do you foresee any problems?" I ask, rather hesitantly. The heavens open up again and we have to speak up in order to hear ourselves above the sound of rain pounding onto the conservatory roof.

"No, it's all straightforward. That bedroom wall will be messy as I'm going to have to knock off all of the plaster. There are too many blown areas to patch it. The boss said he's happy for me to do this job in my own time for cash, if that's okay with you? I could make a start this afternoon. Our office shuts at lunchtime tomorrow for the holiday, so I'll be free again in the afternoon. I expect Lewis won't be chipping the wall tiles off until tomorrow anyway, so I'll do the knocking back today, then I can plaster tomorrow."

"Whatever works best for you is fine by me. Do you know Mr Hart ... um ... well?" I have no idea why I'm asking that question. I'm not usually a curious person when it comes to other people's business, but the comment from Simon about Mr Hart's mother was concerning.

"Lewis? He's a good guy, just likes to be left alone to get on with the job. His mother lived up north, I think. He's not a great conversationalist." Simon points out the obvious, but doesn't offer any more information. It would be rude to question him further, but enough has been said to reassure me that Mr Hart's rudeness isn't personal. Knowing that helps a little; not much, but enough for me to be determined not to let it get to me.

"It's a great place," he adds. "Of course, Aggie's deteriorating health meant that over the last few years less and less maintenance work was carried out. Lewis managed to keep things just about ticking over for her, but she couldn't stand noise or mess. She was in a sorry state at the end. Funny, everyone always assumed that Lewis was going to buy the cottage after she passed on. I think Aggie thought so, too. Anyway, it should only take a few hours to chip off the old stuff and bond the walls ready to re-plaster them."

"That's great, thanks. How was the flooding when you drove through the village?"

He shakes his head.

"They have the pumps running and it is maintaining the level so cars can still get through at the moment. I don't suppose you've seen the news, but the flooding here is nothing compared to some parts of Gloucestershire. Entire communities are cut off, with food and water being distributed by boat. Who would have thought?"

We stare out at that awesome view. It's barely visible through the rain, which is falling vertically in sheets and hitting the ground so hard that it's bouncing back with force. The backdrop of Lewis hammering away in the kitchen shakes the ground beneath our feet as Simon heads back out into the rain.

I sit in the conservatory for a while to warm my toes on one of the heaters. Then I pull on my woolly hat and waterproof to dash up the hill and make a few phone calls. I ring the plumbers and they promise to call in on their way back home tonight, pretty confident it's a fuel blockage. We also agree that ordering a replacement motor seems like the best option. Despite the fan heaters blasting out on full, the dampness seems to infiltrate everything and my toes and fingers are constantly cold.

I'm assured that the bed will arrive today and it turns out that the van driver literally drove straight past the cottage yesterday and it was nothing whatsoever to do with the flood water on the lower road. He simply gave up looking and I suspect the fact that it was a late drop, dark and he was likely to get very wet, was no incentive. I make them write down the directions in full and tell them that the driver should look out for a large sign on a telegraph pole next to a white garage. On the way back to the cottage I remember a piece of board I spotted tucked away in one of the stone store rooms. Retrieving it, I dig out a pot of white gloss paint and in foot-high letters paint 'Ash Cottage'. I leave it propped up against the wall to dry and close the garage doors.

Back inside, Mr Hart is still hammering away and I can hear the sounds of splintering wood. He's a hard worker, that's indisputable. A slight movement to the side of me draws my eye towards the door and, to my utter dismay, I see Jeff standing there with a soggy bouquet of flowers in one hand. Reluctantly, I open the door wide enough for him to step inside. As I remove my own, soggy coat, it's clear I'm not inviting him to stay and I ignore the fact he's dripping all over the floor.

"What are you doing here?" It's probably not the reaction he was expecting and I sound almost as rude as The Man Who Can, who, by the sound of it, has just had an accident. The language emanating from the kitchen seems to fill the space between Jeff and I, as he stands there awkwardly, a shocked look on his face.

I spin around to look in the general direction of the kitchen and Mr Hart appears, blood pouring from his hand. He stops in his tracks when he catches sight of Jeff.

"Um ... that looks bad. I'll get the first aid kit. Mr Hart, this is Jeff, my ... um ... ex-husband."

Jeff shuts the door behind him as I run off to ferret through boxes. I'm vaguely aware of an exchange of words, but I can't hear what they're saying – only the low grumble of two male voices. Returning, I see that Mr Hart has found some blue paper towel to catch the blood.

"I'll be back in a minute, Jeff. You're timing isn't the best, take a seat." As I walk off in the direction of the downstairs bathroom, I leave Jeff eyeing the two folding chairs rather dubiously.

"We need to clean that up," Mr Hart follows me into the bathroom without saying a word.

I turn on the tap and indicate for him to put his hand under the running water. The clear stream instantly turns bright red and I'm shocked at the amount of blood pouring from his index finger. When, finally, I can assess the damage, a slight sensation of queasiness passes over me.

"You'll be lucky not to lose that fingernail. It looks like you've hit it right at the base and it's split. Unfortunately there's nothing to stitch, so all we can do is clean it up and dress it to help stem the flow of blood."

It's rather unnerving standing so close to this man who is, after all, nothing more than a stranger to me. The thought of actually touching his finger feels slightly invasive, if I'm honest, but he can't clean the wound and apply the dressing all by himself.

"You're a nurse, as well, are you?" I look up at him, my arm brushing his makes me recoil slightly. I'm not sure if that's his attempt at humour, or if he's being sarcastic.

"Raising two sons you get used to dealing with minor accidents. If you'd rather pay a visit to the local accident and emergency centre, go ahead."

I immediately regret my tone when I see his expression, as I think he really was attempting to make a joke. For some peculiar reason I'm stressing about having contact with him. I grab a towel with both hands, indicating for him to lay his hand on top. It must be stinging like mad as I wrap the towel around it, patting it gently. His hands are large and I notice there are callouses on his palm. Turning his hand over, still within the towel, I incline my head and he perches on the corner of the bath. He seems to be content to do as I instruct without complaint, and that allows me to lift the towel, and his hand, onto the edge of the sink. Just letting go sends a little wave of relief over me. Honestly, blood doesn't usually upset me in this way and I feel really silly. I pull out an antiseptic wipe, some butterfly strips and a large, waterproof plaster. I tear open the wipe and grab some cotton wool to soak up the fresh blood that is now running down his finger.

"Mr Hart, this is going to sting a little I'm afraid." He doesn't flinch as I mop up the blood and apply the wipe.

"It's Lewis."

His voice sounds almost normal. There's no hint of sarcasm and the bark is missing.

Applying the butterfly strips is the right thing to do and might end up saving his nail, but now I'm touching him, skin on skin. His hands are those of a manual worker, strong and hardened, but his fingernails are nicely cut. They aren't ugly hands by any means, which surprises me. My eyes wander down to his wrist, which by comparison looks strangely vulnerable, although his forearm is solid muscle and looks as strong as steel. I've never really studied a man's arm before. An unnerving sense of something happening in the pit of my stomach shocks me back into the moment. What on earth is going on here? I avoid looking at him as I put the plaster in place, making sure the gauze covers the base of the fingernail and won't stick to the wound if it continues to bleed.

Pulling my hand away, it suddenly feels cold, as if the warmth of his skin had permeated my own. Now I feel embarrassed, so I busy myself with washing the streaks of blood out of the sink and disposing of the debris from the dressings.

I can see he's going to speak and assume it will be a curt 'thanks', but that's not the case.

"Your ex is waiting."

"He can wait, but you're done." I continue washing my hands, dry them and then apply a hand sanitiser.

Our eyes meet for one brief second and I avert my gaze, my eyes settling on his mouth – full lips, slightly parted, showing a row of extremely white teeth. This man might present as a rough, tough individual who doesn't care about anything, but he's particular. That's not a trait someone who doesn't give a damn about anything would have. My head starts to spin and I have to distance myself. As he so kindly pointed out, my ex is waiting.

"I'm Maddie," I say on my way out of the bathroom door.

"I know," he replies, "I'll call you Madeleine."

My hackles are raised without even having to check the look on his face. This man is determined to wind me up for no other reason than the fact that he's an expert at it. Well, Lewis, we'll have to see about that.

"So," I demand, as Jeff looks back at me rather sheepishly, "why the flowers?" I'm in no mood to be messed around by anyone today, least of all my cheating ex.

"Maddie, it's a gesture, that's all. The boys wanted me to check you were okay, it's only natural they're a little concerned. If there's anything I can do ... this is quite a job to take on. I'd assumed you'd pick some cosy little place, not a ..." He doesn't finish the sentence; probably realising he's treading on thin ice.

"To be frank, Jeff, it's none of your business any more. Thank you for the flowers, but I'll be having a word with the boys to make things very clear. My life is now my own and if our paths never cross again, I'll be one very happy woman."

He looks like he's been punched in the stomach as I open the door and all but eject him physically from the conservatory. I immediately turn the key in the lock, pick up the bouquet and march out to the kitchen, from where Lewis has been watching the whole sorry little scene. His eyes widen a little as I literally ram the flowers into the plastic waste bin in the corner.

"Now I'm happy," I mutter under my breath. "Do you have a hammer and a nail?"

A slight frown passes over his face as he duly hands me a hammer and a six-inch nail.

"Big enough?"

I swear there's the merest hint of humour going on in those eyes as I march off to put up my sign.

CHAPTER 14

By the end of day two Lewis has completely emptied the kitchen and chipped off the wall tiles. Only the hot and cold water supply pipes remain, standing to attention like copper soldiers. His disposition doesn't change and he leaves, as he came, with barely a word. I'm not even sure when I'll see him next, as it would be unreasonable to expect him to work on Sunday. As much as it's a relief to see his van pull away, a little part of me also feels a little unsettled as I turn the key in the lock. I have no idea why, precisely, other than he's beginning to grow on me in a rather annoying way. I reluctantly admit to myself that it is nice having a man around, especially one who is so capable. I can't imagine any emergency or situation Lewis couldn't handle.

The plumbers managed to get the central heating working, but tell me that if it cuts out again and it doesn't fire on the third attempt, then it's best to stick to the portable heaters. I might have to accept the inevitable and be patient until the new part arrives.

The house is still chilly, but just that waft of heat circulating around the entire cottage seems to give it a glow. So why do I feel so spooked?

I finger the small stone in the pocket of my fleece. Lewis found it in one of the drawers in the kitchen when he was pulling out the units. He didn't say anything; it just appeared next to the sink in the bathroom. It's something you'd find on the beach and pick up, marvelling at nature's ability to create something so unique. It's a flat, dark-grey pebble that has worn into the perfect shape of a heart. A fluke – a treasure. Knowing that it was something Aggie had chosen to keep made me feel a little sad. Not that I knew very much about her. She was a single career lady who loved to play the piano and who had come back to her family home to nurse her elderly mother. She decided to make Ash Cottage her final resting place and lived here quite happily until her death. The last few years had been increasingly difficult for her and it sounded like Lewis made it his business to ensure she was at least safe and the cottage didn't fall into total disrepair. It's nice to know he does have a heart, buried deep within that formidable, bear-like shell. Clearly Aggie must have thought so, too, as she obviously trusted him. For someone who, at times, can be so very antagonising, I have to admit that there's something about Lewis that fascinates me. I constantly have to fight the urge to watch him while he works, simply because when he isn't talking he's so darned attractive.

As I turn the little heart-shaped pebble over and over in my hand, I wonder if Aggie ever experienced a man's love. Why would an elderly woman have such a wonderful keepsake if there wasn't some distant memory attached to it? Maybe she was simply in love with the idea of being in love and my heart ached to think of anyone filled with unrequited longing.

Have I unwittingly made Aggie unhappy today? Is she here, watching and feeling that her own heart is being ripped out with every hammer blow? Or is she happy that Lewis is here and putting her trust in him, once more? Despite the fact that at the moment all we have are four ugly, blank walls with nails, screws, pits and scrapes like vicious scars. The kitchen feels strangely hollow and hostile, as if it's staring back at me reproachfully. Old-fashioned doesn't mean it's of no use, and it would have been Aggie's pride and joy twenty years ago: newly installed and sparkling. I feel guilty knowing that it's stacked in the garage, now merely a pile of rubbish fit for recycling. Surely she'll understand, though?

Turning Aggie's pebble over in my hand, I wince at the thought of the memories created in this room and hope they remain, even though it's now merely a shell.

"I'm sorry, Aggie. It will sparkle again, really it will. Lewis will make sure of that. You have to trust me when I say I love Ash Cottage, but you need to understand that I'm feeling something here that makes me feel a little scared. Can you help me to get past that? Being on my own is daunting enough, at the moment."

Tears start to roll down my cheeks, plopping onto my fleece. Whether I'm feeling sorry for Aggie, or myself, I don't know. The one merges into the other, as if she isn't a stranger, but someone I knew in life. I walk through into the downstairs bathroom and place the little heart on a shelf in the corner, out of sight, but safe. I have no idea how long Aggie had held onto it, but I would feel terrible if it was broken or discarded in error while the cottage is in such a mess.

Walking back into the conservatory I check my mobile and it's showing emergency calls only again. Then I pick up the telephone handset, but the line is still dead. I know I should take *the walk* and talk to Ryan, but I can't face it this evening. At least the dining room is now painted. I'll do the skirting boards and window sill tomorrow.

They finally delivered the bed at half past four this afternoon, after several frantic calls to confirm it was definitely on its way. I told them a woman of my age couldn't possibly be expected to spend a second night on the floor in a damp cottage. I threatened them with a chiropractor's bill if they let me down again. When the van driver and his mate arrived, they were distinctly grumpy. Manoeuvring the double mattress in through the door, they complained that they had left me a couple of messages updating me on their anticipated arrival time. Obviously the office had been hassling them after each of my phone calls, but no one bothered to explain to them that I can't get a signal. Feeling guilty, I gave them a twenty-pound note as a tip, which the driver took without comment. He looked miserable and wet through; they both did.

The bed frame took a while to assemble using some of Lewis' tools and all I have to do now is make up the bed. Glancing over at the window I remember the blind. If anyone comes to the door and they glance in through the window, they'll see me in bed. However, I'm past caring: all I want to do is make a sandwich in my new, makeshift kitchen in the corner of the sitting room and then snuggle up.

I thought sleep would come quickly, but my mind can't stop processing snippets of what's happened over the past two days. Thinking of Jeff makes me angry, but not because I have any love left for him. Now that I can see him for the weak and selfish man he is, I wonder why I'd chosen to ignore the signs for so long. I do have to make it very clear to both of my sons that my life has to move on. What I share with them is between us, and their father no longer has the right to be involved, as hard as that is for them to accept.

It's probably my own fault that they don't understand the impact of what happened, because I chose not to share the full extent of my hurt and humiliation with them. What point was there in making the situation any worse than it already was? I told them it was regrettable, but that "these things happen". What I should have said was that their father was a cheat, who didn't even have the decency to admit his indiscretion when I first challenged him about it. He slept with my best friend in *our* bed; all those years I'd loved and looked after him swept aside as if they counted for nothing. He didn't even respect me enough to be honest with me. Well, he made his bed and now he can enjoy lying in it – they both can.

I slip into a light sleep until a loud noise awakens me. I think it came from the kitchen. I hold my breath, listening to the eerie silence and fearful that I'll actually hear the sound again. Suddenly, the phone starts ringing and my heart nearly jumps out of my chest. I grab the torch, throw back the covers and shiver as a waft of cold, damp air hits my bare legs. I can't hear the drone of the boiler and as I run towards the phone, goose bumps cover my arms and legs.

"Yes?" In the darkness of the conservatory my mind imagines heavy breathing and a chilling voice that will strike fear into my heart.

"This is a service announcement. We apologise for the disruption to your electricity supply, but localised flooding has caused major damage to one of the sub-stations. We hope to restore the supply within four working hours and we will keep you informed of any further changes to that status. For more information press one, to hear the message again, press two. To speak to one of our service agents, press three."

What? They wake people up in the middle of the night to tell them their electricity isn't working? Is this a joke? Then it dawns on me that the landline is working – Ryan is a star.

I glance out of the window; it's pitch black and there isn't a single light to be seen. It looks as if someone has blacked out the windows, there's not even any sense of depth to the darkness – it's like a blanket. Now my teeth are chattering and I run back, jumping into bed and burying myself deep beneath the covers. It isn't just the cold that hastened my legs, but something else.

"Hello?" My voice is uneven as I call out, shattering the silence. Obviously there's no reply, only an eerie silence that feels strangely heavy. I find myself wishing that Lewis was here. As difficult a person as he is to be around, his presence makes me feel safe and protected. I pull the covers up to my chin, my teeth still chattering slightly as my body works hard to dispel the chill. At least I know why the boiler isn't working, but when the supply does come back on it means going outside to try to re-start it again.

Sleep is now the furthest thing from my mind. I switch on the torch for comfort and it helps a little to dispel the sensation of panic that has begun to rise inside me. I'm here, alone, in the dark and I definitely heard a noise. My fingers lightly brush over the torch, wondering if it's substantial enough to be used for self defence. There's no door to the former dining room, simply because the entrance is narrow and the ceiling in here is lower than the rest of the cottage. This is an extension, added on to what would probably have been a one-up, one-down, worker's cottage. If you carry on down Forge Hill you run into an area called the Lime Kilns and no doubt most of the cottages around here housed workers and their families. A large part of the quirkiness of this type of cottage is down to the differing ages of the extensions, and even the ground floor is on three different levels, each having either a step up or a step down.

I push the pillows up behind me and pull myself into a sitting position. Hoisting the duvet up around me, I shiver slightly as the warm air escapes, replaced by the cold dampness that feels moisture-laden. The phone rings again, not only breaking the silence, but shattering my nerves. This time I wrap the duvet around me as I vault out of bed. The torch falls to the floor with a loud crash, but I don't stop to pick it up.

"Yes?" I'm panting, nervous energy sapping my breath.

"This is an updated service announcement. The estimated time for your electricity supply to be restored is now six hours. We apologise for the inconvenience and the further delay. You will be advised of any further changes should this arise. We thank you for your patience. For more information press one, to hear the message again, press two. To speak to one of our service agents, press three."

Shivering and in the dark I replace the handset and a feeling of total vulnerability washes over me. I've never really been alone before. The number of nights I've slept alone in my married life I could probably count on one hand. Now here I am in what feels like the middle of nowhere, in a freezing cold, damp cottage. Suddenly a tap on the door makes my heart stop and my throat constrict.

There's someone outside, trying to peer in. I hobble over to the door, winding the duvet firmly around me in an effort to retain some of my body heat.

"Hello?" I call out, too fearful to turn the key in the lock.

"It's Terence Darby, Maddie. I've come to check on you." Terence's face looms up out of the darkness, as he presses his nose up against the glass to reassure me. I turn the key and open the door.

"Come in, come in." Just the presence of another person suddenly changes everything. In a split second whatever I felt is no longer relevant, there's nothing to fear.

"I've brought you a storm lantern. I wasn't sure if you had a torch or not. Is everything all right here? Joanna wanted to know if you'd like to come and use our guest room tonight as the power is out. I waited until the rain eased off, in case you wanted to come back with me?"

Terence turns on the lantern and hands it to me, the light cascades around the conservatory with a hearteningly warm glow.

"That's so very kind of you. I have a torch but it's not that bright. I'm fine though, really, but I do appreciate the offer. I should have thought about power cuts and prepared myself."

His smile is warm and his concern is genuine.

"Is there anything you need? It's early days and you must feel like you're camping out at the moment. We have all the mod cons, so if you have to use the shower or anything, you only need to knock. Here's our number, just in case you think of anything. Feel free to ring and I can pop round."

I'm really touched to have two neighbours who are so thoughtful and kind.

"Well, I didn't even know the landline was working until I received a call from the electricity company to say the power was off. It scared me half to death, to be truthful. I've had two calls from them already, which makes me laugh, as most people are asleep and totally unaware the power is out."

Terence chuckles and I bid him goodnight. His own lantern lights the way in the darkness as he retraces his steps.

Making my way back to bed, I lay the pillows back down and give into the tiredness that seems to be affecting every muscle in my body. I decide to leave the lantern switched on, figuring that exhaustion will take over and at least that spooky, unsettled feeling seems to have disappeared. My heart nearly stops when suddenly my phone lights up and a series of pings announce incoming text messages. They're all from Ryan, earlier in the day, just checking up on me. I start typing a quick response, but even before I can finish typing it's showing the SOS status again and the signal has gone. Unbelievable!

How long I slept I have no idea, it's still dark outside when my own voice awakens me; it's a murmur of sheer unadulterated passion. A man's arms are wrapped around me. As he works his way, tantalisingly, across my shoulder and onto my neck with the gentlest of kisses, his face comes into view. I recognise those perfect lips. Sitting bolt upright, suddenly I'm wide awake. As my eyes adjust to the light flooding out from the lantern, the image of Lewis Hart fades away into nothingness.

What I find most disturbing is that I'm left with this satisfyingly warm after-glow. Am I totally losing my mind? It's one thing to fantasize over a larger-than-life movie star, and who hasn't? But Lewis? To him I represent a pay cheque and it's more than a little humiliating to find myself getting hot at the thought of being in his arms. Most women hate to be viewed as purely sex objects and, in this instance, I think Lewis would feel exactly the same way! But that doesn't stop me smiling at the thought...

CHAPTER 15

Tap, tap. Tap, tap. I'm floating up through layers of consciousness, peeling away the covers that seem to be holding me down. Tap, tap.

My head spins around as it dawns on me that the light in the room is coming from the window. Lewis Hart is peering in at me as I lie sprawled across the bed. My first reaction is to feel my face colouring up, as last night's dream creeps into my head like a guilty confession. The second is to hug the duvet tighter around me as I climb out of bed.

Opening the door, he seems completely unfazed by the fact that I'm in a baggy old tee-shirt and he's dragged me out of bed.

"What time is it?" I stifle a yawn as I step back, so he can enter. He has a large toolbox in each hand.

"Six-thirty." His answer is abrupt and it's clear I'm not going to get a 'good morning'. "You need a blind and I've fired up the boiler for you," he throws at me and disappears into the kitchen. That low, comforting drone is back and soon the worst of the chill will disappear, to be replaced by Lewis' mood-dampener. Any thoughts about last night's little fantasy dream have already dissolved. His attitude is a real turn-off, actually. Maybe he shouldn't talk, just *do*. I stifle a giggle.

It's Sunday, I reflect, and how was I to know he was going to turn up today? He really does need to work on those communication skills, but I'm not going to be the one to pass on that little tip.

I disappear upstairs to shower and dress, wondering how on earth I'm going to be able to make eye contact with him today after last night's little episode. What, if anything, did that dream mean? Should I be concerned? Or am I over-thinking this and it's understandable he was on my mind? He's the sort of man who gets under your skin for all the wrong reasons. That thought is cheering, relief flooding through me as the hot water begins to relax my aching muscles. It was probably Jeff's unexpected visit, and everything became muddled, as dreams often do. But the thought that it might have been about Jeff worries me even more. I know I no longer have those feelings for him, as an image of him with Eve flashes through my mind.

What did I do wrong? Even as the question pops into my head, I want to slap myself. I know that I didn't do anything wrong; we fell out of love, that's all. The excitement left our relationship a long time ago, but family ties and friendship created what I regarded as a more meaningful bond. I thought that was the way it was supposed to be, but with hindsight was it really about the comfort that accompanies familiarity? Aren't all long-term relationships the same? Would he have strayed if I was a little thinner, more attentive, less caught up in the boys' lives as they grew up? Was I guilty of complacency: acceptance being more convenient than facing up to the truth of our situation?

You didn't do anything wrong, Maddie, it happens, my inner voice tries to reassure me. And you can't blame him for everything. You are no longer that vibrant, risk-taking young woman to whom everything is a potential opportunity to be grabbed. Worry, self-doubt, disappointment – all of these things have gradually, over the years, worn you down. Acceptance, I decide, is a soul-destroying word. It stands for the very opposite of what life should be all about. Taking the safe option might limit the amount of hurt you feel, but it means you are missing out on the very extremes that remind you that you are alive and not merely existing. Face it, Maddie, at this time in your life all that excitement is in the past.

You've earned the quiet life that is now yours to enjoy.

Turning off the shower and stepping out, the towel feels snug, wrapped tightly around my body. I savour the glow generated by the hot water on my skin. For the first time in two days I actually feel warm inside and out. As I round the corner to go into the bedroom and retrieve the clothes I left in a neat pile on the window sill, I unexpectedly collide with Lewis Hart's back. It's like hitting a wall, his body is rock-solid. To my horror he turns his head and stands there staring at me for a few moments, holding a spanner aloft by way of explanation for his presence. I'm conscious that the towel probably doesn't leave much to his imagination. As I recoil, the look of shock on his face probably mirrors my own. He makes a noise and my jaw drops as he looks – what? Appalled? The door to the landing cupboard, which houses the hot-water tank is open. I seem to have bumped into him as he's tightening something with that spanner of his.

"There's a leak ..."

"Sorry, I had no ..."

Our clash of words peter out, I don't know who feels more awkward. Nervous eyes meet and something tangible sparks between us. Surprise is replaced with anger that he didn't have the decency to announce he was there. Surely he could have shouted above the noise of the shower to warn me!

My legs feel weak and my stomach is doing somersaults. A frisson of excitement kicks my core into touch and I realise that he felt something, too. Was that a groan that escaped his lips? In all of the years I was with Jeff, I can never once recall ever having made him groan.

That's the trouble with human nature; the one thing that every single one of us longs to feel is desired, whether it's appropriate, or not.

"A little help here would be good." Suddenly, there's a cracking sound and the dribble of water turns into an arc. It rises high in the air and bounces off the wall opposite.

"What can I do?" Panic begins to mount in my chest and my personal predicament is pushed to the back of my mind.

"Find something to catch the water. It has to be narrow enough to wedge in here," he points to a round fitting on the side of the tank and there's only about an eight-inch gap between that and the wall. He's trying to adjust what looks like a metal collar, but water is now spraying out with such force that he can't seem to tighten it.

Grasping the towel tightly, I run downstairs and forage through some boxes until I find a plastic waste bin, then I race back, taking the stairs two at a time. Water is now running down the wall and pooling at our feet. I have to tread carefully to avoid slipping.

"Here, will this fit?"

Lewis has stopped the gush, but there's still water seeping out from below the joint. He wedges the plastic bin in tightly and straightens his back.

"Another thing that isn't working," he observes, drily. "I need to drain it anyway while I sort out the hot-water supply in the kitchen. Let's hope re-sealing that joint will do it."

"Um ... thanks. Good job."

We turn and walk off in opposite directions; my heart is pounding so loudly he must have heard it. As I start dressing, I hear the door to the conservatory slam shut. There he goes, off to take shelter in his van to get away from me for a while.

Avoiding Lewis Hart isn't going to be easy. What was I thinking? Stupid, stupid, stupid! At this point in my life I need a builder more than I need a guy who makes me go hot and cold, and weak at the knees. Of course he does all of that, without really having to try. But this is Lewis Hart, not some ordinary guy. He's not in the market for a relationship and neither am I. As tempting as he is, nothing fundamental has changed.

As a soon-to-be fifty-year-old woman, with a body, which – let's face it – looked a darn sight better at thirty than it does at fifty, I don't want any man to think of me as some sex-starved divorcee. We have to get past that awkward moment with our dignity intact. I saw a side of him that rather surprised me. Far from causing the anticipated sense of acute embarrassment, he is actually quite laid-back about it later when I walk into the kitchen, dressed and with my racing heartbeat firmly under control.

"Are we cool?" His voice has a warmth to it I haven't heard before.

"We're cool." I'm surprised to hear myself sounding rather carefree, as I respond.

I put on the kettle to make a cup of tea. As the morning rolls on, Simon arrives and the reality of living and working in what is effectively a building site, becomes a harsh reality. There's one other thing that is a bit of a revelation, too. Despite my head telling me it's utterly ridiculous, I'm attracted to Lewis on the most dangerous level possible. I'm old enough to know better and, let's face it, these are feelings I'm just not used to handling. Is there a wanton side of me that could throw caution to the wind to enjoy a little unbridled passion with no strings attached? That's the trouble with knowing yourself only too well. My conscience looms up inside me. It's refusing to be ignored and won't allow me to let go of a lifetime spent trying to do the 'right' thing. Sadly, I know I would just end up feeling used and disappointed in myself afterwards. Damn it! I'm vulnerable and now I know that, I'm going to have to be very, very careful. If Lewis is the sort of man to take advantage of a woman, then I'm probably giving off all the right signals without even knowing it. That thought leaves me wondering what the heck is wrong with me, that I'm terrified at the thought of simply 'letting go'. Sometimes facing up to who you are isn't easy. I've become this reserved and cautious woman who is too scared to drop her guard and have some fun. The problem is that there are moments when I'm pretty sure Lewis is feeling that connection, too. If it's just lust, I'd still be flattered, but if it's pity… now that's another thing entirely.

LEWIS

CHAPTER 16

I know I don't spend much time in the company of women these days, other than in a work situation, but this woman is like no one else I have ever met. You don't know where you are with her from one moment to the next. She veers from being friendly and trying to get me to talk, to jumping every time I walk past her. Sometimes she gets under my feet and I just want to tell her to go away and let me get on with the job. Then she disappears and when I do need her input, I sense a kind of standoffish attitude. As if she thinks every problem is something I'm creating on purpose just to annoy her.

My mobile kicks into life and it's Pete, an old army buddy, who moved here a few years ago.

"How's it going, mate? I wondered if you were up for a festive night out with the lads?"

It's so tempting; it's been a while.

"I can't. I'm on this job and it's a tight turnaround with Christmas looming."

"Lewis, my man, we were banking on you joining the party. You sound like you need to let off a little steam."

"Yeah, well, that might be the case, but I have the client from hell. I'm not used to having the home owner around on a job that requires this much demolition and renovation. It shows what a stubborn and foolish woman she is to think she can live here without some of the most basic facilities. It's the middle of winter, for goodness' sake."

"Then walk away from it for a few hours. All work and no play, you know what they say."

"It's the morning after that wouldn't work for me, as I have to really motor on this one. I need to get it done and get out of here."

"Sounds bad. Is there something else you're not telling me? I'm guessing this is a single lady, by the sound of it. Is she coming on to you?"

"Not intentionally. She's not that sort. But take today, for instance. She boldly walked out of the shower room wearing nothing more than a stupid towel, without checking it was all clear. I had my head in the cupboard, trying to loosen a valve that was refusing to budge and as I straightened up, we collided. She almost jumped out of her skin, as if I was some sort of predator lying in wait. She knew there was a virtual stranger in the house – where's her common sense? It's hardly my fault she won't do the sensible thing and take herself off to a B and B for a week or two."

"Be careful there, mate. This is getting to you, isn't it?"

He's right and he knows that usually I'm more than capable of handling any situation, so there has to be a little more to it than I'm willing to share.

"She's not my type; too intense and difficult to read."

"I'll leave you to it, then. Maybe we'll catch up in the New Year."

"Sounds good."

I catch his laughter moments before the line disconnects. This situation is anything *but* funny. From what I saw today, Miss Madeleine Brooks has a great body and she's not the sort of woman who calorie-counts. She's cuddly in all of the right places, but seems to have no idea how sexy she is. I can't stand complicated women like her who over-think every little thing. They are hard work to be around and I have to watch out that I don't get caught up in anything.

When my arm touched her skin, the warmth sent a ripple of

desire through me that rooted me to the spot. Then I came to my senses and realised this was a customer, and a difficult one, at that. I made an excuse and took myself off to the van for a breather while she dressed. It's the only place I feel I can sit for a quiet moment and relax. Terence was on his way out and stopped for a chat.

"You look harassed," he commented, frowning at me. "Problems?"

"Plumbing and wiring. Nothing is in the right place for the new layout and I'm not a magician. I can only do the best I can, especially with the deadline she's given me."

"Oh, sorry to hear it's like that. But then it is a big job. How, um, are you getting on with Maddie?"

This might be paranoia, but it strikes me it's a rather odd question for Terence to ask. I wonder if the delightful Miss Brooks has been talking about me.

"I'm trying to keep the social chatter to the minimum, to be honest, Terence. It's unlikely we have anything in common other than Ash Cottage. I need to get this job finished as quickly as I can and move on. I realise now I should just have said 'no', but I needed something to really get my teeth into. First Aggie and then my mother; it's a lot to get my head around at the moment. Losing people you care about leaves a hole and it's a reminder nothing lasts forever. At least redesigning the plumbing for the new kitchen layout Miss Brooks is insisting upon, requires complete concentration and all of my problem-solving skills. What she doesn't seem to understand is that while it isn't easy to move the cold supply from one wall to another, it's do-able. But it's virtually impossible to move the drainage unless you start digging up concrete floors."

That came out in a rush and Terence looks rather surprised.

"Well, keeping occupied is good, but maybe you need to explain the nature of the problems to her. If it doesn't mean very much to me, it will probably mean even less to her. I'm not being sexist, but I doubt she's ever really given it any thought."

I nod. He might have a point there. However, I'm the plumber and it's not a part of my job to educate her. Terence means well, but she isn't some young, naïve lady who hasn't owned a house before. Maybe her problem is that she's just a control freak and if that's the case, then sorry, lady, but you've picked the wrong man.

MADDIE

CHAPTER 17

The phone isn't working again this morning and I have to do *the walk* to ask Ryan if he can ring his contact and see if they can send out an engineer.

When we speak he's concerned that the heavy rain has continued and the number of flood warnings being issued each day is growing. It means that this isn't a little problem that is going to go away soon. So many houses are now completely cut-off – little communities stranded and acre upon acre of fields disappearing under ever-growing lakes that seem to stretch out endlessly.

Walking back to the cottage I pass Terence, who tells me that down on the lower road it's now restricted to one lane as a team endeavours to clear out the culvert. Apparently, the local paper indicated it's likely that the only solution is to rebuild the area that has collapsed. The pumps are working around the clock to keep the water level as low as possible. Driving through the swirling, muddy water, he says it comes halfway up the wheels of a car and even at low-speed it's hard not to create a series of waves that seems to drag even more soil from the quickly eroding bank. Thankfully all of the properties along the route are now well sand-bagged and beginning to dry out. The sheer misery this has caused is heart-breaking and I realise just how lucky we are, high up here on the hill.

Inside the cottage things are progressing, although I'm keeping well away from Lewis. With the newly-plastered wall in the main bedroom drying out nicely now the heating is back on, Simon told me to open the windows an inch or two, to stop it drying out too quickly and cracking. Lewis is now working on the kitchen floor. He has laid a levelling compound, so the downstairs bathroom is out of action today. I have to say that it's a little bit awkward knowing that every time either of us visits the upstairs bathroom it's a reminder of our little mishap.

The rain eases off mid-morning and as I put the final coat of paint on the dining room window sill, Lewis walks past with a dirty trowel and a bucket. He disappears, returning a few minutes later after visiting the outside tap. I look up once more and the merest hint of a smile passes between us.

"You have another problem," he calls out as he walks back into the conservatory.

I thought it was too good to be true to anticipate a whole day without something going wrong.

"You'd better come and take a look at this."

I put down the paint brush and follow him outside. The sky is still a mass of ominously grey cloud, but for the moment the rain has stopped. I notice that the paving stones leading around to the terrace in front of the conservatory now have a pale-green hue. The algae make the surface extremely slippery underfoot. As if reading my mind, Lewis extends his arm.

"Careful, mind you don't slip."

The contact is purposeful and I'm relieved that his motive is genuine. This isn't touching just for the sake of it.

"Thanks. What exactly are we looking at?"

He nods his head in the direction of two, rather large, Calor gas bottles that stand tucked away in the corner, to the right of the kitchen window. Above one of the bottles, which are chained to the wall, is a mass of something.

"What is it?" I ask, moving closer to get a better look.

"Squirrels have chewed through the pipe. It means that when

the new range arrives today, only the electric oven will work until it can be replaced; might be best to consider a reinforced one next time."

"They chew pipe? What on earth is the point of that?"

As Lewis begins to explain that squirrels will chew absolutely anything, the sound of Ryan's voice makes me look up.

Lewis spins his head around, following my gaze.

"Ryan, what a surprise, you didn't mention you were going to call in. This is Lewis Hart, my contractor. Lewis, this is my boss, Ryan Fielding."

Ryan steps forward and they shake hands, weighing each other up as men have a tendency to do.

"I just wanted to see the extent of the flooding for myself and check that you were okay. Is the phone line still down? I've booked an engineer anyway, but apparently some lines were affected for a while overnight. I couldn't try ringing you on it as I don't have your new number. When you gave them permission to talk to me to sort out your installation, apparently that didn't extend to them divulging your new number. Data protection is seriously getting out of hand these days.

"Oh, I see you have a problem with squirrels. Better watch out if you leave any windows open, the little blighters can do a lot of damage."

Lewis nods in agreement and heads off back inside.

"How's it working out?" Ryan asks, as soon as Lewis is out of earshot.

"Good. The kitchen has been stripped out and the white goods will hopefully arrive later on today. When the actual units arrive tomorrow, Lewis has said he will make sure I have a working sink and at least one fitted cupboard with a worktop before he finishes on Christmas Eve. The main bedroom has already been re-plastered and Simon did a good job of making good after Lewis chipped off those dated wall tiles in the kitchen. We're on target. Come and take a look."

The kitchen now looks slightly less hideous, with flat, clean walls and the dark-grey levelling compound on the floor is already starting to lighten as it dries. Lewis is in the conservatory sorting out a pile of timber that was delivered first thing. He's going to start work on the framing for the fridge and freezer until the floor is safe to walk on, in about three hours. The walnut flooring also arrived yesterday and that was a relief. Most of it won't be laid until the New Year, but Lewis has to lay the boards in the kitchen area before the units can be fitted.

Ryan seems genuinely surprised at the progress. The former dining room is now white and bright, a little oasis from the chaos of the rest of the cottage.

"You're starting to feel at home here, but you really do need a blind up to this window, Maddie. A woman alone, in an out-of-the-way location like this! There are some weird people about."

"Stop worrying. It's in the garage. I just haven't had time to put it up yet."

"I'll unpack the modem so you can plug it in once the line is up and working again. You find that blind and ask Lewis if I can borrow his drill. That's an order, not a request."

This is so out of character for Ryan that I find myself puzzling over his behaviour as I walk away. Is he really concerned that I'm at risk, and if so, should I be worried, too? Lewis has also made a couple of comments about the blind, but then it's in his line of work. However, I can't recall Ryan ever getting involved in do-it-yourself. I didn't even know he knew how to use a drill!

By the time I've located the blind, taken it out of the wrappings and walked back to the cottage, Ryan already has the modem unwrapped and plugged in. There are no lights flickering, so obviously the line still isn't working. I fetch a box with my laptop and printer and put it down on the corner of the coffee table, leaving Ryan to sort out the leads.

"I'll keep chasing for that engineer's visit, Maddie. I'll feel better once I know you are more easily contactable."

I saunter off in search of The Man Who Can.

"Lewis, are you using your drill? Ryan has offered to put the blind up for me in the temporary bedroom."

Lewis finishes marking up a piece of timber, running a pencil line against the spirit level, which is wedged beneath his knee.

"No need, I'll put it up before I go."

Immediately his head is back down and he's marking off another measurement.

"Um ... great. Thanks."

Is this an awkward moment we're having here? Are men protective of their tools – really? Ryan's reaction surprises me even more.

"That's ridiculous. It would take me ten minutes tops. What's wrong with the guy? It's not like I'm taking work away from him. He already has his hands full."

I'm not sure who, out of the two of them, is acting more ridiculously.

When Ryan leaves for home, my laptop work station is all set up awaiting the internet connection. He scowls as he passes the window, which is still blind-less. Walking alongside him, I sense his annoyance.

"If you have any concerns at all, no matter what time of the day, or night, I want you to head up that hill and ring me, right? I'll come straight over. Remember, it takes a long time to really get to know someone. And even then, they can surprise you when you least expect it. Besides, I'm not happy for you to spend your birthday here, Maddie, if I'm honest. I'm sure your sons would feel the same way if they knew."

"Don't fuss. It's one birthday and one Christmas – next year will be amazing."

Why is he suddenly so worried? We have our customary hug before he climbs into the car, then he plants a kiss on my cheek. I feel myself colouring-up.

As he reverses out onto the hill, there's a frown on his face, which disappears behind a smile when he finally raises his hand in a wave. I thought he'd be pleased to see the progress, but maybe I'm fooling myself and he thinks things should be moving along faster.

Walking back down the path I feel a little deflated. Ryan usually cheers me up. He's been a tower of strength and he's the only person in whom I feel I can confide. A cold sensation begins to fester in the pit of my stomach.

Ryan is my boss and a good friend; would he feel slighted if he felt there was something I didn't think was his business to know? And what about the kiss?

Lewis looks up as I close the door behind me.

"So, he's your boss?"

I raise my eyebrows, in sheer frustration. Not you, too, Lewis. If there's going to be any muscle-flexing around here, you'd both better do it when you're off my property. No one owns me, I'm a free woman and I no longer have to spend my time keeping men happy, or explaining myself. Whether that's ex-husbands, sons, hired help or bosses. This woman is doing it for herself!

CHAPTER 18

I try my best not to become increasingly paranoid about the remaining deliveries. The fridge, freezer, cooker and washing machine are all due to arrive sometime today from The Appliance Store and at least Ryan is proof that the main road is still passable. The postman, who doesn't appear until late-morning, explains that a number of smaller roads through the Forest have experienced subsidence problems and the weight limits have been restricted. One by one, the routes through to our little part of the world seem to be ruled out and I'm keeping my fingers crossed that they don't have to shut the main road.

With Christmas just three days away, I've also placed a large order to stock up the new fridge and freezer. That will be one more worry off my mind and another big item ticked off the to-do list if that, too, arrives today. At least I won't have to worry about food until the end of January, at the very earliest. Plus I'm already fed up with eating sandwiches.

Lewis pops out to pick up a new pipe to replace the one the squirrels chewed up and to collect some fittings he's ordered, ready to install the new range cooker. Earlier in the morning he'd looked quite serious when he was sitting cross-legged on the floor making his list.

Of course, deliveries are great but every time something is delivered it presents a problem. The cottage is small and Lewis needs room in which to work. I was a little dismayed when the flooring arrived yesterday, as the huge mountain of boxes and rolls of foam underlay now mean my temporary kitchen is reduced to a very tight corner. But it feels good to know it's here and it's one thing less to worry about. Plus the new white goods will at least be in situ and working by the end of the day, and I'm excited about that. It will be a big step forward.

There's a knock on the door just as I'm about to put on the kettle and have a break from sanding the stair spindles. I'm surprised to see Sarah from the estate agents standing outside with a box in her hands, trying her best to shield it from the rain.

"I come bearing gifts," she laughs. "No, not really, but I think this will be of interest to you."

"Great, come in. I was just about to make a cup of tea. Do you have time to join me?"

She nods and I notice that she isn't wearing her usual suit, but she's casually dressed in black jeans, beneath her soggy top coat.

"It's my day off. I've been to visit a friend who lives about ten minutes' drive away. You won't believe what I've had to drive through!"

I stare at the package in her arms; it's about the size of two shoe boxes and has a faded pattern on the outside. It looks old and rather fragile.

"The company who did the house clearance auctioned off a lot of the furniture. Obviously whoever emptied out the personal contents of the house missed this. It was in a dressing-table drawer. The relatives didn't want it and it looks like it's full of receipts and stuff to do with the house. The auctioneers asked me to pass it on to you. I thought you might want to go through it, in case it solves the mystery of the land at the back. You never know, the answer might be right here." She places the box down on one of the folding chairs and then slips off her coat.

"Thanks, that's thoughtful. Spread your coat out over that chair, it might dry off a little. I did think it was strange there weren't many documents with the deeds. People of that era kept absolutely everything. Unlike today, when it's all electronic, in bygone years at least snail mail left a physical record. Goodness, even I can't find things on my laptop, let alone anyone else carrying out a search. I guess in this wonderful age of technology and communication overload, a lot is going to get lost in the future."

Sarah chuckles as I hand her a mug of steaming tea.

"This already feels like a different place," she comments, looking through into the former dining room.

"I'll give you the tour – not that there's much more than basic building work being done at the moment. It's more about ripping it apart and making good the walls. My temporary bedroom is cosy, though, come on through."

Seeing it through Sarah's eyes, it does look inviting. The white room feels more spacious than the size would give credit for, and with the blind and matching bedding in a zingy white with over-sized green and pale-yellow leaves, it feels very country with a contemporary vibe.

"Wow, I wasn't expecting this. At least it's a little sanctuary while the work is going on around you. That low ceiling certainly works to give it a cosy feeling now there's some furniture in here."

We walk through to the kitchen and Sarah does a double-take.

"Goodness, for a tiny kitchen, now it's stripped out it looks twice the size. What colour units are you putting back in?"

"Here's the 3D plan," I pull a few sheets of paper out of Lewis' tool box. "Sorry about the dirt and dust, it's not the best filing cabinet."

I smirk and she laughs.

"How's it working out? He seems to have done a lot in a short space of time."

This is my chance to ask a few questions, but I don't want Sarah to feel I'm quizzing her. Ignoring any hint of a dilemma, I say the first thing that pops into my head.

"Great. I've never known a tradesman work Saturdays and

Sundays without having to twist their arms. I get the impression he's not from around here, which was a surprise."

Sarah sips her tea then frowns slightly.

"He isn't, although he's looking to settle in the Forest at some point. I don't think it's a secret that he's looking to buy something to do up."

"Oh. Why didn't he make an offer on Ash Cottage? I would have thought it would have been a perfect project for him."

She nods, taking another sip.

"In strictest confidence, he was going to. I had a message on my desk to call him urgently when I arrived back in the office after your viewing. If he'd phoned through on my mobile, as my colleague suggested, he might just have beaten you to it. He wasn't here when the *For Sale* sign went up, his mother died unexpectedly and he had to go back home for a couple of weeks to sort out the funeral. A case of unfortunate timing, I'm afraid."

That's awkward and sort of confirms my suspicions. I don't know what to think now about the fact that he's bending over backwards to help with a renovation that could have been his own.

"He must have felt gutted to come back and find he'd missed out on Ash Cottage. I feel sad knowing that."

Sarah hastens to reassure me. "He will have been grateful to have a job to keep his mind occupied, no doubt. I don't know how close he was to his mum, but a death brings out all sorts of emotions – especially at this time of the year. He's on our mailing list and something else will come up before too long. In his line of work he'll no doubt hear on the local grapevine if someone's thinking of selling, so he'll be one step ahead. It's a small community here. This case was complicated because of the number of beneficiaries involved. Everything took a little longer than expected to set up."

"I'm glad I asked. I'd hate to say anything to upset him in any way. His mother's death must have been tough to deal with. He isn't the sort of man who finds it easy dealing with emotion, is he?"

I wasn't expecting Sarah to respond to that, I was simply voicing my thoughts.

"I think he's lonely, to be honest. I don't know why as he's made a few hearts pound among the single females and widows around here. I know Joanna next door is one of his biggest fans. The gossip-mongers are watching his every move." She laughs, raising her eyebrows at me, knowingly.

I feel the heat rising up from my neck, gulp down the last of my tea and muster up a laugh that sounds suitable dismissive. A cough alerts us to the fact that Lewis Hart is standing in the doorway and the fact that he's soaking wet might not be the only reason why he looks like thunder.

"Well, maybe the gossip-mongers need to mind their own business," he scowls and I'm surprised that his tone isn't quite as angry as I feared. Sarah gives Lewis a melting smile.

"Oh, Lewis – you know what it's like in the Forest. Everyone knows everybody's business. It's a pastime. You aren't a local if someone, somewhere isn't talking about you."

He smiles back at her and I wonder if there's something going on between them. The look of thunder disappears without a trace.

"Well, you can start a new thread of gossip. After I've finished helping out Madeleine, here, I'll be disappearing for a while. My mother's house will need a lot of work doing to it before it goes on the market."

Sarah looks disappointed and I try my best not to follow suit.

"You'd better keep your fingers crossed," he glances in my direction. "That water level is rising faster than the pumps can shift it. What time are those deliveries coming today?"

"They couldn't give a time for the white goods, only that it would be after twelve o'clock and I've booked the groceries for early this evening."

He shrugs off his jacket, throwing it in the corner. "I need you ladies to move into the conservatory to continue gossiping, I have to finish off the framing for the fridge and freezer, now that the floor appears to be dry." He looks down at our feet, checking we

118

haven't done any damage.

We exit quickly and it feels as if we've just been told off. He's right, of course, we shouldn't have been walking on that floor and we definitely should *not* have been talking about him.

As Sarah pulls on her coat, I notice she's wearing a wedding ring, so maybe that wasn't a look of interest that passed between them. Unless she's stuck in an unhappy marriage as I was, only I didn't appreciate that fact at the time.

As she leaves, she looks at me with concern on her face and leans in to whisper something.

"It's none of my business, but Lewis likes you, I can tell. He's abrasive, but sometimes it's a way for someone to hide their feelings. Don't let that put you off."

As she straightens up and steps outside, I nod my head in thanks.

"Hope you find some useful documents in that box," she adds, raising her voice slightly. No doubt keen to let Lewis know the purpose for her visit wasn't just to share a little gossip.

I turn around, considering how to apologise to Lewis and he's standing there, in the kitchen doorway, staring at me.

"Documents?" For starters it's unusual for anything to pull him away from his work. The other mystifying factor is that very little of what goes on around him seems to spark his interest.

"The box. Apparently it was in one of the drawers when the house clearance people took the furniture away. They contacted Sarah, who asked the bank if any of the relatives wanted it. They said no, so she thought I might want to go through it in case there were any documents to do with the house."

He looks rather shocked; his face starts to redden, as if he's angry.

"Well, I'm not sure I'd want a total stranger going through my personal effects."

He looks directly at me, as if he's challenging me.

"I don't regard myself as being a total stranger, Lewis. I live in Aggie's cottage now and that gives us a real link. Her memories

119

are between these walls and always will be. I'll be adding my own to those. We're all caretakers in this life, Lewis. We can think we own brick and mortar, but we are merely passing through."

His jaw is set at a stubborn angle. I think he was expecting an argument and my answer surprised him.

"You believe in all that stuff?"

"Some of it. I've felt her here; it's subtle, but I talk to her to reassure her that we will put Ash Cottage back together and it will look lovely."

I wonder if he's going to laugh or mock me. Instead he raises his hand to rest his chin between his index finger and his thumb, his elbow leaning on the arm wrapped around his waist. He looks rather like a Greek statue. I almost laugh, but restrain myself, as now is not a moment for hilarity. It's a classic thinking pose, although the body language suggests he's not comfortable with something. Maybe it's the topic of conversation or maybe it's being around me.

"It's still an invasion of a person's privacy. I suggest you are mindful of that." He turns and walks back into the kitchen.

I simply cannot understand this man who acts like a bear but has a side to him that is almost an unbelievable contrast. He's complicated, that's for sure. It makes me wonder what has happened in his life that he finds himself alone, putting up barriers and living far away from friends and family. It sounds as if warning bells should be ringing, but the reality is that I feel very safe when he's around.

CHAPTER 19

The day continues to go downhill. I climb the hill to talk to Ryan to see if there's any news about the house phone and check if there are any messages about the imminent delivery. Ryan hasn't heard anything, but I see there's one message. It's from Sarah to say that a wall has collapsed and the top road is now impassable. It took her over an hour to get back home, though, as down on the main road the fire brigade has brought in extra pumping equipment. They are only letting a few cars through at a time, now. I walk back down the hill feeling miserable and damp, wondering what else can possibly go wrong.

Lewis has hardly said a word since Sarah left and I don't like to disturb him. I decide to take him in a cup of coffee and if he looks as if he's approachable, I'll pass on the news. It doesn't work and when I put the mug of coffee down for him, he nods in the direction of the window sill, dismissing me without a word.

Walking back into the conservatory, there's movement outside and a bedraggled man with sack trucks and a pile of crates is approaching the door. Oh great, the food has arrived, but the white goods still aren't here. I hadn't realised it was five o'clock already – and that doesn't bode well. Food without a freezer is a disaster.

"Hi, um ... I have a slight problem. Can you hang on a moment while I find a key to the store room outside?"

I grab my coat, woolly hat and the keys, as the poor guy struggles to turn around and follow me, the driving rain making everything much harder.

We stack the contents, most of which has been bagged-up, in the corner and he ventures out for another load. I root around in my pocket for a tip. I have three pound coins and that's all, but it's better than nothing. Once the second lot of crates are empty he accepts the coins with a grateful smile.

"How's the road? Are they winning?"

"It's breached some of the sand-bag defences, so they've called in some more volunteers to help out. They are still letting traffic through at the moment, but it's slow going."

"Well, I hope your deliveries are finished soon."

He gives me a look that indicates that's unlikely.

"The van is full," he says, dourly. "No one wants to go out in this and people are beginning to stock up, expecting the worst." Shoulders slumped, he turns his sack trucks three hundred and sixty degrees and disappears into the wet, murky darkness.

Where is this lorry? I now have almost two hundred pounds worth of food, half of which needs to go into a freezer within the next couple of hours or it will spoil. It's rather like a cold store in here, but it's only going to delay defrosting, not stop it.

"Was that the food?" Lewis calls out, as I rush back into the conservatory.

"Yes, it's in the store room. I'm going to ring the delivery company. I can't even contemplate the freezer not arriving ..."

It's too windy for an umbrella as I climb the hill, so I pull my hat down even further and trudge along miserably. They reassure me that all of my goods were loaded this morning and the lorry will make the delivery. He's keen to clarify whether the lane is large enough for the lorry to get through and there's enough room for it to reverse onto the drive. Why leave this sort of thing to the last minute, I wonder, although I'm pleased that at least he's in contact with the driver. He suggests that I wait another twenty minutes and then go out to wave them down in case there's any

122

chance they'll miss the sign in the dark. It occurs to me that what they should have done is made my delivery the first one of the day – not the last.

By the time they arrive I'm soaked to the skin. Even sheltering with my back against the garage door, I have to keep popping my head out every time I hear a vehicle. Three cars go by and each time just that few seconds of exposure and the rain seems to seep into every little crevice. Then a large white apparition looms up and I run out, frantically waving my hands.

To say they aren't the most cheerful of delivery guys is an understatement, but they have due cause. Not only do they have a lot of appliances to deliver, the path down to the cottage is rather steep, even if it is flat. However, it winds back on itself, which effectively doubles the walking distance.

They take the large, larder fridge down to the conservatory and then wheel the freezer across to the stone store room, as directed.

"I hope that pile of food isn't for the fridge or freezer, Miss," the driver's mate nods in the direction of the stack of plastic carrier bags. "You have to allow at least six hours before you turn them on, to let the coolant settle."

He leaves me standing there, open-mouthed. He's kidding, surely? If he isn't, then why didn't I know that? I poke a hole in the plastic covering of the freezer to fish out the instruction manual, which is taped to the side, and hurry back to the cottage with it.

I can't even watch them when they begin to manoeuvre the range cooker down the slope on a wheeled dolly. There's a six-inch step inside the entrance to the conservatory, so they have to put straps underneath it and, with Lewis' help, they lower it onto the tiled floor. I paid for the unpacking and assembly service for the range, simply because it looked as if it was going to be complicated. As they begin unpacking it I make a well-deserved round of tea. Everyone except Lewis is damp and cold. When I walk back in with the tray I can't believe what I'm seeing.

"That's not the one I ordered. It's the wrong colour!"

All three guys turn to look at me. The lorry driver and his mate seem to think I'm joking.

"That's forest green and I checked several times that this wouldn't happen. The one I ordered is olive green. I'm really sorry, guys, but I simply can't accept it!"

Lewis turns on his heels and disappears into the kitchen. The two guys take their tea in silence. It's an awkward moment as they stare at me, unable to comprehend what I'm saying.

"If it was black I'd probably accept it, but I hate forest green and I wouldn't have that colour if they were giving it away. It was the colour of my school uniform when I was at school, you see, and ..." There I go, justifying myself when I've already told them it's not acceptable.

"So what does olive green look like?" The driver is scowling at me as his mate begins a conversation I can only assume is going to be aimed at trying to get me to change my mind.

"It's a soft green, a cream, really, with a hint of green. I've based the whole colour scheme of the cottage around it. That's why it's more expensive than the other colours and why I checked and double-checked the order code. I'll show you."

I pull a notepad out of my bag and leaf through until I find the page with the order details. I hand it across so they can check it against the code on their clipboard.

"Yep, yours is a different code. But we have the right cooker for the code we have on our delivery sheet."

I'm still panicking about the frozen-food problem and this guy has the audacity to imply that I ordered the wrong one?

"I have an order confirmation here somewhere that lists the code on that notepad. You'll have to take it back."

Two sets of eyes peer at me as if I've lost my mind.

"Well," the driver throws in, "we're not allowed to take anything back without the consent of the office."

"Then you'd better give them a call. Mobiles don't work here," I add, guiltily. "You'll have to walk up the hill to get a signal."

He looks at his mate and rolls his eyes, grabbing the clipboard from him rather roughly and heading out. After a long twenty minutes spent in total silence, he returns.

"They need your authorisation," his tone is curt. "You'd best follow me back up to the top."

I'm still damp from earlier on and longing to get out of these clothes and under the shower. Reluctantly, I pull on my coat yet again. The walk seems to get longer every time.

"Hello?"

"Good evening, Miss Brooks. It seems you aren't happy with the forest green range that has been delivered this evening?"

"That's right and that's because I ordered olive green. I obtained the code from the manufacturer and I phoned twice to confirm that you had it in stock. On both occasions I was told that, yes, there was one in stock and it had been reserved for me."

"One moment while I check your records."

Food spoiling, food spoiling ....

"Ah, yes, you're right. The problem is that we don't have an olive green range in stock and it will take up to sixteen weeks to get one from the manufacturers because they are built to order. It's not a standard colour."

"I know that, that's why I was so particular about the code when I ordered it. I understand forest green is a stock item and if I'd wanted that colour I could have bought it elsewhere at least a hundred and fifty pounds cheaper. I ordered from you because your organisation said they had one olive green range in stock."

A trickle of water runs off my collar and down my back, under my tee-shirt.

"So you aren't happy to accept delivery of the forest green range?"

"No and please cancel my order. I'm really annoyed about this, as it has wasted six whole weeks and now I won't have any cooking facilities over the Christmas and New Year period. I've been misled and I certainly won't be recommending your company to anyone in the future."

I pass the handset back to the driver, who listens and makes a few grunting sounds.

"We have to pack it back up and lift it up over that step again," he informs me, scowling again.

I'm so mad that I have to walk on ahead. It's not fair that I should be made to feel guilty when none of this is my fault. I wonder how often they do this and get away with it.

Returning to the cottage, I leave the two men to re-pack the cooker and seek out Lewis.

"I have a problem."

I hoped that he would dismiss the 'letting the coolant settle' comment and say that of course the fridge and freezer can be switched on immediately. That will still leave a couple of hours for them to get to the required temperature before I have to really worry about the condition of the food. It is freezing out there today.

"I think you'll find they're right. Check the instructions."

"Why on earth didn't you think to mention that?"

Lewis looks at me, puzzled.

"I never interfere. You're a fearsome lady when someone upsets you, do you know that?"

He turns back to what he's doing and I'm left feeling exasperated and rather like a fool. Think, Maddie, think.

"So," the driver levels at me, "are you keeping the rest of the delivery?"

I pull my woolly hat back down over my ears and, still dripping, walk up to him. He takes one step back.

"If you need my signature I suggest you get it now. I'm off to visit my neighbour."

He marks 'x' in a couple of boxes on the sheet and thrusts the board and a pen under my nose. I duly sign and head back out into the cold, damp night.

"Terence, I'm really sorry to bother you, but I have a big problem and I don't know what I'm going to do."

"Come in dear lady. Joanna, we have a visitor."

So far I've only waved at Joanna in passing, usually when she accompanies Terence on one of his walks, and I've spotted them from the conservatory as they turn to venture down Forge Hill. I'm careful to remain standing on the coir matting just inside the door, mindful that I'm in danger of creating a puddle.

"Nice to meet you, Madeleine. It's a pretty name and a shame to shorten it. Goodness, we're beginning to think you're a jinx! It hasn't stopped raining since you moved in."

We shake hands and I have the distinct feeling that Joanna doesn't approve of me for some reason. Terence seems oblivious, though, as I find myself starting to squirm a little.

"How can we help?" Her voice implies that I must want something, and I do, but her reception is so cold it makes me hesitate.

"I'm ... um ... well."

Whenever I've spent time talking to Terence he's so warm and welcoming that this is one surprise I didn't expect. What an odd couple, to say the very least. Like hot and cold ...

"Yes?" Joanna peers at me, suspiciously.

"Well, the truth is that I have to wait until morning to be able to use the new fridge and freezer. As I've had a large shop delivered to tide me over until the end of January, I wondered if you had any suggestions. I'm desperate and maybe there's a local farmer you know who might have freezer space ... or something."

Terence immediately jumps in.

"That's not a problem. We have several freezers in the outhouses. You have to stock up for winter when you live in the Forest. I'll grab my coat and we'll see what we can fit in."

"As I said, nice to meet you Madeleine." Joanna turns and walks out of the room without another word. I feel as if I've been dismissed.

Terence is back within moments, looking like someone who has just stepped off a fishing boat. But I think that's more to do with his grey beard.

"Come on, Maddie, before that food spoils."

Terence reorganises the freezers while I go back down to begin carrying up the bags. I notice that Lewis has unpacked the freezer and has moved it back into the corner. The lorry has already left and I realise that I totally forgot to give them a tip. I feel guilty, but I'm past caring about niceties now. I'm tired, wet and hungry; my back is aching and I have a niggling headache that keeps giving out a stabbing pain over one eye.

With a flourish my lovely neighbour fits in the last item, a packet of croissants, and closes the lid. I feel grateful, but very, very awkward. I had the distinct impression that Joanna doesn't like me and I hope she doesn't give Terence a hard time for coming to the rescue.

"Terence, thank you so, so much. I really appreciate this. It was stupid of me not to realise I couldn't just unpack the freezer and switch it on. Goodness, I didn't even give thought to allowing time for it to reach the right temperature! I'm afraid all of this has been such a learning curve."

"Hey, what are neighbours for? It's not a problem and you can leave it here until you are ready. If it's pouring tomorrow don't rush around first thing. In fact, leave it to me. In between showers I'll bring the carrier bags down to you."

"The forecast for tomorrow is the same, then?"

He shakes his head, looking worried.

"It's the worst I've ever known it in nearly thirty years. I think you did the wise thing stocking up now, Maddie. If we think we've had it bad, parts of Tawkesbury have been cut off for a couple of weeks now. The only way in and out is by boat."

"We're lucky up here, Terence. And thank you, this is really appreciated. Say thanks to Joanna, too, for me."

He looks at me with smiling eyes.

"Her bark is worse than her bite, you'll get used to her. She's also a bit annoyed, as she wanted Lewis to paint her study before Christmas and he wasn't available. Seems he had another job on."

Terence smiles and gives me a wink.

"Oh, I'm sorry. I didn't realise he'd been quite so accommodating ..." I should have realised he didn't have a completely free diary.

"Joanna will get over it; she's also not feeling very well at the moment. I hope she doesn't come down with something this close to Christmas."

He raises his eyebrows, acceptance written all over his face. I can't help thinking that this man is used to putting up with quite a lot of hassle from a wife who seems to be unduly demanding at times.

CHAPTER 20

When I walk back into the conservatory, Lewis has already moved the larder fridge into the kitchen and it's sitting neatly inside the frame he's built. The only thing left to unpack is the washing machine.

"Thanks for sorting that. It's getting late. You must be tired and hungry. I can't offer anything hot unless I use the microwave," I stare at the blank space where I thought the range would now be in situ. "How about I order a takeaway?"

He straightens, turning his head from left to right until something clicks, ominously, and our eyes meet. It's a curious moment, as if he's giving it a great deal of thought. It's a takeaway, not an invitation to move in. Or am I, unwittingly, giving out unknown signals that turn this into a yes/no decision for him. The thought sends a flush of warmth up through my core; this is stupid and I have to stop looking for signs that he's interested in me.

"The Indian down in the village is good. Do you have the number?"

I want to laugh at myself, because obviously he is in the mood, but clearly it's for a curry.

"It's in my notebook," I begin walking away to make the call, "I'm the woman who likes to be organised, remember?"

The trudge back up the hill isn't much fun. Within ten minutes I'm back in the kitchen and Lewis looks up, then immediately stops what he's doing when he notices my expression.

"What's up?"

"They've shut the main road. Nothing can get in, or out."

"No problem. Microwave food isn't the best, but at least it will be hot. I'll shoot off straight after though and use the top road."

I feel the colour rising in my cheeks. "Um ... the top road isn't open, either. Sarah mentioned a wall has collapsed, or something, and it's going to take a few days to clear it."

He narrows his eyes and his forehead wrinkles up in a frown. "When did she mention that?"

"She left a message. I should have said something, but I had no idea they would shut the main road, too. I mean, we're stranded. Can they do that?" The note of disbelief in my voice is very real.

"Guess you weren't to know. Last year the road was closed for a while, but the water rose quickly and it was mainly the debris left behind that delayed re-opening it. But the rain didn't last very long – it wasn't anything like this."

We're in the conservatory now, looking out into the darkness. Without the lights on, the only clue to the bad weather are the trees, which are frantically swaying back and forth as the wind picks up.

"Tinned stew and new potatoes?" He looks at me soberly, as it dawns on us that he's going to be a house guest. I'll have to be careful I don't get a reputation. Lewis will be the second guy I've had sleeping over since I moved in.

"Sounds interesting." He turns and begins packing away his tools.

We sit in the conservatory on the not-too-uncomfortable folding chairs. Having eaten the least-appetising meal you could ever imagine, I kick myself that I hadn't thought to order some cans of beer.

"Is wine okay? I'm afraid I don't have anything else, aside from soft drinks. That's the problem with online shopping; it's easy to forget something."

"Wine is fine. I'm not a huge drinker, anyway."

I scurry off to grab a bottle and find some glasses, the best I can come up with are two tumblers, but I figure it's better than drinking out of mugs.

"Thank goodness for screw tops," I mutter. Finding a corkscrew would have been impossible.

"Cheers," he says, raising his glass and we chink. "To better times."

That feels a bit derogatory. I mean, we're very lucky to be sitting here where it's warm and dry; we've eaten and there's enough food to last a while. I'm not sure whether all of it is microwaveable, of course, but beans-on-toast is a great fall-back option. I can only assume Lewis isn't too pleased about having to spend his relaxation time with the person who's employing him to do a job.

"Thanks for everything you've done today, Lewis."

He jerks his chin up in acknowledgement.

"Olive green, eh? Bet you wished you'd settled for the other one, now."

I'm just about to explode, when I notice the tiniest hint of a smile playing around the corners of his mouth. Okay, two can play that game.

"I know what I want and I'm not prepared to settle any more."

There's no venom behind the words, it's simply a statement. Silence reigns; the sound of the gusting wind against the conservatory roof is a reminder that flooding isn't the only concern. What if one of these huge trees topples over onto the cottage? Is it possible to survive something like that?

"I reckon you'll be able to switch on the fridge and freezer about one in the morning and then you should be okay to use it around breakfast time. At least the storeroom is like the old-fashioned cold house and the fresh stuff shouldn't spoil."

I'm surprised at his attempt to make conversation. My eye was on the clock and I'd already worked that out for myself.

"I'm just relieved and grateful to next door. Was I rough on

132

the delivery guys? I didn't tip them and I feel awful. It wasn't their fault."

Lewis holds out his glass for a refill.

"Nice wine. I don't usually drink this pink stuff. They just wanted to make their drop and get off home. Range cookers are heavy beasts and it wasn't the best of days to find out they'd been given the wrong one. I did tip them a twenty-pound note, by the way. I knew you'd feel guilty that you'd forgotten."

I don't know how to take that. A part of me is grateful, because they did deserve it, if only for the hassle due to the location. But I'm in charge here. A glance at Lewis' face confirms he thinks it's not a big deal.

"I'll reimburse you, thanks. Even that doesn't seem like very much for such a lot of lifting. That was a thoughtful thing to do."

"It's okay. I can add it onto your bill. I was going to, anyway."

As I'm mulling over whether I should be worried about what must be the rapidly escalating costs, given the hours he's working, it suddenly hits me.

"Oh no, I think the heating has stopped working."

The wall lights are still on, so it's not a power cut. Lewis and I, rather reluctantly, drag on our coats and armed with Terence's storm lantern, we step out into the darkness. The boiler cover isn't heavy to lift off, just awkward. It's wall-mounted and can only be reached from halfway up the ramp, which is directly in line with it, albeit there is a two-foot gap between the ramp and the side of the cottage.

"I can smell oil, so that's a good sign," Lewis comments. I raise the lantern up high to shine down on the length of clear pipe that feeds directly into the motor. He puts his finger on the button to kick-start it. Nothing. He tries this again. Nothing, other than a small splutter that immediately dies.

"The plumbers said three attempts if it goes out again and if that doesn't do it, it will probably mean the motor has completely seized up."

Lewis fiddles with something, the smell of oil gets much stronger and then he presses the button again. Nothing – not even a splutter this time.

"I'm sorry, Madeleine, I think they're right. The motor has finally given up."

Once we're back inside the chill very quickly begins to take a hold and what was basic, but cosy, is already beginning to feel rather bleak and dismal.

"I suggest we get ourselves sorted for the night. I'll set my phone as a reminder to get up and switch on the freezer and the fridge in the early hours. Do you have extra bedding? It's going to be a cold night."

"Plenty, not sure how many pillows I can find, though. Do you prefer blankets or a duvet?"

"I'm good. I'll pop out to the van and grab my army-issue sleeping bag and all the gear. I was thinking more of you."

He can see the puzzled look on my face.

"I'm used to sleeping on the job. This is luxurious accommodation compared to some of the renovations I've had to sleep in. The van is like my home on wheels. I have a small camping stove I'll bring in. And don't worry – I won't be wearing the same socks tomorrow. I'm covered on that front, too."

I have to give the guy his due – he comes prepared. By the time he returns I've pulled out a pile of blankets and found two spare pillows. My bed now has two duvets and I manage to locate the box holding some warm socks and a really thick, hooded, cream dressing gown.

I try not to watch, fascinated as Lewis begins unpacking his kit in the sitting room, opposite the door to my temporary bedroom.

"Is it okay if I settle myself down here? I suggest you have two of the electric fan heaters going all night in the conservatory. The heat will drift through into the sitting room and dining room. The other heater ought to go upstairs to help the plaster dry out. If you need anything, just shout."

I think he's dismissing me. I hand him a bottle of water from the makeshift kitchen and grab one for myself. I head off to gather up my night things and a fan heater, then make my way up to the shower room. I leave Lewis sorting the heaters for the conservatory.

It's a nuisance having no door on the dining room, but then I didn't dream I'd ever have a house guest sleeping on the floor just a few yards away. I clean my teeth and get ready for bed, unable to face showering and exposing my naked body to the chilly air, even for a few minutes.

Walking back down the stairs, I probably look like a misplaced Eskimo in my cream dressing gown with the hood up and a pair of cream and grey woolly socks with snowflakes on them. They were a present from last Christmas; the sort you open and then have to paste a smile on your face while you say 'thank you'. It was the present I swore I'd never use. Lewis is, thankfully, nowhere to be seen and then I hear a noise from the downstairs bathroom. I run through the sitting room and am in bed under my double duvets in a matter of seconds. My heart is pumping and it's not just from the exertion.

CHAPTER 21

Birthdays are supposed to be special. I check my phone for what feels like the hundredth time and as the small hand clicks on the twelve, it confirms that I've officially hit the big five-o. Happy birthday, Maddie. They do say we get the life we deserve. You must have done something very, very wrong to find yourself in this mess. This certainly isn't how I envisaged my life at this point in time. What could be more depressing than lying in the dark, the air so cold I can't bear to even have a hand outside the covers and knowing that my kitchen probably isn't going to arrive today? This is it for the entire festive period. Ho! Ho! Or rather, bah humbug! No heating, no cooker and only the worst Christmas on record to look forward to. As far as firsts go, I think any one of them on their own would have been rather unfortunate. Come on universe! I've spent a large part of my life sending out good karma in one way or another – isn't this just a little unfair?

I pull the hood of my dressing gown in tighter, the cold air not only makes everything feel slightly damp to the touch, but it seems to infiltrate down through any little gap or crevice it can find. Lewis hasn't made a sound, so I'm guessing he's asleep. I roll over, trying to encourage the duvets to tuck in tightly around my body, but they're too thick and a new channel opens up for the cold air to investigate.

A little while later I hear a movement and realise Lewis is

pulling on his coat. I hear the door and then hollow footsteps as he walks past the window. His shadow floats across the blind and then a minute or two later he's in view again. It's so quiet I can hear the click as Lewis flicks the switch to turn on the fridge in the kitchen. As he walks back into the sitting room, the light from his torch flashes across the doorway into the dining room. A sudden tickle in my throat provokes an involuntary cough and I freeze, not wanting to draw attention to myself.

"Are you asleep?" his voice is barely a whisper.

"Yes," I reply.

"Sounds like you're awake to me. Would you like a cup of tea?"

"I thought you'd never ask. It's freezing and I'd love one, I'm just too cold to get out of bed. Aren't you cold?"

"No, years of army training and field ops discipline your body to withstand the elements. It's only when you're wet and cold that it becomes a problem." His voice is raised slightly, above the sound of the kettle heating up. "Have you slept at all?"

"Hardly. The kitchen isn't going to arrive, is it?" I sound as depressed as I feel.

"No."

A few minutes later he's standing in the doorway and I can just about make out his outline and the fact that he's carrying two mugs. He wants to talk.

In the gloom it looks as if he's dressed in a dark navy, or possibly black, sweat suit and I can see the top of what looks like a white tee-shirt visible at the neck line. He doesn't seem too sure about what to do next. The bed takes up most of the room and all I have is a small coffee table in the corner.

He steps forward, I assume to head for the table to put down the tea, when he stumbles over something.

"Damn it!"

"Sorry, watch out for my shoes. Hang on, let me sit up and I'll take it off you."

It's scalding hot, but I pull my dressing-gown sleeves down

over my hands and nestle the cup between them. The heat is welcome and it's cheering. "Why don't you sit on the end of the bed for a moment?"

I'm surprised when he does just that – I thought he'd feel awkward.

"Thanks for plugging in the appliances. I'd like to get the food back out of Terence's freezer first thing. I don't think Joanna approves of me, for some reason. I wouldn't like to cause any trouble between them."

"Joanna's a cold one. She's probably worried you'll crook your little finger and Terence will be there helping out. He has no idea his wife walks all over him, poor guy."

I wasn't expecting that comment and I don't know quite what to say.

"That's a bit judgemental. I think she felt this might be too much of a project for me to take on, that's all. I should have known about allowing the coolant to settle, she was right to be a bit put out. Poor Terence had to work hard to fit everything in. It is nearly Christmas, after all."

"Oh, come on! We'd all help out a neighbour in a similar position and we wouldn't make them feel uncomfortable. Do *you* think you've taken on too much?"

"At the moment, yes. When the heating is blasting out and I have a working cooker, ask me again and you'll probably get a different answer."

"If you ever want to walk away from it, I'm a willing purchaser."

I'm glad of the cover of darkness, so he can't see the look on my face.

"Sarah said that you intended putting in an offer the same day that I saw the cottage."

There's a moment's hesitation.

"Sarah shouldn't have told you that – it's confidential information. As it happens, I messed up."

"Was that why your diary was free? You thought Ash Cottage

138

was going to be yours?"

"Yep. Although I do have other jobs waiting, including one for next door."

We sip our tea, respectively, both considering the implication.

"I'm sorry your ... um ... circumstances meant you missed out. You think I won't get through this?" My voice sounds edgy in the darkness, as if it's an accusation.

"Look, it's none of my business what you do, but if you change your mind about living here on your own ..."

It's surreal. I don't know this man who's sitting on the bottom of my bed; I only know that people seem to trust him. It's true to say I don't feel unsafe with him here. His body heat has already made a difference to the room and just having that solid human bulk sitting there, talking to me, means more at this particular moment than he could ever know.

"I'm not afraid of anything – except failure." I have no idea why I'm admitting that, or even what it means. Have I already judged myself as having failed? Hitting fifty, single and living in a wreck, in a place where I don't know anyone? At first I thought gaining my freedom was liberating, but maybe poor decision-making will be my undoing. I could be living in a cosy little flat in Bristol, within walking distance of old friends. Friends? Well, people who now feel uncomfortable around me because they've only ever known me as one half of a couple. A tear starts to trickle down my cheek and I wince to think that I've probably never felt sorrier for myself than I do right now.

Lewis leans forward, his forearms resting on his knees and his hands cradling the mug. He's unaware that he's feet away from someone who just started a new decade in her life. Fifty is the new forty, or so they say, but I'm sure as hell depressed by the number.

"Failure, now that's a dangerous word, Madeleine."

His voice is soft, but shows no emotion whatsoever. Curiosity begins to encroach on my self-pity.

"Which means?"

He spins his head to look at me, although we are merely shapes to each other and there's no way I can read his expression.

"Sometimes failure is the difference between life and death. One little mistake and that's it, a life is lost forever. But it gets worse. It ripples outwards and a family is torn apart by their grief; the word 'hero' makes no difference to their loss. It's cold comfort for changing their lives forever."

Now I understand.

"Where?"

"Afghanistan. But that's irrelevant. We're talking about you. So your marriage failed – what's new? Your sons are grown and you're free to do what you want. Who are you going to fail?"

"When you're used to having lots of people around you, all fighting for your attention, it's hard to adjust to having no one. Maybe you can't understand the feeling of loneliness, because from where I'm sitting it feels like a kind of failure. Everything I thought I had has slipped through my fingers so easily I now wonder if I ever had anything at all. I always braced myself for the time when the boys were independent and I'd see less of them, but I thought I'd have someone by my side. Someone who wanted to be with me."

What am I doing? Lewis doesn't want to hear all this ... stuff, that's whirling around all jumbled up inside my head. For goodness' sake do yourself a favour and stop talking, Maddie!

"You don't think you're attractive any more?"

"I'm fifty and frumpy."

"Fifty? Really?"

"Fifty and oh, one hour and twenty-seven minutes."

He starts laughing.

"Happy birthday, Madeleine. Here's the thing – you're anything but frumpy, just ask that boss of yours. Guess I'd better leave you to get some beauty sleep, then."

The bed lifts as he straightens and I watch the hazy shape of him disappearing through the doorway, a chuckle breaking the silence. Is he being sarcastic?

I put down the mug, roll onto my side and scooping up my pillow I punch it twice in quick succession.

Just as I lay my head down, my mobile phone kicks into life and a series of pings announce incoming text messages. Why is it that any surge in signal happens in the early hours of the morning?

"What *is* that?" Lewis calls out.

I turn my phone around and look at the screen.

"Happy birthday messages from the boys and two from this morning announcing the appliances are on the way," I throw back at him, anger reflected in my tone and volume.

"No need to shout," he replies in a tediously fake hush, "you might wake the neighbours."

CHAPTER 22

If you're going to be stranded with someone and you get a choice, pick a man who's an ex-soldier. Lewis insists on cooking me a birthday breakfast of scrambled eggs on his camping stove. The toast is slightly burnt because he didn't check the setting on the toaster, but I was so hungry I would have eaten anything. The thought was touching, even if I was still annoyed with him from last night – for laughing at me.

The rain eases off and there's even a hint of blue sky behind the clouds, so he suggests we walk down to the main road to see what's happening. The fresh air is wonderfully cold and sharp. It's refreshing and welcome after the dry air that the fan heaters have been pumping out. They are efficient if you stand within range of one, but the moment you walk away the cold pockets of air seem to drag any residual warmth out of your limbs. My fingers, toes and nose seem to be constantly cold.

As we're about to head out Terence appears, wheeling a small trolley filled with carriers bags. He looks tired.

"Terence, thank you so much. I now have a fully functioning fridge and freezer. Are you feeling okay? You look rather tired."

Lewis lifts two carrier bags in each hand and makes his way to the stone store room.

"Awful night. Joanna has the 'flu and I'm not feeling too bright myself. To be honest, I'm going straight back to bed."

"I'm so sorry to hear that. I do hope you both feel better really soon. Awful being poorly at this time of the year. If there's anything you need, please do let me know. If I don't have it, I'm sure one of the other people around here will. I know I have painkillers and Vick's Vapour Rub." Goodness! I sound like an old maid.

"Very kind of you, but I think Joanna has a little stock of winter medicines. Things like this tend to run their course. Looks like it's going to be a quiet Christmas."

I commiserate, thinking that makes for two of us, as he wearily heads back up the path.

As we casually walk down to the main road, my mobile rings and it's Logistic Solutions doing just that and explaining that their vehicle can't get through to deliver my kitchen units. Thankfully they are only shut for three days and will try again on the twenty-eighth.

Lewis takes the news in silence and doesn't attempt to make any sort of conversation. I decide I'm not going to let him get away with it any longer.

"Failure doesn't really apply to war, does it? Things are taken out of your hands."

He stops, abruptly. When I look at him and our eyes meet, he looks like thunder.

"What sort of a comment is that to throw at me?"

"Sorry, I was thinking about what you said last night. I shared, so I think it's only polite that you do, too."

"You're paying for my skills, not my memoirs." The words are sharp and his mouth snaps shut. There's visible jaw-clenching going on there.

"Do you know how rude you are, sometimes? You blow hot and cold. How on earth are people supposed to know how to deal with you?"

His eyes flash, annoyance plastered all over his face. I feel my cheeks beginning to flame, instantly regretting my attempt to explain why he's so hard to talk to at times.

"Look, lady, my private life is just that. Private. I'm alone because I choose to be. People tend to get on my nerves and you're doing a good job of reminding me why that is."

So talking about anything meaningful is out of bounds, unless he says so.

"You were serious, though, about wanting to buy Ash Cottage. The problem is, I don't intend selling it. Everything will come together and I will be happy here." Even I have to admit I sound way more convinced than I feel.

"Whatever. Time will tell." Both his comment and his body language are dismissive; clearly he doesn't think this is going to be the life for me.

We trudge on in silence and I'm glad I've at least made my intentions clear. I wouldn't want him working on the cottage under false pretences. This isn't a project to fix it up and sell it on, in the hope of making a profit. This is going to be my home for the rest of my life. There's a part of me that is gutted by his words and his general attitude. Why I should feel any connection at all to this ... Neanderthal of a man, who is not simply rude, but obviously emotionally repressed, I have no idea. Unless ... was I naive enough to think that the reason he was beavering away was because he liked me? Unease shifts in the pit of my stomach. His comment about Ryan didn't go unnoticed, but he's wrong. Perhaps a man like that can't understand friendship in all its hues. Maybe he's so hardened and embittered by the career he chose to follow and the feelings he's had to cut off, he can no longer feel much of anything, any more. Can he only relate to comradeship? That struggle to survive when faced with danger and barking orders at people who have been trained to obey without question? How do you integrate back into a world that must seem as unreal as Disneyland in comparison to the battlefield?

As we round the last bend in the road, the full extent of the flooding is clear to see. It's impossible to get closer than about thirty yards to the main road, but from our vantage point further up the hill we can see along the road in both directions. There are two fire tenders and an assortment of vehicles blocking one end. Clearly, the turn-off for the hill is in a dip; something you hardly notice when you are driving. Looking at it now, all that is visible is a lake of muddy water as far as the eye can see. A whole row of buildings, from the pub at one end to the cottages and houses at the other, are knee-deep in water. In the middle, and at the lowest point in the dip, there is a commercial car-repair centre and you can just about see the tops of the cars that are standing on the forecourt. I'm speechless and Lewis shakes his head in disbelief.

To the left, if I stand back a little, I can see the heads of a group of workers who appear to be digging.

Lewis climbs up onto a wall to our right and drops down the other side. He's now on church land, or maybe its common land, as there's a children's slide way up on the bank. The grass slopes gently down to the stone wall, which has probably been there for hundreds of years. The drop the other side of it, down to the road, is probably about twenty-five feet.

"How's it going?" His voice travels back to me, caught on the wind.

I can't hear the response from below, but he spends a few minutes talking to the firemen. There are pumps going and the sound seems to fill the air, replacing the usual drone of traffic you'd expect at this time of the morning. He points back up to the top of the hill, nodding his head.

A few minutes later he makes his way back across the muddy field and, using one hand to steady himself, vaults over the wall to land on the tarmac.

"It's about five feet deep at the worst point, which is just around the bend," he points back up the road to our left. "It was much higher last night, apparently. The section of culvert that has collapsed means that the water running off the hill can only get so far along the pipe. It's spewing out of a hole in the ground just as you hit the approach to the village. The force of it is eroding the bank alongside the road, carrying a huge amount of soil and stone with it. There's nowhere for this water to go and if they weren't pumping, all of this would be under water, too." He indicates the area where we're standing.

I'm horrified at the thought of the people whose homes and businesses are filled with that murky, swirling water that seems to have a life of its own.

"They are going to bring in earth-moving equipment to start digging out the culvert, but it's not going to be easy to replace that pipe."

We start walking back up the hill just as the sun peeks out for the first time in well over a week. The heavy, grey clouds are menacing and there's more rain to come, of that I have no doubt.

"What about the top road?"

He shakes his head.

"A garden wall and bank have collapsed, apparently, and it's blocking the road. Once the debris is cleared they are going to have to shore it up with gabion cages. It's doubtful the road will be re-opened for at least a couple of days."

I look in horror, unable to believe what I'm hearing. How can there only be two ways in and out when so many homes are affected? I just can't take it in.

"Forest life is like that, Madeleine. You can't live in this sort of terrain and not expect problems. Large rock falls aren't common, but it happens in extreme weather conditions. I expect there are quite a few trees down, as well, and a few of those will have fallen across the tracks that traverse the landscape. Fortunately there aren't many access roads to keep clear, but that's also a negative. If one does become blocked, as with the main road through Bybrooke, things begin to grind to a halt."

"It's frightening. How will those people manage?"

I was surprised that most of the men milling around seemed to be firemen or workers wearing high-viz jackets.

"Most of the locals will have been evacuated. A handful might

146

have decided to camp out on the first floor of their properties, but the fire brigade will have tried their best to dissuade them. It's too dangerous, although unlikely the flood water could rise that high. This isn't something they're going to fix today, or tomorrow, Madeleine. If it stops raining then remedial work will speed up once the worst of the flood water is drained away, but it's going to take a week or two to clear the debris that's been carried along the length of the road."

"And there's no other way out?"

"Not until that top road is reopened. We're lucky that the water supply hasn't been affected. General supplies are being brought in later today. Is there anything you are going to need?"

"No, it's just an unsettling feeling being trapped."

"I hope you weren't planning on having a birthday party."

One glance confirms he's trying to lighten the moment, but to me this whole thing is alien and shocking. I hate to admit it, but if Lewis wasn't stranded here with me, I don't know how I would have reacted to this news.

"Don't worry. I have a plan," he looks at me sideways, his mouth curled in a relaxed smile. It really is like being with Jekyll and Hyde. I never know what to expect next.

"You aren't going to have a kitchen in time for Christmas, but we might be able to get the main bedroom sorted for you. No more sleeping in the dining room."

My mobile starts to ring, startling me and I stop while I dig around in my pocket to find it. Lewis strides on ahead, seemingly oblivious.

"Hello?"

"Mum, happy birthday. How's it going? I've been online reading about the floods. You are safe, aren't you?" Matt's voice is full of concern.

"Thanks, honey. Another year older, as they say. It probably sounds much worse than it is – the flooding, I mean. I live at the top of a hill, remember?" I make my voice bright and breezy, trying to shrug off any worries.

"There's a parcel on the way from Nick and me, but at the moment we've been told they can't give us a delivery date. It was a bit of a shock. Apparently you are officially cut off. You do have food and stuff, don't you? To be honest, Nick was on about paying you a surprise visit to check up on you."

"He texted this morning and didn't mention that. Tell him I'm fine and he's not to make the trip. It's too far and too close to Christmas. I don't want his plans upset when there's nothing he can do at this end. Besides, he'd have to leave the car quite a distance away. Really, I'm fine and, thank goodness, fully stocked-up with food. The builder is also here, so it will be a working Christmas. Maybe not so much fun as I'd expected, but it's more important to tackle some of the big jobs at the moment. How's Sadie?"

There's no point in telling him how awful things really are, and that has nothing at all to do with the rain. But the last thing I want is Nick driving the best part of two hundred miles to end up sitting in a freezing-cold house.

"She's doing well, but the morning sickness is on and off all day still, so she's finding that a struggle. Her parents are coming over for Christmas Day lunch. I'm cooking – poor them. I miss you, Mum. It doesn't seem right not seeing you on your birthday and it's a landmark one, at that."

A little tear forms in the corner of my eye as his words touch my heart. Be strong, Maddie. I kick a large tuft of grass with my wellington boot, anger over this whole situation threatening to erupt. I take a deep breath before continuing. Lewis is now almost at the top of the hill.

"I'm fine, really. It was always going to be a difficult first Christmas here, with so much work to be done. But things are beginning to shape up and working through the holidays will mean another room completed and one less to tackle in the New Year. Fifty is only a number and you know me, I've always thought birthdays were over-rated once you hit twenty-one." The laugh at least sounds light and breezy. It's true, of course; age has never really meant anything to me. But, fifty! I want to turn back the hands of time, because it's a number that scares the hell out of me.

"Well, it's good to hear your voice. When we catch up we'll have a belated celebration. We put your Christmas presents in with your birthday parcel, so I hope they manage to get it through in time. I wish we'd sent it off a bit earlier, but we had no idea how extensive the flooding was in your area. Thanks for your pressies, by the way. It's way too much, as usual, but Sadie will enjoy spending the vouchers. She's going to use them for the nursery."

"You're welcome, Matt, and thank you for the parcel. I'll let you know when it arrives, but I suspect that will be after Christmas now. It will be something to look forward to, to brighten up that lull between Christmas and New Year. I'll ring Nick later, but please speak to him and make sure he doesn't attempt that trip. I'm cosy here, everything is fine."

He clears his throat, an air of awkwardness in his hesitation.

"Has Dad phoned?"

I close my eyes, wrinkling up my face as Matt's words hit me in the stomach, like a blow.

"Darling, your dad called around to see me and I made it very clear that my life is now my own. When you divorce someone, the ties are cut. That doesn't wipe away the memories, but it means they are no longer a part of your future. I know that's hard for you to accept, but that's the reality. Whatever I choose to do now, your father isn't a part of it and it's none of his business."

"You sound bitter," Matt's voice is full of disappointment. I'd hoped he would understand.

"No, I'm not and I wouldn't want you to think that. What I am is happy. I need you, and Nick, to be happy for me, too."

"Fair enough. But, Mum, you will look after yourself, won't you?"

"Of course. At the moment it's all an adventure and every day brings something new." Well, the essence of that is true, although

149

the 'something new' is usually yet another problem. I'm just glad Matt and Nick don't know that.

I begin the climb again, thinking that Lewis sounded like a man on a mission and I guess that's what he's been trained to do. Take a bad situation and make the best of it. As my chest starts to burn and my breathing becomes laboured, I realise I'm nowhere near as fit as I thought I was. Pride won't let me fall too far behind, though, and I put my head down and plough forward with determination, as the first drops of rain start to fall once more. It might be the twenty-third of December, but there isn't one single vestige of Christmas spirit in me.

CHAPTER 23

After I throw off my muddy boots and hang up my wet coat, Lewis appears with two mugs of hot chocolate. My own mood is rather sombre as I come to terms with the idea of being stranded. My body quickly acclimatises to the blast of heat that initially hit me when I first walked in. I'm back to having cold toes and hands within a few minutes, and knowing that this is going to last for the foreseeable future is depressing. The part is on order; as yet there's been no confirmation of a delivery date. Most factories and warehouses close for a two-week period over Christmas and New Year. The added complication is that the company's main delivery depot is also on a flood plain and access is severely restricted at the moment. The last I heard, with the backlog, it's unlikely to arrive before the end of January.

I assume Lewis will head back into the kitchen, but instead he takes the seat next to me. Will he think I'm weakening if I say I'm going to shut up the cottage for a while?

Looking out, even with the heavy, gun-metal grey clouds and the relentless rain, it's a scene in which you can lose yourself. It's like a painting, where every time you look at it you spot something new. But what's the point in being trapped here over the holidays with so few comforts, when out there many people are still leading a normal life – floods and landslides something they can't even comprehend?

"What's up?" Lewis can see I'm preoccupied.

"I'm cold." Ironically, I'm the one now who doesn't feel in the mood for talking.

"That wasn't another problem, the call?"

"No. That was my son, Matt. The boys are concerned, but I hope I've convinced him everything is fine. Nick was going to make the journey down, but it's a long way to come when there's nothing he can do."

"It's nice to know they care. I guess that's what families do." He sips his drink, a slight frown hardening his face. "I don't mean to bark at you. That's the trouble with being a loner, you get used to your own company. I spent too many years away from friends and family, in a job where I was paid to issue orders. It's a one-way communication stream. I have a confession to make and it's a peace offering, so don't take it the wrong way."

He leans forward, forearms on his knees and mug cradled in his hands. He looks straight ahead, as if he's scanning the view, but I think it's more to avoid my gaze.

"That first time I met you here, I said I was checking you out. Some people are a pain to work for and hover all the time, or keep changing their minds. What I said was true in a way."

He pauses and a few seconds pass before he continues.

"I wanted to see if you were the right one, you know, to take over Aggie's cottage. Aggie sort of expected me to buy it. She knew I was looking for somewhere to settle and I promised her that, when the time came, I'd restore it to its former glory. When I received the call informing me that my mother had died, naturally I dropped everything and headed back home. With hindsight I kick myself. I should have contacted Sarah before I left, leaving a full asking price offer on the table. The price was irrelevant to me, as this is where I wanted to be. But when the bank was finally ready to put it up for sale, I was a couple of hundred miles away arranging a funeral."

I'm frantically thinking of a suitable response that won't upset him, or sound patronising, when he continues.

"Of course, I know Aggie isn't still here, because I don't believe in ghosts. However, I've seen enough of death and been exposed to things I don't fully understand, to freely admit it's an unknown to me. But I do think that between these walls, the life that went on leaves some sort of impression behind. I've walked forests, fields and towns, where the stench of death plays tricks with the mind. Your skin prickles with the aftermath of horrors not necessarily witnessed, but a trace of something very negative is tangible in the air – places that are blighted forever and where even courageous battle veterans think twice before stepping.

"It's time I put down roots. The truth is that I envy you this place. In the meantime, I'm more than happy to help out here."

I blink, my eyes watery as I imagine Aggie sitting here and looking out: year in, year out. All those memories and that heart-shaped stone, telling me that love leapt in her heart, even though she never found her one true love.

"I'm sure you'll find the right place for you, Lewis," I try to keep my tone light and not reflect the emotion he's drawing out in me.

"Plus, a guy has to earn a living. Now, let's take a look at the master bedroom. If you're happy to help out we can probably turn the room around in just a few days. It's not like you have anything else to do."

I have to make a split-second decision. A few minutes ago it was my intention to ring Ryan and ask if I could go and stay with him until the roads are open again. We might not be able to drive out of Bybrooke, but on foot we could get out and it seemed to make sense. I know what I told Matt, but that was simply to stop him worrying. If I do this, am I doing it for myself, for Ash Cottage, or for Lewis?

"Well, I have all the materials, so I guess it's going to be a working Christmas."

After a quick inspection Lewis manages to expose four layers of wallpaper, each like a snapshot going back in time. I can see the seventies, eighties and nineties staring back at me. He then points to the ceiling.

"The ceiling tiles are going to be a nightmare to get off. Then I'll fill in the holes from scraping off the glue. Under normal circumstances I'd suggest getting a plasterer in to skim it, but I'm sure I can do a passable job of it. I have a steamer in the van. If you use that, then I'll start peeling off some of the outer layers. They should come off quite easily. It's the bottom layer that is going to be time-consuming if it's stuck fast."

We work in silence and I find myself wishing I knew where the radio was, but it's in a box somewhere. However, I'm not sure Lewis would approve – he seems content to be left alone with his thoughts. I wish I felt the same way. I'm not sure I want to face up to the things that are whirling around inside my head.

Do I want to settle and grow old gracefully, ending up like Aggie? Was she happy being on her own? Did she feel fulfilled, or were there times when she doubted some of the decisions she had made? Maybe fate won't allow us to stray too far from our allotted path. Maybe I need to take each day as it comes and try not to think about the long-term future. The thought of being alone forever makes me tear-up; the thought of getting to know another man in all senses of the word is daunting. I'm not sure I have the confidence, or the desire, any more. What if I never find anyone who is right for me, ever again?

As I stop for a minute to sweep some of the debris on the floor into a pile, I glance across at Lewis. My eyes travel over him from head to toe and I have to admit that a little quiver of something flashes through me once more. He's a stocky build, but it's all muscle. As he reaches out with the scraper, his muscles flex and tighten; he sure looks good for his age. Then I think about the wobbly bits around my middle and the laughter lines that are now seriously way beyond a joke. They're only supposed to crinkle nicely at the outer edges of your eyes, not work their way across

154

your entire face.

I can still recall the excitement and attraction when Jeff and I first met, even though it now seems as if it was in another life-time. We were so young. When did that all-consuming love start to fade? I have no idea; we settled into family life and there was never a moment to stand back and think about our relationship in that way. I force myself to think about Jeff. Did he make me feel special? I suppose the truth is that he hadn't for many, many years. Yes, we made love, but when he held me it was because that's what you do. I can't remember the last time he actually *held* me, as in, drawing me close with no hint of sexual gratification. I've always been a hugger and the boys followed my lead. But they never hug Jeff – it's always a handshake. It worried me for many years; I didn't want them to think that was normal. Men should hug their sons, no matter what their age. It's how you show someone you care, really care, and each one is a special moment.

"Shall I make some lunch?" It's too hard to be in the same room with a man I don't know and have these things running through my head. There are many ways to spend a fiftieth birthday, but this isn't one of them. Maudlin, miserable and scraping walls is unlikely to make the list.

"If you want. I'm happy to work through, but you probably need a break. Shout when it's ready." He doesn't stop what he's doing, just throws the words over his shoulder.

I wonder where Lewis' thoughts take him when there's nothing to distract him, his hands automatically going through the motions of the task in hand.

Downstairs, even with the two fan heaters blasting, it's chilly in the sitting room. The back wall is set into the hill and it's inevitable that the chill will come through. I suppose I just have to be very grateful that the water doesn't find its way in. Ryan was right; I should have had a survey. However, I know it wouldn't have dissuaded me, no matter what it threw up. Lewis has already hinted that the downstairs bathroom is likely to pose a few problems, but

155

I'll face that when we get there.

Well, lunch is basic – cheese and ham sandwiches and a packet of crisps. I make double for Lewis, who seems to have a large appetite, although I think he prefers to eat at the end of the day. Who knows? With him everything is a guessing game.

"It's ready!" There's no response, so I sit down in the conservatory and assume he'll join me when he's ready.

LEWIS

CHAPTER 24

It's difficult working with Madeleine Brooks constantly under my feet. She's doing a reasonable job and she's a tidy worker, but I could whip through this a lot quicker if I was on my own.

Why on earth am I bending over backwards, when every task just serves to remind me that Ash Cottage isn't mine? I suppose it's because of Aggie, and knowing how disappointed she'd be that this isn't going to be my home. Sometimes life really sucks!

Terence seems to wander out whenever I take myself off to the van to have a break. There's another man who spends a lot of his time finding excuses to get away from a woman. However, I'm beginning to enjoy our chats and this morning I felt able to share a little of what I've kept bottled-up, with him.

"Were you close to your mother?" His question had surprised me, coming out of the blue.

"My mother had been ill for a long time, but her death was sudden and unexpected. If it had happened just a few days later I would have been here when Ash Cottage went on the market. That sounds cold, but everyone has to die, and in her case it was a welcome release. She was a good woman, if strict, and in lucid moments she hated not being her usual self. My mother had high standards and was a very private woman. Sometimes it was hard to know if you had succeeded in pleasing her. You always knew if you'd done something wrong, though."

"It's a generation thing, Lewis. Don't take it personally. My mother was similar, a great character but you knew if you'd upset her."

"When the call came I took off, dreading what was to come. Although that house was home to me during my early teen years, when I was seventeen years old I joined the army. My mother was happy to sign the papers and, I think, a little relieved I would at least be 'off her hands'. My army career was an excuse to keep visits home to the minimum and I know it's wrong, but I don't have any regrets. She never looked to me for anything, but I was grateful for the upbringing she gave me. My chance to pay her back came in the latter few years of her life. I made sure she was taken care of and that she could remain in her own home for as long as possible. Aggie, on the other hand, was mentally fit as a fiddle, but it was her body that began to fail her. Unfortunately, she had no one close at hand to help her out."

"I'm sure Aggie was very grateful for the kindness you showed her, Lewis. Sometimes it's easier dealing with a stranger than it is with your own family. Family can be complicated." Clearly, Terence understood that a part of this was all about guilt.

"My mother and I struggled to find things in common. She wouldn't have understood my working environment; few could understand the life of an active-serving member of the forces. Being on the frontline isn't something you want to talk about; it's bad enough when your dreams drag you back there. When I did go home, we'd exchange pleasantries and I'd catch up on the local news, but we never talked about anything meaningful. Of course, when exactly the dementia started, I don't know. She was an insular woman all of her life, never recovering from the shock of being widowed so early in her married life.

"At the point where she stopped recognising me, I knew that moving her into a facility, rather than having carers in to look after her at home, was inevitable. I also knew that she would have hated it if she had been aware of her surroundings. The house remained as it was the day I took her to Leyton Park nursing home and I paid the bills out of my army pension. Now it's mine, there is no one else and I can't feel sad that it holds no interest for me. It's a house full of the woes of a woman who never managed to stop grieving. That's life."

Terence had leaned forward and placed his hand on my shoulder.

"Sometimes it's hard to let go of the past. You're handling it well, Lewis. It can't be easy. Especially being here, now."

What I couldn't tell him was that I felt Ash Cottage was different. It will always be Aggie's no matter who lives here. She was a vibrant, intelligent and kind woman. Everyone seemed to think she had an easy life as a single professional woman. But as an only daughter it fell to her to give up her career, and her life, and move back home to nurse her widowed mother as she fell into decline. She was a lady who made sacrifices, always driven by other people's needs or principles. Alone, Aggie was free in a way she had never been before. It was at that point that we met.

"Why Madeleine Brooks should come along and happen to be in the right place at precisely the right time to buy Ash Cottage, fails me. This place is totally wrong for her and I bet she'll be moving on within a year. It's too isolated and too different to the city living she's always known." It had been hard for me not to sound bitter.

"I'm not so sure, Lewis. Doesn't everyone deserve a second chance when something goes wrong in their life? I don't think her life has been easy recently."

Terence's words stuck in my head as I went back to work. The problem is that I know Madeleine is out of her depth and there should be a sign on her back with a big warning triangle. The other concern is that she has absolutely no idea how attractive and desirable she is, and that's a real problem.

I'm a loner by habit and women are a bit of a puzzle to me. Old people I can understand. Their needs are driven by the basic requirements of life. Aggie needed help with her shopping, fetching things from the doctor's and little things that I could fit in around the jobs that needed doing to keep the cottage ticking over. Madeleine is used to having a set routine and a family to look after. She might have organised this project to death, but where did it get her? Nature is no man's servant and that's how I came to find myself in this impossible situation. I should have said I was too busy to take the job on and let her sink from the start. It would have been quicker and less painful.

But there are times when she catches me unawares; when her vulnerability becomes a draw. Before I know it I have to fight off the mounting attraction. There's something about her that keeps grabbing my attention, even when I'm trying my best to ignore her. Just when I'm about to lose it and walk away, she'll start talking and I find myself watching that kissable mouth, mesmerised. And she's a hugger. Wouldn't you just know it! Okay, we're strangers and she's rather a reserved lady in many ways, but when she manages to get me to lower my guard I see that look of hers – the one that tells me to shut up before that nurturing instinct of hers kicks in. If I find myself with her in my arms, I'm not sure I could hide the attraction I feel.

As a teen my mother found it hard to control me at times. I was hot-headed and had nothing to absorb all the energy that seemed to constantly set me on edge. I did what many teenage lads do and I drank too much, stayed out too late and behaved as if each day was going to be my last. Going into the army saved me from myself, because you can't talk back to a drill sergeant. The physical training exhausted me, but it also built me up and turned me into a fitness fanatic. Every goal I achieved spurred me on to set the bar higher and higher. I was completely focused when many of my peers had other things going on in their lives to distract them. I didn't. With personal success came promotion and responsibility made a man of me. Enough to understand that if I couldn't connect with my mother emotionally, then I could at least make sure she had everything she needed.

And then I met Aggie. That made two people who, for very difference reasons, needed help. Have I now, unwittingly, collected a third? Madeleine Brooks isn't my responsibility, but it seems that something won't let me walk away and leave her to learn this lesson the hard way. Maybe life really does reward those who are good, and she's a life-long do-gooder. I'm being dragged in as the solution simply because I was in the wrong place at the wrong time. Well, for me, anyway. I doubt if I count for much in the overall scheme of things. A few good deeds don't wipe out a lifetime of self-absorption and then there's warfare ... does anyone ever come out of that deserving of praise? You kill, or get killed – that's not heroics, it's basic survival.

So, here I am; caught up in something that scares the hell out of me. I don't want to feel sorry for anyone or get drawn into their problems. But creating a flood is a pretty drastic act of God if you ask me, so I guess hiking through the woods in order to get away from her might not be the answer. Believe me, I've considered it! Annoyingly, if this is where I'm supposed to be right now, then I just have to put up with it and get on with the job. The sooner it's done, the sooner I can walk away with a clear conscience. I can only hope whoever's up there is listening and this time I score a few points. You never know, they just might come in handy one day.

Without warning, my mind is thrown into confusion. A memory, buried deep down inside, begins to re-play inside my head like watching an old, familiar movie. It was the day three of my men died in an ambush, slaughtered like dogs before the rest of the unit could get to them. I saw a red mist, nearly lost it before the training kicked in and I was barking orders again, making sure the bastards didn't get anyone else. It had been a textbook operation; none of my men had put a foot wrong. During debriefing it was plain that the ambush wasn't planned at all. Two of the enemy had deserted, knowing that they would soon be beaten and they were simply running away from the conflict. As they stumbled across our guys they started shooting, fear taking over when all they had to do was lie low. I doubt they even stopped to consider whether they were killing their compatriots or the other side. I was at a low ebb, even for me, and that day I felt helpless and confused. I wanted to cry out to the universe over the senseless waste of three good lives. All were family men; all had children.

By comparison, I don't know why I'm whinging over babysitting Madeleine Brooks. This is the reality that I now have to live with and it's short-term. But she makes me feel helpless and confused in a different way. I guess that's the trigger, the thing I can't move past because it's my Achilles heel. Except that I'm not responsible for the knee-jerk decisions she's making. That includes buying a property she can't handle and the fact that she's a townie who can't comprehend life in an isolated area like the Forest. I was responsible for every action taken by my men, because they did as they were told to the letter. So it makes no sense that I should feel obligated to help out here, unless there's a chance she'll end up selling Ash Cottage to me. I suppose it's the same streak of vulnerability that I saw in my mother and Aggie. They were strong women who suddenly found themselves floundering and alone. It taught me something; something I'd lost touch with in terms of having a normal life – well, normal by most people's standards: people who haven't been to hell and back, or had to face the consequences of squeezing a trigger and ending a life. Survival for some is about how to make sure there is food in the cupboard when they aren't mobile, or who to call when something goes wrong in their home – the things that can become almost impossible to handle because of age or circumstance. When it comes to responsibility, you don't always have the luxury of making a decision about whether or not you want to take it on.

I have to draw the line somewhere, though, and it's not my job to shake some sense into Madeleine Brooks. Or to be the one to tell her that running away from everything she knows isn't any sort of answer to the mess her life is in at the moment.

MADDIE

CHAPTER 25

By early evening the walls are stripped and half of the ceiling tiles are now tied up in a stack of black sacks. I head off to shower, leaving Lewis to carry the bags out to the garage. It has rained on and off all day, but it's a lighter rain and, thankfully, it has warmed up a degree or two.

I had to stop because I'm aching all over. Lewis is like a machine and if I wasn't here I think he'd still be working. The man never seems to tire.

The back of my arms and neck are sore to touch and my knees just can't bend – even one more time. The warmth of the water is soothing and slipping into a clean pair of jogging bottoms and a thick, fluffy white jumper makes me feel almost human again.

Lewis doesn't come straight back in after carrying out the last load of rubbish and I wonder if he's sitting in his van again, grateful for a little peace and quiet. It's clear he prefers to work alone and sometimes his facial expression is enough to inhibit conversation of any sort.

Tonight it's tinned curry reheated on the camping stove and microwaved rice. Lewis returns as I'm just about to plate up the food and the aroma, at least, is mouth-watering. But then, I'm so hungry I could eat anything.

"I'll be two minutes," he says, indicating a rolled-up towel and some clothing tucked beneath his arm. He climbs the stairs two at a time as I turn the heat down low beneath the saucepan and take the knives and forks through to the conservatory. I carry through the small side table from the bedroom and place it in front of the two folding chairs. Then I dig through some boxes to find a couple of candles and I come across the contents of my former drinks cupboard. There are half a dozen assorted bottles, but I doubt Lewis is into aperitifs or dessert wine. There's a bottle of vodka that's barely touched and I figure at least it will warm the parts the fan heaters can't reach.

When he returns he looks relaxed, wearing a grey tracksuit and the conservatory has the distinct smell of his and hers shower gels. I can tell he's feeling uncomfortable, so I pour a finger of vodka into two tumblers and hand one to him.

"I know you said you don't drink much, and I'm not a drinker myself, but I figure we've earned this."

He accepts the glass, raises it in the air and mutters, "Happy birthday, even if it is the big five-o," before downing it in one. My eyebrows shoot up in surprise and he looks at me, rather blankly.

"I said I wasn't a great drinker, that's not to say I haven't had a few sessions in my time. That hit the spot! Could I trouble you for a top-up?"

"Help yourself while I dish up the curry."

When I carry the plates back through the candles are lit and the smell is distinctly Christmassy; a mixture of mulled wine with a hint of vanilla. Lewis is sitting down, his glass refreshed but he hasn't touched it.

"Thanks, it smells good."

Coming from a guy who is used to living off a camping stove, I suppose that was a compliment. We eat in silence; the candlelight is soft enough to allow a peek into the darkness outside. It's inky black, but the outline of trees and the hillside still draws the eye. It's also something to focus on, making the quiet at least bearable.

I think back to this time last year; all of the family sitting around a table at my favourite restaurant. A pile of presents I didn't really need in front of me, but it was about the love I saw reflected in their faces as they watched me opening them. Except that maybe I hadn't really looked at Jeff's face or connected with his emotions. The boys were laughing and joking around, content to think that I was happy. Jeff was a little more reserved and, with hindsight, maybe it was because he'd become detached. And now I'm wondering whether or not I, too, was truly happy way back then.

"I said – can I take your plate?"

Lewis' hand is extended and he's standing to the side of me.

"Sorry, yes, thanks."

I can hear him flick on the kettle and the chink of mugs. He comes back with two strong coffees.

"You did well today, keeping up."

His voice is gruff, even though his words are surprisingly kind.

"I'm using muscles I don't normally use, so I suppose I have to expect a bit of stiffness."

I pick up the tumbler and take a swig of the vodka. It's not a taste I find that palatable and I go in search of something to soften it, returning with a box of orange juice.

"That's better. It certainly does warm from the inside out, though."

Lewis says nothing, but leans forward to add juice to his own glass, then settles back in his chair with his coffee mug.

"Aggie loved the view. She spent hours looking out across the valley."

I'm hesitant to ask any questions, but it's going to be a long evening if I spend the entire time worrying about saying the wrong thing.

"Did you know her well?"

"Not really. I came here about fourteen months ago, by accident really."

"Oh, I assumed maybe your family lived here at some point and had moved away. So you aren't a Forester?"

"No. My mother lived up near the Lake District."

167

"So how did you find yourself in this part of the world?"

I can see he's annoyed at himself for the slip, giving away a little personal information without thinking and now he feels he can't ignore my questions.

"Pete, an old army friend settled here and he needed a favour. I came to help out and before I knew it the jobs came rolling in. How about you?"

When the shutters come down you can see it in his eyes and he's leaving me in no doubt at all that the questions have to stop.

"I needed to start afresh." Two can play at that game.

"A dangerous thing when you get safely past the mid-life crisis, relax and then have a meltdown."

I immediately take exception to his tone and anger raises its head. He thinks I'm fickle.

"When your husband sleeps with the person you've called your best friend for more years than you care to remember, it's ... devastating, actually. Ironically, I wasn't upset about losing Jeff; I was more upset to think that we'd been living a lie. The hardest part was facing the reaction from friends and family. Being the subject of people's pitying glances reduces your self-esteem to zero. By the way, how's the finger?" I rather threw the words at him and he stops short, his coffee cup an inch away from his mouth.

He looks surprised and I'm mortified. I can't believe I just blurted that out. What's wrong with me? I don't have to justify myself to anyone, least of all Lewis Hart. He holds up his finger, which now sports an almost black nail, but it's intact.

"Hiding yourself away here is the answer, is it?" He gives me a dismissive glance, then downs the remainder of his coffee.

I'm speechless at his lack of ... I don't know ... compassion? I pick up the glass tumbler in front of me and take a large gulp of the vodka and orange.

"I'm not hiding. I just don't want to be constantly reminded of the past. There's no going back and somehow I have to make a new life for myself. I admit that it hasn't been easy so far, but I'll survive." I pull my chair a little closer to one of the fan heaters and a little further away from Lewis. If only the heating was working everything would feel a lot less grim.

"Knee-jerk reaction. I bet a modern little house in Bristol must seem very appealing right now."

I turn to look at him, wondering what's behind the sudden softening in his voice. Oh. I'd forgotten.

"You won't talk me into giving up, you know. It's one miserable Christmas, that's all."

He makes a noise that sounds rather dismissive.

"Did you go through that box of Aggie's? I wondered if you found any documents or letters about the lane at the back."

It's obvious why he's interested and I'm rather disappointed he's not even trying to disguise his motive.

"I haven't had time." It's true, but even if I had learnt anything, I wouldn't tell him on principle.

Lewis leans forward to top up our drinks. Watching him in this setting, candles flickering in the background as he dispenses the drinks, it's easy to overlook the fact that this isn't by choice. I am feeling a little more relaxed, suddenly, but maybe that's the alcohol beginning to take effect. He sits back down, handing me the tumbler and holding out his own.

"I know I'm not the best company. I'm used to spending a lot of time on my own, so I'm sorry if I say the wrong things. I wasn't fishing for information, just fumbling around for conversation."

Why does he do that? Suddenly throw in something that makes him sound almost human. Now I feel guilty.

"I was being offhand and it was unnecessarily rude of me. I realise that while your van is stuck here for the next couple of days, you could easily find a way out on foot through the Forest and back to civilisation. You could be in your own place rather than sleeping here on the floor. I hope this isn't messing up your plans for the holiday."

He settles back in his seat, the expression on his face is hard to read.

"Christmas means nothing to me. Anyway, I'd planned on working through the holidays, if I'm honest." He can't hide the telling grin that begins to creep across his face.

"Oh, yes, of course. Look, I am sorry about what happened. That's why I really appreciate you helping me out. I'm not sure how I'd feel if I had to stay here on my own ..."

The moment the words leave my lips I regret them. Lewis Hart isn't going to appreciate being regarded as anyone's crutch. He's probably biting back a strong retort because there's no one to blame but myself for this mess.

"Hey, it's your birthday. So I'm not going to point out that only an insane woman would move into a cold, damp cottage, surrounded by forests and floods, in mid-winter. For a sensible woman, you are full of surprises."

I feel myself beginning to colour-up. The heat rises slowly up from my neck and now my cheeks are probably glowing. Is he paying me a compliment, or is he questioning my sanity? Maybe he has a point there. Why didn't I exchange with a completion date after the holidays? I could be snuggled up in a warm bed in a centrally heated hotel, or in someone's spare room. But the latter would mean endless conversations about Jeff and the affair. While I'm over it, unfortunately our friends, or ex-friends, aren't. I doubt any of them will know whose side to take and I've seen situations like this before. One by one they desert you, simply because the dynamics have changed. They can't accept new partners and it's hard to swap loyalties, or even apportion blame. How dare he judge me when he has no idea what I've been through?

"And for an intelligent man, I can't believe you left anything to chance if you really wanted Ash Cottage so badly."

Damn it! That was mean and bad manners, but I can't bring myself to apologise for stating the obvious.

"My mother had dementia but she wasn't sick. The call was unexpected."

His tone is curt and I cringe, inwardly. For a man with such a tough exterior, there's still a heart beating beneath it. If I say I'm sorry now, he'll brush it off.

"Then maybe it wasn't meant to be for a reason." My words are gentle and I feel sure he'll understand it's a peace offering.

"And what do you suppose that reason was, Madeleine?" His voice is hard, unforgiving and the intonation is mocking.

I've rather backed myself into a corner here and my mind is a total blank. I take a large gulp of vodka and orange and then say exactly what I'm thinking.

"Maybe I needed a dose of reality, to put things into perspective and you needed to ... chat to someone."

Did I really just say that?

"What is it with women like you, who feel the constant need to interfere whenever they meet someone they don't understand? I don't want your sympathy, or your help with anything. You're the one who is needy, lady. I'm doing just fine." He stretches out his legs in front of him and crosses them, as if to make a point. I'm the one shivering and worried about being on my own in a stripped-out cottage. He is right, he's at home here and I'm not.

My head is feeling a little fuzzy with tiredness and alcohol, and I feel upset by his words, which were spoken in anger. My brain is telling me in no uncertain terms that he's being totally unfair and, for the first time in my life I find myself wanting to slap someone.

"Now who's being judgemental? Who knows what the reason was? Aside from the fact that just maybe I deserve my little slice of heaven? I was being empathetic and trying to put myself in your situation."

I empty the remainder of my tumbler in one swallow.

"You'll excuse me, but I think it's time I went to bed."

I immediately stand up with such force that it sends the folding chair in one direction, while my body begins to topple over in another. Lewis is on his feet just as fast and catches me before I even know what's happening.

"I think you need to be more careful about what you drink," his words end up being spoken into my neck, as he deposits me into an upright position. His breath is warm and his arms around me are surprisingly gentle for such a powerful man. For one second I close my eyes and savour the moment. What if he wasn't steadying me, but this was a genuine hug and I look up into his eyes to see real desire?

"I'm sorry this deteriorated into ..." I can't resist glancing up at his face. What I see looking back at me isn't anger. Before I know what I'm doing my face is moving towards his and our mouths meet somewhere in the middle. It's fierce, as our lips clash with hungry desire that seems to be overtaking us and gathering momentum by the second. His arms tighten around me and I can feel his heart beating wildly in his chest. My head begins to spin and my legs don't seem to be able to support me, as I melt into him. What is the price of a dream come true? Am I capable of doing this?

He pulls his head away, staring at me with a look of total shock written all over his face.

"I don't take advantage of single, lonely women." He groans as he begins to pull away.

"Well, that's a pity then, because I was rather hoping you were the sort of man who follows through once they start something."

Suddenly, I've never felt more clear-headed, or surer about wanting something. As I head off in the direction of the temporary bedroom, I half-turn towards Lewis and give him a look that leaves him in no doubt at all that this isn't one-sided.

"The choice is yours, Mr Hart."

CHAPTER 26

It's Christmas Eve, but more importantly it's the morning after the night before. Aren't you supposed to wake up feeling awkward and ashamed when you indulge in an unexpected night of passion with someone you least expected to fall into bed with? Especially when he's very attractive in a rugged, rough-around-the-edges, sort of way and not at all like any man you've ever met before? A little thrill makes my stomach do a somersault, acknowledging that, at the grand old age of fifty years and one day, I've just had my first one-night stand. It's incredible – if not almost unbelievable. Well, hopefully my only one-night stand, as this really isn't my style, but what a night! I can feel myself blushing, but I wouldn't change one second of it.

If I thought I'd made love before, scratch that – this was hot passion, unleashed slowly and skilfully. Lewis Hart smoulders when he's not talking. You could say that his talents lie elsewhere. There isn't a part of me that doesn't ache, but in a good way, aside from the muscles in my arms that are still grumbling from stripping wallpaper, of course.

I've been touched in places that I had no idea were erogenous zones, and others where it feels like something new was awakened in me. And I've touched ... Lewis Hart ... and felt intense desire behind that solid, muscular bulk. He's a man who has two extremes – if only he could talk with the same level of emotion

173

and passion with which he makes love!

We connected physically, on a level that touches the soul and to say that was totally unexpected is a huge understatement. Last night he was a different man, someone I haven't yet glimpsed. How sad, if that's the only time he can allow himself to completely let go and tap into his inner feelings. I had the distinct impression he rarely trusts anyone enough to allow them to get close to him. I don't know what his demons are, but it's very obvious they are deep and complex. His battle scars don't show on the surface. For all I know, he may even be nursing a broken heart that will never mend. A part of me aches for the pain his life has inflicted upon him and the person he's become in order to deal with it. He doesn't want to be fixed, as tempting a challenge as that seems to me this morning. But if last night left me feeling this way, then I can only hope that it gave him something exceptional, too. I put my trust in him, followed his gentle direction and didn't hold back. I knew I wasn't merely being used, that was obvious. How much he cared about me in the process was humbling, as if he wanted me to understand I was special. In return, I wanted him to know that I glimpsed the remarkable man at his core, the one who can feel emotion and handle it.

The bed next to me might be empty now, but there's a space recently vacated by his body and I feel exhilarated still by the thought of that. Why? I'm fifty – my life was over and now it's not. He's made me realise that there will be surprises ahead and some of them are going to be as unexpected and wonderful as last night. He made me feel wanted and special. When my desire threatened to take over, he slowed me down and showed me how to savour every little sensation. I never knew that touching alone could be that sensual, and at one point he was telling me how to breathe, his words spoken softly against my neck. As he breathed in, I breathed out and that simple collaboration made it feel as if we were working as one. His iron-strong arms around me cradled me with a gentleness it was hard to comprehend.

I want to lie here and reflect, but the smell of bacon wafting through the doorway means breakfast is on the go. I can hear him walking about in the sitting room and he's whistling. Whistling – that's a first! When his footsteps head out into the conservatory and beyond, into the bathroom, I decide it's time to run up to the shower room.

Looking in the mirror I see bed hair that reflects a tumultuous night; a night of sensual discovery, where touch of hand and mouth suddenly became a thing of wonder. Who would have guessed that a man like Lewis could be capable of ... finesse! As the hot water slides down over my body I feel renewed. I'm smiling and I can't seem to stop, but I have to get myself back under control, or I'm going to scare off my builder. Maybe Miss Brooks will survive after all and if he's expecting me to be embarrassed this morning, then he's in for a surprise!

"Why do you keep looking at me?" I give Lewis a meaningful glance, taking a moment to relax my left arm, which is aching worse than a toothache. The steamer pad is heavy when you have to hold it up above head-height. Still, the final wall is nearly stripped and Lewis is already starting to make good the first two walls.

"I was checking on your progress. It seems a bit unfair to expect you to work on Christmas Eve," he mutters, but I know that isn't what's on his mind.

I turn my head to hide a smile, still unable to understand his reaction this morning. Did he think I'd wake up totally appalled by our behaviour and ask him to leave? The shocking truth is that while I've only slept with one other man, sex isn't something foreign to me. Of course, it was very different ... if I giggle now, he'll be mortified.

"I like being productive and it's not as if there's anywhere really comfortable to sit and relax. Anyway, I'm nearly finished; another twenty minutes and this final strip will be done. Do you think filling in the worst of the digs and dents will make the walls good

175

enough to paint?"

He kicks into work-mode, standing back and assessing the result of his efforts.

"It depends. If you are looking for a smooth, flawless finish then, no. If you are looking for a more rustic look with a bit of character, then I think it will be just fine."

"Rustic does it for me," I catch his eye, holding his gaze for a few seconds before he looks away.

"I don't feel awkward and I don't think you should, either. If we're going to be working together until Bybrooke is accessible again, then we have to put last night behind us."

He shakes his head in disbelief. "Look, I feel bad. It was out of order and even if you weren't being sensible, I should have known better. And I suggest next time you drink vodka and orange you stick to just the one."

I feel like I'm being told off for bad behaviour.

"Point taken. Helpful," I reply with as serious a tone as I can muster. "Lewis, um, this is out of sheer curiosity, but where did you learn how to ... um ... make it less about the *act* ..."

"It's called tantric sex and it's about connection and celebrating the body. The word means *woven together* and I had a good teacher. Let's just say that it was an experience I had shortly after I joined the army, on my first trip abroad and something that once learnt, you never forget."

"Oh, Sting and his wife ..."

"Madeleine, this isn't going to become a topic of conversation between us. Let's just leave it at that and, yes, I know Sting is infamously linked with it, but it's been practised for thousands of years. My teacher happened to be a Japanese woman who was twenty years my senior. She taught me that lovemaking is an art and not a race. If you are going to do something, then you should do it well."

It's hard not to laugh – not because I find it amusing, but because I feel so happy today. And, as anticipated, Lewis has made it sound as though last night was simply another task for The Man Who Can, and his execution was faultless. If he's half as good at installing kitchens, I'm sorted!

Lunch is an uninspiring cheese and pickle sandwich, with a large glass of apple juice. Lewis doesn't want to break off for very long and we eat quickly, in silence. When we go back upstairs I vacuum up the remaining bits of paper off the floor and he begins work on the wall I've just finished stripping.

There's nothing else I can do in this room without getting in his way. If I begin sanding the skirting boards we'll no doubt trip over each other. He keeps going back to lightly sand each of the spots and then apply another fine layer of filler to make them as smooth as possible.

I decide to go down into the conservatory and begin sorting through that box of Aggie's. A lot of the documents are yellowing and there are receipts for things that make me smile. I find one for a navy woollen coat, purchased in nineteen seventy-two and some gold earrings from a smart jeweller's shop in Clifton, Bristol. It feels wrong to be looking through her belongings and it's sad to think that when we die we all leave behind clutter. Things that someone else will have to sort through and throw away. Oh, Aggie, how I wish you'd had someone very close who could have done that for you. But I hope you understand that someone has to do it. At least I have a vested interest in ensuring that Ash Cottage remains as secluded and peaceful as when you lived here. It simply wouldn't be the same if someone laid claim to the track at the back and I know Terence would be devastated.

An hour passes and I feel humbled as I piece together a life that wasn't ordinary – by any means. There's a hand-written letter from a lady named Mabel, who commended her for being the first young woman from the Forest to attend university. She was a clever woman, who loved playing the piano and many of the cards so lovingly stored in the box featured pianos or musical notes. She also loved gardening because there were empty seed packets with the date of planting hand-written on them. The growing pile of items on the chair next to me looks a lot larger than it did inside the box, but nearer the bottom are thicker, older-looking documents. There's the architect's plan for the conservatory, and that's a pleasant surprise. It's only eight years old, so it must have been added shortly after her mother died. The death certificate, too, lies inside the box. I'm only halfway through and I realise that the afternoon is slipping away. Time to give some thought to tonight's dinner, but first I'm going to shower and change into something a little more feminine. There's only so long you can live in jeans and jumpers covered in paint and general building grime.

A tap at the door takes me by surprise. I look up to find Ryan staring back at me through the glass. I'm stunned and it's a moment or two before I leap up and unlock the door to let him in.

"Belated birthday wishes – I hope you picked up all my messages?"

I realise that I have no idea when I last saw my mobile.

"Thanks, and sorry, I've been stripping wallpaper ..."

"You were absorbed there for a moment," he nods in the direction of Aggie's box, "problems?"

"Um ... no, just sorting some papers to do with the cottage. You look like you're going hiking, or something. What on earth are you doing here? Is the road open?"

It's not raining, but he's wearing a thick ski jacket and stout walking boots. He leans in to give me a hug and a kiss on my cheek.

"No, both roads are now closed. You really do need to check your mobile. I've left you over a dozen messages, so I gave up and decided to come on foot. I see the heating isn't working again, poor you!"

I usher him inside and close the door.

"Sorry, I've been up and down that hill so many times in the last couple of days that my calf muscles think I've become a gym addict. Seriously, you won't believe what it's been like. But why aren't you at home watching some cheery Christmas movie and getting ready for tomorrow?" I know he likes to celebrate in style and there will, no doubt, be champagne to accompany the turkey, with all the trimmings.

"Because I can't possibly settle down and indulge knowing you're stuck here, under these circumstances. It was awful enough you missed out on any sort of birthday celebration yesterday and, I'm sorry, but the line has to be drawn somewhere. I'm parked further along the main road, just before the bend and there's a guy with a small boat ferrying people across the worst of the flood water. I've come to take you back with me for a few days and I won't take *no* for an answer. I've been invited to a couple of parties and you can be my plus-one. But tonight I'll be cooking for you. I wanted to come over yesterday, but I had to wrap things up at work."

At that precise moment Lewis appears in the doorway. Ryan's face registers surprise, which he quickly replaces with a smile.

"Lewis," he offers his hand and they shake. "Merry Christmas. I didn't realise you were stuck here too. I wouldn't have been quite so worried about her, if only she'd answered her mobile. I've come to take Maddie back to warm up and share a little festive company this holiday. The offer extends to you, too. I have a spare room and a comfortable couch."

Lewis looks unimpressed.

"That's a kind offer, but it's easier for me to work through as I'll be heading back home at New Year. I need to get this job finished as quickly as I can."

He nods in my direction, his eyes searching my face for a few seconds before he turns back to Lewis.

"To be honest, this isn't the right place for Miss Brooks to be staying at the moment. As soon as I've finished the main bedroom I'll start laying the laminate flooring and that's going to be easier if I can be left alone to get on with it."

Clearly, Ryan now believes that I've been getting in Lewis' way.

Am I a distraction? My head is whirling with random thoughts and a series of little out-takes from last night. His arm sliding down my naked back ... What would Ryan think if he knew our little secret? Suddenly, the boost to my self-esteem begins to dissipate. I was fooling myself that I'm the sort of woman who can make rash decisions and then take it in my stride. We are each accountable for our actions and now it looks like I have no choice but to let Ryan rescue me. It wouldn't make any sense to say I want to stay, especially with Lewis making it quite plain he wants me out of here.

"I'll put some things together, if you're sure, Lewis? I feel awful leaving you here with the mess, and I was just about to plan dinner ..."

"It's not a problem, Miss Brooks. I should be able to finish the bedroom and lay the flooring before the kitchen units arrive on the twenty-eighth. I'd like to be heading back up north on New Year's Eve, so it's going to be tight but I'm sure I can do it. A few days' break away from all of this will allow you to recharge your batteries. And you need to make up for yesterday."

Yesterday? Oh, he means my birthday.

Is this the same man I've been holed up with the past few days, or is he saying this to reassure Ryan? I don't expect him to fight to keep me here, of course, but I feel like I'm being thrown out of my own home. If he hadn't joined in I could have persuaded Ryan to stop for a festive drink and then sent him off with a 'thank you'.

Anger starts to rise up, making me feel hot and a little tearful. I walk around picking up things and begin stuffing them into the only holdall I can find. Ending up back in the conservatory, the two men are now in the kitchen talking about the layout. Lewis actually has the 3D plan in his hands.

I quickly pick up the remaining documents from the bottom of Aggie's box and stuff them into the side pocket of the holdall. Then I ram the pile of papers lying on the chair back inside the box and push the lid on.

Ryan comes to look for me and as soon as he spots the holdall he gives me one of his dazzling smiles.

"Right, Cinderella, you shall go to the ball. I hope you've packed a couple of cocktail dresses, the fun is about to begin."

Dresses? I dive into the sitting room and grab the first few garment bags hanging on the temporary rail. Throwing them over my arm I'm feeling, rather bizarrely, extremely disgruntled.

"That's it. I'm ready," I croak, my throat suddenly very dry. Lewis doesn't reappear from the kitchen.

"Just to warn you, I'll be raiding the shopping and I'll pop the keys through the letterbox if I'm done before you get back," he calls out, rather sharply.

Ryan has already picked up the holdall and is holding the door open for me, as I do up the buttons on my best winter coat – the one with the faux fur collar.

As we trudge up the hill and then down the other side it all feels very surreal. One moment I'm with Lewis and the next I'm with Ryan. I know Ryan is my boss and a great friend, but something tells me not to bare all. He keeps smiling across at me as we walk and it's obvious he thinks he's rescued me – but from what? And why?

CHAPTER 27

After we left Ash Cottage every step I took made me want to turn around and go back. It wasn't about the intimacy, well, not really – but, like it or not, I couldn't stop thinking about Lewis. Not only had I snatched the cottage out from under his feet, I'd abandoned him in a cold, damp environment with roughly the same level of facilities that you'd have if you went camping. And who would be stupid enough to do that in the middle of winter? The more I thought about it, the more I realised there were only two possible explanations. The first is that he needs the money to fund the work on his mother's house to get it ready to sell. He said as much, in a roundabout way. The other reason is rather sad to contemplate. If he doesn't have anyone left at all, and his army buddies are probably scattered around the country, perhaps he's lonely. Christmas is the hardest time of the year for people who are old, sick, homeless, alone ...

Ryan's mood is bordering on excitement and my mood is slowly pulling me into a depressive funk. Come on, Maddie, Lewis isn't some abandoned mongrel. He's a man who makes his own decisions and if he's alone, then it's by choice. I think he mentioned that, too. So it's unlikely to be the latter, and if it's about the money then you've done him a favour. He obviously enjoys what he does and, besides, I think this is something he's doing for Aggie rather than a stranger he doesn't know. Yes, of course! By the time we reach the boat I have convinced myself that it is the right thing to leave. Even if it's just to placate Lewis, I'm horrified to think that all I had been was an unwanted distraction. But I can't ignore the fact that he has made me feel good about myself again, in a way that is totally unexpected. For that, I am very grateful. There are no strings attached, I knew that before we shared our first kiss. I can't help wondering, though, about what might have happened tonight if we had spent another night alone together? One night of passion can be construed as a moment of madness; two nights mean there's a real on-going attraction and that would have been out of the question for him. Wouldn't it?

The evening turned out to be amazing. Ryan had prepared a wonderful birthday celebration dinner and as soon as we entered his vast kitchen/diner, I saw that the table had been laid with great attention to detail. Cut-glass wine glasses gleamed alongside the beautiful place settings. This was not a case of grabbing a few festive things, but everything was colour-coordinated and tasteful. The centrepiece on the table was a selection of reds and greens; from the holly, with bright shiny berries, to crimson roses – it was the result of careful planning.

When it was time for dessert, Ryan disappeared and came back a few minutes later with a small birthday cake with one red candle on the top.

"Happy birthday, lovely lady. Make a wish and blow out the candle."

This was no off-the-shelf supermarket item – he'd obviously had this made to order. I'd been to Ryan's house many times, but as surprised as I was by the effort he'd made, it somehow didn't seem out of character for him. He's the type of man who has always enjoyed a little luxury; he works hard, earns a good salary and lives well. I was touched by the gesture, though, because it was totally unexpected.

"Now you're spoiling me. But I like it!" It's a refreshing change to be in the company of a man who is making an effort to please *me*. I play the game and pause for a moment, then blow out the flame.

Afterwards, we retire to the sofa to look out at the courtyard garden as we sip our espressos. The outside lighting, combined with the large wall of glass sliding panels, make it feel as if the garden is a part of the room. It's decadent, as outside it's raining and windy: inside it's toasty. Magical, even, you might say, and it reminds me how easy city living is in so many respects. I wonder if I've made a mistake, and maybe Lewis was right when he accused me of hiding myself away.

"So what did you wish for?" Ryan looks at me expectantly.

"Just a chance to pull off this fresh start that isn't turning out to be quite as easy as I thought it would be."

"You weren't the one in the wrong, Maddie."

"I know, but Jeff's affair humiliated me in front of all of our friends and acquaintances. Most of them knew it was going on and I understand that no one wants to meddle in someone else's business, especially in that sort of situation. He'd done wrong, but because I've been on the receiving end of the sympathy, it made me feel inadequate in some way."

Self-esteem is so easy to knock down and so very, very hard to build back up.

"You can't dwell on it. Moving on means letting go, Maddie. A few days of city living will do you the world of good and when you get back to the cottage it will be looking a whole lot better than it does at the moment. That's bound to be pulling you down. It's like living in a hovel and in winter that's no fun."

"Thanks for rescuing me." Our eyes meet for a second and suddenly I'm not seeing just my boss.

For a woman who has decided she doesn't want a permanent man in her life again, it seems that two knights in shining armour have come to my rescue and saved me from myself. One might be doing that for money, but the other one... well, I'm beginning to look at Ryan in a whole new way and that is a real surprise.

"We've been invited to a drinks party the day after tomorrow, at Nathan and Arlene's. I mentioned I was hoping to talk you into having a break away from the cottage and they said I had to persuade you to come. I hope that's okay and you don't feel I've overstepped the mark?"

Ryan smiles, but I can see he's a little anxious about my reaction. I've never socialised with Nathan outside work and I only know his wife, Arlene, from the Christmas party each year.

"That's a nice gesture, I'm sure it will be fun. I'm very grateful to you, Ryan. It's tough getting through the first Christmas. I thought that being at Ash Cottage would take my mind off it, and it did, but with the flooding and the lack of heating…"

"Hey, that's what friends are for. Besides, I had an ulterior motive." He shifts in his chair, his body language indicating that this might be some sort of confession.

We've just eaten a wonderful breakfast of French pastries, fresh fruit and muesli. I'm reading a book on my Kindle and Ryan is leafing through a magazine. It's like something out of *Homes and Gardens*, you know, the idyllic setting and everything is shiny, pristine and screams life and style. I could get used to this.

"Really? Is this something you can share?" Ulterior motives aren't his thing; he's the sort of guy who is usually very upfront about everything. He can see I'm amused, but he's captured my interest.

"I don't quite know how to say this and, believe me, I had no intention whatsoever of bringing this up now. I know the timing isn't good, but when a complication crops up you have to react and deal with it, then change your plans accordingly. You know me – I like a challenge."

As he raises his head and our eyes meet, I see something I've never seen before. Why is he so hesitant? Whatever it is, he's concerned about my reaction and he doesn't know how to deliver the news.

"Maddie, your life has been turned upside down and anyone

going through that would understandably need time to adjust to the changes. You've done well with the decisions you've made so far and I have been keeping a discreet eye on you. I would have stepped in if you'd announced you were running off to foreign climes or taken up some absurd sport. However, I don't think it's wise to wait any longer to be straight with you about something. Especially given recent ... umm ... developments."

What a fool I've been, wallowing in my own problems. Ryan is going to sack me and I can't blame him. My head has probably been all over the place during the past few months. I thought I was coping and managing to function, at least on the basics like work and finding a home. The cottage has turned out to be a bit of a disaster and maybe I've been fooling myself that my work and our clients haven't been affected.

"Look, Ryan, I'm really sorry to have turned into such a liability lately. I know we are friends and we go back a long way, but you have to do what you have to do."

I can't look him in the eye any longer. My head falls forward as I busy myself with turning off my Kindle and placing it neatly alongside the coffee cup in front of me. What am I going to do? Now I'm on my own this is the worst possible thing that could have happened.

"Jeff was right and I should have acknowledged that."

I freeze, then my head jerks up, questioningly. Ryan has been one of my strongest allies throughout this entire mess and now he's changing sides? I might be guilty of a lot of things relating to my marriage, particularly in terms of not facing up to the fact that we'd grown apart. But does that mean I deserved to be cheated on and lied to? I look at Ryan aghast, the breath knocked out of me as if he'd delivered a physical blow.

"When he told you men don't have women friends unless there's an element of attraction, I remember how we laughed at that. It hurt a bit, if I'm honest, although I couldn't let you see that. It was a ludicrously generalised statement, of course, but I'm afraid in my case it was true."

I'm frozen, unable to speak or move. What?

"You see, I could never understand what you saw in Jeff. He took everything that you did for granted and I never, even once, saw him really value your role; either as a wife or as the hub of the family."

Ryan turns to look out of the window, feigning distraction and, no doubt, awaiting my response. I'm speechless, unable to take this in. After a couple of minutes he turns back to face me.

"I always felt you were special, Maddie, but it took me a while to work out why that was. When I started up the business, of course I wanted you to be a part of it, because you're a well-motivated and hard worker. But it was much more than that. I needed you, somehow, to be a part of my life and I settled for what I could get."

I'm not sure how to react because I can't process what I'm hearing.

I always thought of Ryan as the eternal bachelor, believing that he enjoyed the freedom of not being tied down. His lifestyle and interests give him what many would covet. He's 'the catch' we all thought didn't want to get caught. Goodness, over the years I've tried to set him up, rather unsuccessfully, with every single woman I've come across. Few lasted beyond one date.

"But you never said a word: never indicated for one second how you felt!"

"How could I? You were with Jeff by the time I realised and when you left to have the kids, I thought that was it. You have no idea how I deliberated over the ethics of getting in touch with you a few years later. I justified my actions by telling myself that it was purely a business decision. I needed good people and there was a possibility that the boys would be starting school and you'd be looking for a job. But the truth was that I missed you like crazy."

I'm still reeling from this revelation and I'm not too sure what I feel about it. I trust Ryan: I always trusted Ryan.

"I appreciate your honesty, really I do, but I like to think I know you pretty well. You're comfortable with me because I understand you, maybe even better than you understand yourself. A traditional relationship would bore you to tears. You weren't made to be a family man, Ryan. The thought of that makes me want to laugh out loud!"

"But even your life has moved on now, don't you see? Yes, you will always be a parent, but it's no longer the focal point of your life. This is the time when you get to think about what *you* want for a change. I'm not offering that staid life you had with Jeff. I love you, lady, and I'm offering you a future that promises excitement and a lot of fun together. I love you and I think I always have."

He shifts in his seat, as if he's going to stand, then changes his mind and extends his hand to me across the table. Our fingertips touch.

"Seeing you with Lewis Hart made me panic. After watching Jeff walking all over you and then tearing you apart with his callous lack of respect, I wasn't about to let anyone use you. You are an attractive woman, Maddie, and you're vulnerable at this particular moment in your life. Okay, I admit jealousy reared its ugly head. I'm sure Lewis finds you attractive, heck, who wouldn't? He's biding his time but, trust me, he'll make a move on you.

"This is my one shot and I'm not going to miss out on grabbing your attention. It hasn't been easy all these years settling for being a listening ear. I want *you*, Maddie, everything – and I'm not prepared to settle for less any longer."

When I tell him what happened last night, what will he think of me? I knew it wasn't going to lead anywhere, but I still let it happen and a part of me has no regrets. Am I still that same woman Ryan is talking about? I wonder if he realises I've changed and each day I change a little more?

We stand – three steps and his arms are around me. I bury my head into his shoulder and what I want more than anything is to let go of any lingering doubt that I could ever be enough for him. Has he really outgrown his bachelor lifestyle and there's no chance he will end up losing interest in me, like Jeff did? The only thing in my life that gives me any sense of worth at the moment is the fact that I'm a mum and a soon-to-be grandma; everything else feels like one complete and utter mess. Will being with Ryan undo all of that? I don't even know what I feel any more. I remind myself that this is real, not some fantasy in my head. I draw back to look up at him.

"We've lived our lives so differently and I never, for one moment, thought that a serious relationship would ever appeal to you."

Ryan stands back a little, so that his eyes can search my face.

"Because I couldn't have the one woman I've always wanted. Hey, did you ever consider that while my life has been fun, it's also been incomplete? That when married friends envied me, I actually envied them back?"

He smiles at me for one heart-stopping moment and then lifts my hand to kiss the tips of my fingers.

"But you came back from your holiday enthused and with plans to get away again very soon."

He clears his throat, holding my gaze with his own.

"Confession time. I was hoping that you'd look up and say how much you missed me and beg me not to head off again. I couldn't understand why you were unable to see what Jeff saw: we always had something special going on."

Ryan pulls me into him again and hugs me gently in his arms. It's strange being held by him in this way. I can't stop Lewis' face from flashing through my mind out of guilt, even though this suddenly feels so right. Ryan and I have shared a lot over the years. I always knew he understood me so much better than anyone else. What a fool I was, ignoring everything around me and escaping into my safe little world of domesticity as if it was a haven. The boys kept me sane and gave me not just a sense of purpose, but also a focus. It wasn't empty-nest syndrome I felt when they left home; it was the reality of being left with something that wasn't real. I didn't love Jeff and hadn't loved him for a long time, so gradually my work filled the cavernous hole in my life. And who was I working alongside, day in and day out? Ryan. Who did I call whenever anything happened? Ryan. Whose opinion did I seek about Ash Cottage? Ryan's.

"I've messed up everything, haven't I?" My voice is little more than a whisper.

Ryan inclines his head, his mouth hovering over mine. Then he smiles and as our lips touch, suddenly I'm opening up to him and the sweetness is replaced by hungry desire.

"Judging by that reaction," he drawls, "I have nothing to worry about. The past isn't relevant. We are drawing a line and I don't want either of us to look back. I tried to find someone, you know that, but I can assure you there is no one in my thoughts apart from you. We can make this work, Maddie. All I need is for you to give *us* a chance."

"One day at a time?" As I gaze up at him, it's like seeing him for the first time. I know every single thing about his face; every line and every expression. What I haven't seen before is the look of excitement he can't contain any longer.

He lowers his face, nestling his cheek against my hair and I hear a soft, "Yesss..." as he wraps his arms tightly around me. I feel as if he has no intention of ever letting me go and that feels so good.

CHAPTER 28

Christmas Day was brilliant, we had such a good time that we hardly noticed the fact that the rain continued throughout. Several times during the day I found myself wondering about the poor people who had been evacuated from their homes. What sort of Christmas celebrations were they enjoying? It was heart-breaking to think of the misery the flooding had caused. The moment my thoughts moved on and I began to think about Ash Cottage, and Lewis, I immediately reigned myself in, determined not to pursue that line of thought.

Ryan, too, was the most relaxed I'd ever known him. Usually he talks about work a lot, as in every other sentence, and it's something I've come to expect from him. He didn't mention work once and with each passing hour he opened up to me, more and more. He seemed intent on proving something, trying to convince me that there was more to him than work and living it up. It was rather curious because I would never pass judgement on anyone's chosen lifestyle and, anyway, shouldn't it have been the other way around? My life has been very sedate, really, everything revolving around the family and work. Jeff said one of the reasons he strayed was because he felt his life had become mundane. Mundane? What did he think it was like for me, constantly having to pull myself away from working online to make sure his meal was on the table and the house was running smoothly? After the boys left home it should have been easier, but it was actually worse because they at least brought a sense of life and energy into the home. Jeff would come home in a mood and then bury his head in his Kindle, while I had to second-guess whether he expected me to be quiet or encourage him to share his problems. There never was much time for *me* and I never questioned that, even when it was just the two of us.

When it came to Ryan, what was there to criticise? He had surrounded himself with the things that go hand in hand with hard work and success, which was only natural. He deserved the comfort and tranquility he had created.

The sound of footsteps in the hallway confirms that he's up and there's a gentle tap on the bedroom door.

"Morning. Are you awake?" His voice is a mere whisper.

"Yes, I've been awake for a while."

He swings open the door and his head pops around. I can't see his expression in the gloom.

"I did wonder, although it's very early. I'm making some tea, would you like a mug?"

"Thanks. Yes."

Ryan closes the door behind him and in the darkness a smile creeps over my face. We're old friends and yet there's a sense of newness about everything now. It brings with it all the uncertainty and hesitancy of getting to know each other all over again. He's a gentleman and I wonder if he realises how endearing that makes him to me. It's a long, long time since the main man in my life paid attention to my needs, over and above his own. Being looked after is a novelty after a lifetime of looking after other people.

When I rang the boys yesterday to tell them I was staying with a friend for a few days, they both guessed to whom I was referring. They know Ryan quite well from his many visits to the house on business, and their main concern was that I was safe and no longer cut off from the outside world. I thought it might be a problem and that they would quiz me about it, but both seemed quite calm and accepting. Truthfully, I think anything is an improvement on the constant rows Jeff and I had been having on and off for years. I don't think either of them is happy to think of me living alone, though, and Nick, in particular, is quite vocal about that. I can't see anything changing in the immediate future and I did my best to reassure Nick that things were going well. What will they make of this latest development with Ryan, I wonder.

The sound of footsteps and the rattle of china make me jump out of bed to open the door for Ryan. In the murky darkness I feel around for the sidelight and switch it on, realising my pyjamas aren't exactly flattering. How I wish I'd given more thought to what I was throwing into that holdall, but then everything happened so fast. I brush off my concerns as needless vanity when Ryan appears with a roguish smile on his face.

"I didn't mean for you to get up. Go back to bed and I'll put your tea on the side table."

"No, that's fine. I've been lying here for a while, thinking. You know how it is."

He places the tray down on the dressing table and steps forward, putting his hand on my shoulder to give it a gentle squeeze.

"Hey, you're a survivor. Not even the floods could keep a good woman down." He's laughing at me now, his eyebrows raised as he surveys my cosy, but distinctly unglamorous, nightwear. He's looking very suave, wearing silver-grey designer pyjama bottoms and a tee-shirt that hugs his body like a glove.

He carries a mug over to me as I sit up and straighten the pillows. He places it down on the table next to the bed, sporting a wry smile.

"What?"

"This is weird, isn't it? If you were anyone else I'd expect to be jumping into bed beside them. We aren't quite at that stage yet, are we?" He looks down at me, his gaze is searching and makes me flustered. No, I'm not ready, but I offer up my face for a kiss and he immediately obliges. That really makes him smile.

"We're still the same people underneath, nothing has changed," I reassure him.

"But everything could be about to change."

Lewis' face immediately springs into my mind and I quickly push it away. Ryan grabs his mug and comes to sit at my feet.

"We need to talk a few things through," he's serious, although I'm having a concentration problem, not aided by this surreal setting.

"Fire away."

"Look, I spent so long thinking of you as someone else's wife that it's difficult for me not to feel that I'm carrying out some heinous crime here. For starters you haven't actually told me how you feel. I just wanted to be straight with you and though I'm trying to be patient, I need to know what your answer is going to be."

Am I attracted to Ryan? Well, the honest answer is, yes, I suppose there always was a little undercurrent going on in our friendship. I simply hadn't realised it was there; I was too busy juggling family life. What happened with Lewis was an aberration, so I have to put that out of my mind.

I pose the question that has been worrying me. "I've always been your number-one fan, you know that, but how do we cross that divide between being just best friends and two people in a relationship?"

"I thought we could use tonight's party as a starting point."

"How?"

"I think we should regard it as our coming-out party."

I almost drop the mug of hot tea into my lap.

"Which means?"

"I want to announce to our friends and colleagues that we're seeing each other. If the world begins to regard us as a couple, then I think the transition will be easier. Let's just put it out there and see what the reaction is to the news. Worst-case is there will be a little bit of gossip about when exactly we became close. As neither of us has anything to hide, that doesn't worry me one little bit."

"This is it, isn't it? I guess I'd better get used to a new role. I won't be sorry to let go of the betrayed-wife label, I'm heartily sick of it. I only hope I can rise to the challenge of being the love interest in Mr Ryan Fielding's life." I look up at him from beneath my eyelashes, hardly vampish, given my attire, but it's a start.

"Hmm ... I'm really looking forward to this evening. I think there are going to be a few shocked faces, that's for sure."

More and more I'm noticing a hint of playfulness mingling with his words and accentuating his low, dulcet tones. I guess the changes are happening already and we've crossed the line into the unknown.

Why, oh why, did I just randomly pick up items and stuff them into the holdall that day, letting anger take over and pushing out any sensible thoughts about packing? Unease settles in my stomach as I know the answer only too well – I was upset that Lewis was in such a hurry to see the back of me. Well, that was then and this is now! I want to look my absolute best tonight for Ryan and, fortunately, I grabbed the right dress to do that. I seem to have thrown in some shoes that will do and all I'm missing are a few accessories.

"What's wrong?" Ryan pops his head around the door, checking up on me. I've been in here a long time.

"I could cheerfully scream at the moment. I'll never pack a bag in a hurry again."

Stressed doesn't quite describe a feeling that is now beginning to develop into a bit of a panic attack.

"Hey, calm down. That dress is amazing and I love it when you pin your hair up like that."

I stare at my reflection in the mirror, acknowledging that the hair looks good, which is rather a miracle, given that I didn't bring half of my hair products. Ryan's guest bathroom is rather well stocked and thoughtfully so, from a female perspective. There was even a small can of hairspray and I try not to think about the woman who forgot to pack it after her overnight stay.

"Well, the shoes will do, although I have a fabulously sparkly pair back at the cottage that would have been perfect. But I didn't pack anything to put around my neck and with this neckline it looks as if I'm half dressed. Why didn't I think to throw in some jewellery or a small scarf?"

I'm moaning and Ryan looks rather wary, no doubt seeing a side of me he hasn't seen before. A woman about to flip because she doesn't feel her best when it's time to shine.

I shoot a look at him in pure exasperation, a part of me wanting to say I can't do this tonight because I want everything to be perfect – and it isn't.

"Hey," he approaches slowly, but doesn't take his eyes off my face. With great care he places a hand on each of my shoulders, making sure he doesn't disturb my hair. Those familiar, gentle eyes crinkle up into a heart-warming smile.

"I have just the thing, well a few things actually. Come with me." He drops his hands down and reaches out for my hand, leading me off in the direction of his bedroom.

I've been in here once before when he was showing off the new decor. It's very minimalist, with a soft cream carpet that must have cost a fortune and glossy doors running along the length of one wall that slide open at the touch of a finger. Exposed is a fitted interior in pale oak and everything is so neatly organised it's like being in a high-end fashion store. To the right-hand side, a stack of narrow drawers extend from the floor to the ceiling and Ryan flips out a small ladder, concealed at the side. He places his foot on the second step and reaches up to pull out a half-drawer, level with his shoulders.

"Here," he climbs back down and indicates for me to look inside.

At first I have no idea what I'm looking at. Is it a keepsake drawer? There is a small stack of what looks like cards, the sort you give at Christmas and on birthdays, plus six or seven boxes varying in size and shape.

"Embarrassing, eh?" A nervous smile plays around the edges of his mouth. He looks at me intently, awaiting my reaction. "Go ahead."

I pull out the top card, wondering where I've seen it before and when I flick it open, it's my own handwriting I see staring back at me. I check the next card in the pile – and the next. They're all from me. I look up at him, questioningly.

"Every card you've ever given me. You always made me feel special, Maddie. Each card wasn't just plucked from a shelf, but thought was put into choosing the right one. Always a work of art or a scene you thought I'd enjoy and even links to places you know I've visited. And I thought of you in a special way, each birthday and Christmas."

"I know. Flowers are my favourite gift, because no one but you ever bought them for me." At the time I don't think that had really occurred to me. I just assumed it was the gift that was easy to give a woman who was your employee and a friend. Not too personal, and yet a lovely gesture.

"These are the gifts I couldn't give you," he places the small drawer down on the bed and withdraws one of the boxes, holding it out to me.

I take it from him, feeling bewildered. He nods his head, inviting me to open it. As I ease off the lid, inside there is an exquisite necklace. The delicate chain is offset by a leaf held by its stem and the detail is simply wonderful.

"It's stunning. But, why?"

"Because I wanted to give you beautiful things, but it wasn't my place. Not then; maybe never. But there didn't seem to be any harm in having them here, in case."

Having taken the best part of an hour on skin preparation and then make-up to look my best for tonight, tears now threaten to undo all the good work. I want to say something, but when I open my mouth to speak, my throat is hoarse with the effort of holding my emotions in check.

197

"Don't be freaked out," Ryan insists. "Just look through what's here and pick whatever you want to wear. These were bought for you and I know we're taking it slowly, but maybe on your next birthday you'll accept them as a special gift from me."

I throw my arms around his neck and, while taking deep breaths to keep myself from tearing-up, I show him how I feel. Hair, make-up ... nothing matters any more. I knew Ryan had a good heart, but I never for one moment thought it was mine.

LEWIS

CHAPTER 29

It didn't take long for Terence to appear after Maddie and Ryan left.

"What's happening? Where's Maddie going?"

I think Terence assumed that I'd upset her in some way.

"That was Ryan, her boss. She's going to spend Christmas with him so I can get on with the work without any interruptions."

"Well, that's a surprise. Guess you're happy about that, then?"

It' a weird question – of course I'm happy about that.

"Do you mind if I sit? It's been an awful morning. Just between us, Joanna isn't an easy woman to live with. She hates to see me being idle, as she calls it."

"Women, eh? No chance of a peaceful life whenever they're around."

"I thought maybe there was something developing between the two of you? I guess if she's gone off with her boss, I was wrong."

That's the thing about Terence, he sees a lot and usually says a little.

"I'm sensing this situation has become a little complicated. Am I right?"

Okay, he's offering a listening ear and that's probably just what I need at the moment.

"I knew she was going to be trouble from the moment I first set eyes on her, Terence. Miss Madeleine Brooks: her name conjures up the image of a formidable ex-school mistress, or a spinster lady you wouldn't want to cross. And there she was, all doe-eyed and fragile after her recent divorce. Hurting and vulnerable, trying to convince herself, and the world, that she's strong, as she tries not to fall apart. So what did I do? I made her feel like the woman she should be, not the woman some poor-excuse-for-a-husband had turned her into. What on earth was I thinking? Why did I allow the situation to drag me into this little world of hers?" I shake my head, unable to believe the folly of the situation. Terence looks appalled.

"Looks like rather unfortunate timing. Awkward, though. This Ryan guy has done you a favour, then."

"Yes, you could say that."

Even as I replied, I think both Terence and I knew that wasn't the case. He gave a shrug and stood up.

"I'd better get back, Joanna will be wondering where I am. And Lewis, it's probably all turned out for the best. Sometimes circumstances dictate our actions. People can end up doing things that take them well outside of their comfort zone, only to live to regret it at a later stage."

I sit for a while, thinking about the past. Yumiko would have understood, of course, because she could see what was inside a person with one sweep of her almond eyes. When I first met her I was a lost soul, just like Madeleine, and having a tough time settling into army life. It was my first trip abroad. I was a swaggering youth, convinced I knew everything, but the reality was that I had a lot of lessons still to learn. Ironically, the posting to Germany didn't seem a big deal, until I was introduced to an oriental lady nearly twenty years my senior. She was quite simply the most beautiful woman I had ever met and in that noisy, smoke-filled bar she seemed so out of place. It was several weeks after our affair began that I learned she was married. Her German husband was a liaison executive for one of the large suppliers of field equipment and he wasn't a nice man. I never really understood why she'd stayed with him, other than he was the man her father had chosen for her.

We had almost three months of illicit meetings and it was a period in my life that changed me forever. She cared for me in a way no other woman had ever done before and made me understand that sometimes life is about having to learn some rather harsh lessons. That doesn't mean to say that people don't care, but sometimes they don't have a choice, or they do, but they make the wrong decisions – even when that ends up causing someone else pain. She told me that disconnecting myself from my emotions in order to avoid confronting the turmoil within was harming me in more ways than I could know. I was doing that to myself, Yumiko told me in no uncertain terms.

"You are the master of your own destiny," she'd said. "Make no more excuses. Make only the right decisions."

As a young child brought up with due care, but shown no real love or demonstrative affection, I came to see that I was bound to feel *unloved*. She wept for me, for the child I was and the man I had become. When I eventually broke down, it was a release.

It's true the army routine was exactly what I needed and it stopped me from getting involved with a group of lads at home who were a bad influence. Wasted potential is a tragedy. It wasn't a surprise to hear that one of them ended up in prison for selling drugs to fund his habit. The training I received was character-building and taught me survival and endurance skills that turned a rather unruly youth into a soldier. Before my training I had no concept of what that would mean.

Yumiko, on the other hand, was the one who taught me how to feel. She also taught me that the body is a temple and you have to respect it. As the first woman in my life who showed me her tears and her joy, she held me to her with a gentleness and desire that was overpowering. The art of tantric lovemaking is not just about erotic skill, but finding within yourself a sense of who you are and laying that bare to the person whose body you honour.

I've made love to many women in my life since Yumiko. Like ships that pass in the night, it's always been a transient thing.

No ties and an instant reaction to a pressing need. Quick, simple and mutually gratifying. I've never looked to rekindle those long, memorable afternoons where time would seem to stretch out endlessly and it was all about the journey, rather than simple self-gratification.

I let this Madeleine into my thoughts for all the wrong reasons and I dropped my guard, so now I'm paying the price. I felt sorry for her and now this damned woman is in my head. Even though she's not here, I can't stop thinking about her.

I have to keep reminding myself that this is Aggie's home and, clearly, I'm helping Madeleine out for a reason. I still can't believe that a stranger came along and, because of the unfortunate timing, I lost out.

Madeleine Brooks made an unwise decision, but she's not a bad person. In fact that's the trouble, she's one of those women who can't stop themselves from wanting to mend the things in life that are broken. She's a nurturer and if she had stayed she would have ended up trying to analyse what's broken inside me. But she also grows on you in an annoying way, with her constant chatter, which draws you out. You find yourself unwittingly telling her things you don't want to share with anyone. Another day and who knows what I would have regretted telling her.

"How's it going, Lewis? Looks like you're nearly there." Terence appears by my side as I'm on the patio sawing a piece of wood.

Madeleine has been gone two days and I've been working flat out.

"Come and take a look. The main bedroom is now finished and all I have left to do is to paint the landing and sitting-room walls. Maddie did all the paintwork and she made a good job of it. Aggie would have approved of getting rid of all of that old, dark rosewood."

I take Terence on a quick tour and it's the first time he's seen anything beyond the conservatory.

"This is probably why Joanna is keeping on at me, then. I can see how much brighter the cottage looks now and it feels more spacious. Joanna doesn't miss a thing, unfortunately. She's probably right, of course, as usual."

"Do you believe in spirits, Terence?"

"Funny you should ask."

I wait, expecting him to continue, but he doesn't.

"There are times I wonder if Aggie is still here and I'm wrong to dismiss what a lot of people believe to be true. But, me, I can't get my head around it. I've felt the negativity of bad karma, well, that's how I think of it. Anyone who has seen death in battle will know what I mean. Whatever reservations I had at the start, after Madeleine moved in, have disappeared. The atmosphere here now is very different, but even I felt spooked that first couple of days. I can't imagine how Madeleine must have felt. There was something tangible here and I know that sounds crazy."

"I wouldn't admit this to anyone else, but I don't believe dying is the end of it. It is a shame, though, that all of this couldn't have been done when Aggie was here to fully appreciate it." He shakes his head, soberly.

"I tried my best to persuade her to let me take my time and, at her pace, turn back the clock on Ash Cottage. But we could all see how tired she was, mentally and physically. Illness is draining and I knew that she would struggle to cope with the upheaval, even though the thought made her eyes shine. So we talked about how it would look, as if her illness was a temporary thing, and she knew I would strive to make her vision come true. The only potential problem was that strip of land to the rear of the cottage and I knew Aggie worried about it, fearing one day someone would lay claim to it. She was adamant that there was no documentation to prove ownership, but always said that her father had purchased it shortly after her grandfather had died. She said, 'You will sort it, won't you, Lewis?' and I'd reassured her that I would. It's none of my business, now, but I hate breaking a promise."

"She'd understand, given the situation. You've more than honoured her memory, Lewis."

"Well, it's certainly a weird twist of fate that a stranger ended up being the vehicle for bringing Ash Cottage back to life. While it's unlikely I'll be asked to do the whole project now because of Ryan, that doesn't matter. There's nothing Madeleine is planning to do that Aggie and I didn't visualise, or that would have made her unhappy. I'll admit a part of the reason I felt uncomfortable here at first was because my motive was two-fold. I couldn't see this woman struggle on her own with something she should never have taken on in the first place. The other reason is that I wanted to be around in case she changed her mind and decided to put it back on the market. I still feel that Madeleine doesn't belong here. I was meant to be a forester and live here; she was meant to be living in the city with a man who enjoys the finer things in life."

Terence and I both shrug our shoulders at a situation that should never have happened. Perhaps it's true that everything happens for a reason. The truth is that without the money from the sale of my mother's house it would have been difficult to have borrowed what I needed to buy Ash Cottage. At least there's a chance it might eventually go back on the market, so as soon as I've laid the walnut floors and installed the kitchen, I'll be putting all of my efforts into getting my mother's house ready to sell. I have a purchaser already lined up and I figure a couple of weeks will be enough to redecorate it throughout and upgrade the kitchen. By then Miss Brooks will be totally wrapped up in her boss's arms, for good. I'm secretly hoping that Ash Cottage will become a memory that turned out to be more of a nightmare, and she'll be only too glad to walk away from it.

When I realised that Maddie had left Aggie's box of papers underneath the coffee table in the conservatory, I tried my best to ignore it. It unsettled me, though, and every time I walked through into the kitchen it was the first thing I saw. Eventually I grabbed a coffee and sat down with one thing in mind. If anyone had a right to go through Aggie's things it was me; we'd spent so much time together over the months and I know for a fact there wasn't anyone else that close to her. Several neighbours popped in from time to time; after all, her family had lived here for a long time. There were some relatives who probably called in at Christmas and maybe on her birthday, but I can imagine the conversation was mostly pleasantries, reminiscing and local gossip.

Aggie and I talked, really talked about everything and anything. If she asked me a question I was honest with her; she asked because she was interested and that meant a lot to me. She once asked if I could help sort through her papers, but at the time it didn't feel right. I didn't want anyone to ever have any reason to think I was taking advantage of a lonely old lady. More often than not, when I popped in for a chat there was nothing she needed, so we'd sit and have a cup of tea and she'd talk about the past. If she wasn't well, then I'd sort her shopping. On good days she'd have a list of jobs she wanted me to do and I did them without charging her, just because it was a pleasure to help.

Leafing through the papers it was the history of the cottage and how it had turned from a simple forest worker's dwelling into the extended version it is today. Receipts from local tradesmen now long gone reiterated the fact that Ash Cottage had always been loved. Like the layers of wallpaper Madeleine and I had stripped off the main bedroom walls, here in black and white was the proof that each decade had seen the cottage having a refresh. Even the original invoice for the kitchen, which had been hand-made by a local forester, was there. Interspersed were more personal documents, the death certificates of her father and mother were a reminder that this cottage has seen everything life has to offer. I raised my head and stared around at the silence, wondering if they were all here watching me.

And then I found the one document, the missing link, and I knew that Aggie would be pleased that I was the one to find it.

My conscience wouldn't let me simply fold it up and pocket it, so instead I slid it in between a sheaf of drawings that turned out to be the plans for the conservatory.

We're nearly there, Aggie. A few months and I'll be living here as we originally planned.

MADDIE

CHAPTER 30

If I was nervous in the car on the way to Nathan and Arlene's, it was nothing compared to walking into their beautiful, open-plan extension, purpose-built for entertaining. What was supposed to be a cosy supper party had turned into a large gathering and a sea of faces greeted us as we entered. I turned to Ryan with a look of shock, tinged with horror, on my face. He looked determined and merely shrugged.

"I thought I'd better give them advance warning and Arlene said to leave it to her. I certainly wasn't expecting this ..."

We were a little late arriving and it seems some of the partygoers might have been here a while, because as Nathan ushered us in a little cheer went up and there was lifting of glasses. I started to sweat a little, uncomfortable about being the topic of everyone's conversation. I could imagine it, 'Have you heard? Maddie has snapped up the gorgeous Ryan. Can you imagine that?'

"What on earth did you tell them?" I whisper out of the side of my mouth, as we follow Nathan further into the room.

"Only that we are now officially seeing each other and that I've never been happier."

Arlene approaches with a champagne flute in each hand and instantly moves in to air-kiss in her inimitable style. Ryan lifts them out of her hands, leaving her arms hovering somewhere behind me. She closes them in a warm, and very positive, hug.

"Merry Christmas! And we were so thrilled to hear your news. About time, too!" There's a general muttering of approval from those watching us and it seems that everyone we work with, or have ever worked with, are here with their partners. The reaction seems positive and not the expression of disbelief that I'd expected.

I take a sip of champagne to cover my initial embarrassment and the fact that I've been rendered speechless. Ryan jumps in, like the gentleman he is.

"Patience is a virtue and I have waited a long time." He raises his glass to me and smiles, intimately, as if we are standing here alone and not being watched by a crowd of eyes.

Nathan immediately raises his glass, too. "You officially wear the badge of the most infamous bachelor I know and then spring this surprise on us! I have to say, though, it couldn't happen to two nicer people. Maddie, here's to you, and may I add that you look absolutely gorgeous tonight!"

I feel the heat rising up my neck and into my cheeks and I'm so glad that I spent time fussing over my appearance tonight. Everyone in the room has their eyes firmly fixed on me and it's nerve-wracking, but for all the right reasons.

"He's a dark horse, that's for sure, but he's so irresistible. And he rescued me in such a dashing fashion – how could I possibly reject a man who crosses a flood to take me to safety?"

There's a ripple of laughter and suddenly the tension begins to dissolve. I realise that the negativity is all in my head and that people who know us don't seem too surprised to hear we are a couple. A cosy, warm feeling begins to wash over me and Ryan seeks out my hand to give it a reassuring squeeze.

"So, how is the flooding? Is the cottage safe?"

I turn to look at Martin Howell – Ryan's right-hand man – as he approaches with his wife, Chantelle. We all shake hands, Ryan has met her before, but this is my first time.

"The cottage is rather cold and damp, but dry. The flood has closed the top road due to a landslide and the only way in via

210

the flooded main road is by boat. No deliveries were able to get through, so aside from the fact that the central heating isn't working, there's still no kitchen. It's pretty grim, I'm afraid."

"That's why I charged in to rescue her." Ryan looks like a very happy man, with a big smile on his face as he glances from Martin to me. "A little bribery to get the guy with the boat to hang around and a bit of a hike – it's not an easy walk up that hill – and she was mine."

There's another ripple of laughter as the little circle we're standing in begins to grow.

"It's so romantic." Shelley, who works in accounts, has joined us.

"Well, I should be back at the cottage helping out. I've left my handyman there finishing off one of the bedrooms and laying flooring. Fingers crossed the flooding subsides enough for the kitchen units to be delivered, because he has another project starting very soon. It's difficult enough that the cottage is so cold, but with no kitchen as well it's not easy living there."

"Then you'll just have to remain as my house guest until he's finished. No point in going back until the heating is fixed, either. January is going to get even colder, apparently, and there could be snow." There's a lot of nodding of heads at Ryan's words. It sends a little shock through me. Not go back until the end of January? Confusion wraps around me, stifling my thoughts and Lewis' face appears from nowhere. Suddenly I'm back in the conservatory and we're having coffee together. It seems I missed something.

"I said that you're lucky to find someone who is prepared to work over the holidays. It must be costing you a fortune, though. Do you have any regrets, Maddie? It sounds like it's a huge renovation project. And rather isolated, too. Wouldn't you rather be back in the middle of city life?" Shelley, bless her, is probably horrified. She's the sort of lady who wouldn't stay in anything less than a four-star hotel, and would think that was slumming it if there wasn't a spa on the doorstep and a hairdresser.

Her words remind me that Lewis has an ulterior motive.

"Well, the guy who is doing the work thought he'd be the new owner of the property. He just missed out, so his diary was unexpectedly free. Besides, his mother died recently and it must be tough to get through the Christmas period when you don't feel like celebrating." As I say the words it tugs at my heart. Of course he wanted to be on his own and no wonder my inane chatter frayed his nerves.

"Sounds like he'll step in with an offer if Ash Cottage is suddenly on the market again," Martin looks pointedly at Ryan, who immediately responds.

"Hey guys, ease up. I told Maddie we'd take this slowly. I think she's fallen in love with the cottage and I can't blame her, it's in a beautiful spot."

I'm beginning to feel a little uncomfortable that people are already making assumptions. I understand that our situation is unusual: we know each other very well, but as a couple we are still brand new. That's what they don't see, the unknown territory that lies between friendship and a full-blown relationship. Ryan is trying to deflect the questions, but what will happen in the future? I love Ash Cottage and yet I know the appeal just isn't there for Ryan, no matter what he says to stem the conversation. His house is just that: his. I feel like a guest in it, which I am. He would never move to the Forest, but would I move back to the city?

I tune back into the conversation and Ryan has managed to change the subject. He's talking about work and there's a heated discussion going on. I hope I smile and laugh in the right places, because I'm not really listening. My mind can't stop thinking about the future and what's to come.

When we eventually leave it's late and walking out into the chilly night air is refreshing. I let out a deep breath, drawing in another to clear my head. I didn't even finish my first glass of champagne, but I suppose all the nervous energy has an effect. It's not raining and the stars are out, a reminder that there's so much more to the universe than the little bubble we live in. In the grand scheme of things, tonight is just one tiny step.

"Sorry, that wasn't such a great idea, was it? I hadn't thought it through properly."

Ryan stops, folds his arms around me and looks down at me with eyes that melt my heart.

"It's just that I want everyone to know that you're mine, now. I keep talking about taking it slowly, but in here," he raises my hand and places it against his chest, "I want to move you into the house and keep you there forever."

I lean into him, my forehead nestling just under his chin.

"A little cottage in the country isn't your thing, is it?"

"No, if I'm honest with you. Great for a holiday one week every year, but it's a big, wide world out there. So many exotic locations to visit – so many wonderful places. I want to revisit them with you by my side."

At last I have someone in my life who really does care enough to worry about what I'm thinking. I'm so used to being taken for granted that I'd forgotten what it felt like to be the centre of someone else's world. I know I can make Ryan happy and fill that sense of loneliness that was always there, lurking just beneath the surface. He masked it well, living a life so full that there wasn't time to dwell on it and that's why it was never really visible. He's ready to make a commitment sooner rather than later.

"The thought of letting Ash Cottage go is hard for me."

He inclines his head, tilting my chin with his finger so he can look into my eyes.

"But you'd let it go to be with me?" It's a question, but the forcefulness of his tone means it's also a prompt.

"Yes, because it's my dream, not our dream. But your house doesn't feel like *our* home, either. I know how long and hard you've worked to turn it into a beautiful statement and a place that is truly stunning. I'm enjoying my stay, it's wonderful, but I'm only a house guest and I don't think that feeling will ever go away."

"It's only bricks and mortar, Maddie. To me it's an investment,

213

no more, and no less. I'd give it up tomorrow for you. We need to plan our future together and that means every little thing, including where we're going to live."

"But it's complicated, Ryan. I have the boys and, next summer, a grandchild. The cottage is my investment for their future, I'm just the custodian."

He pulls me in close, hugging me tightly and with an intensity that almost takes my breath away. When he releases me, the look I see is one of determination.

"Heck, give them their inheritance now and I'll take care of you for the rest of our lives. I have elderly parents, no siblings and no children. Unless I get married, I have no one to whom I can leave the trappings of my life's work. Sad, isn't it?"

"This isn't what we should be talking about, Ryan. I'm sorry I brought it up." I wasn't looking for assurance that he'd support me, quite the reverse. I'm not sure I want to give up my independence when it's still so new.

"No, don't do this to me, Maddie, don't put up barriers. You've just been through a horrendous divorce and freedom is scary, but liberating. Of course, I understand that. You gave up everything for your family, but this is the stage in your life when you can finally think about what's best for *you*. Your sons are grown and they want you to be happy. Whatever happens going forward, we have to be in complete agreement about it. I'm laying my cards on the table, here. I want to marry you because it's the one thing in life I've always longed for, someone to come home to at the end of the day. I want to build a life with you because I love you and always have done. I only ask one thing. Don't tell me you love me until you are completely, and unequivocally, certain about how you feel. That's why we are going to take this one day at a time and that's why I won't make love to you until I know you are certain, too. You have a little catching up to do on that front, my darling. But mostly I feel it's about confidence, because Nathan was right. You are absolutely gorgeous, only you don't know it."

He searches for my hands, raising them in his to keep them warm and lifting them to his lips for one brief moment.

Suddenly I'm no longer this fifty-year-old, sad woman whose husband cheated on her and whose figure will never again be described as svelte. Ryan is honouring me with his love and leaving me in doubt whatsoever that he's prepared to make a long-term commitment. I couldn't feel more alive than I do right now, as we aren't just two young, inexperienced kids, giving something a try. We're seasoned veterans of life, who have a good idea of what we're looking for when it comes to a partner. This really is going to be the next chapter for me and – surprise, surprise – this has turned out to be the best Christmas ever!

All thoughts are waved away as he holds my face between his hands and his warm, loving kiss seals the deal.

CHAPTER 31

The days between Christmas and New Year fly by, each a little better than the one before. Ryan and I concentrate on simply getting used to being around each other twenty-four-seven. I know it would drive many people mad, but we find ourselves laughing a lot and relaxing without the eyes of the world upon us.

There's only one problem. I still haven't told him about Lewis, even though I've tried – really I've tried. Every time I make the decision that now is the moment to reveal everything, something happens to send the conversation off-course.

I've left several messages for Lewis on his phone, but he never replies. They are basically checking he's okay and apologising for not being able to say exactly when I'll be back. I thought maybe he would want to let me know what was happening and whether the kitchen units had eventually arrived. If they haven't, then I suspect he's already locked up and gone on his way, eager to make a start on his mother's house. I wouldn't blame him, but I owe him quite a lot of money and I feel uncomfortable about that. What if he needed it to buy materials for his own job – and here I am, selfishly playing house with Ryan. I have to stop myself from thinking about Lewis, Ash Cottage and renovation hell. It's the only way I can deal with it for the moment. Besides, Ryan is the best distraction.

It's New Year's Eve and we are curled up on the sofa as Ryan searches for a film for us to watch on his sixty-inch TV.

"Murder, horror, sci-fi, romance ..." He flicks through from section to section, pausing briefly as I shake my head. Then up pops *Love Actually* and I must have blinked or changed my expression because he's looking at me, knowingly.

"I could go for a bit of romance, I suppose." He sounds begrudging, but I notice he's quick enough to press start and turn up the volume. He points the remote at the full-length curtains and they gracefully sweep along the track, blocking out the wintry sunshine.

As the music strikes up and the opening credits start to roll, something about all of those images of people meeting and greeting – hugging as you do when you've really missed someone you love – brings tears to my eyes. In the gloom I assume Ryan can't see them.

"You're eyes are glistening and it hasn't even begun yet. How many times have you watched this particular film?"

I nestle a little closer to him, letting his arm drape around my shoulder for comfort.

"Maybe once or twice, or perhaps a dozen times – I lose count. How about you?"

"This is my first time, so I hope it's not a tear-jerker. I'm a sucker for a sad ending and it's not true that real men don't cry. I've watched *The Sixth Sense*."

The way Ryan says that suddenly sounds extremely funny and I have no idea if he's joking or not, but I can't stop myself laughing.

"Hey," he pulls me into him in an attempt to quell my peals of laughter. "I'm trying to get into your good books, so I can get you into bed."

I know he's only half-joking and I decide that now, under cover of darkness, and with only the lights from the TV screen flickering, is the time to confess.

"You said we were putting the past behind us and what went before didn't matter. But what if there was something ... recent?"

"Look, when I went away on holiday, yes, you were on my mind. But I had no idea if there would ever be a right time to let you into my dark secret. And what if you'd rejected me outright? I'm not the sort of person who sleeps around for the sake of it, Maddie, but we're adults and we've both had other partners."

Ryan thinks I'm questioning *him*.

"Um ... I wasn't talking about you, actually."

His arm slips slightly as he adjusts his position.

"This is about *you*?" There's a note of incredulity in his voice that makes it waver.

Now his arm slips down off my shoulder and he fumbles for my hand, turning to face me, sideways-on.

"You were seeing someone else while I was away?" All I can hear is disbelief and shock in his voice now.

"No. It wasn't like that. It was just the once and it was one of those mad moments that could so easily not have happened at all. But it did, although it didn't mean a thing. It was just two lonely people thrown together under a weird set of circumstances."

We're facing each other, barely eighteen inches apart, and while I can't make out his expression, his eyes are cold.

"I won't pretend it doesn't hurt, or surprise me, Maddie. But while I might be capable of jealousy, I'm not a hypocrite. We have no choice but to put the past firmly behind us and all I want from you is confirmation that it didn't hold any meaning."

My hand is still wrapped up in his and his grip around it increases.

"If I could undo it, I would, believe me. I knew you'd be upset and the last thing I want is to hurt you. It was a meaningless lapse that was so out of character, I can't really explain it to myself."

"As long as it wasn't that damned Lewis Hart. There's something about him I don't like. That's one of the reasons I came for you, if I'm totally honest. Hopefully he'll be gone by the time you return to Ash Cottage."

Suddenly it feels like I've been stabbed through the heart with a shard of ice. What can I possibly say to Ryan now? I've been such a fool. Didn't Sarah, from the estate agents, mention something about Lewis that referred to women falling all over him? Does he play the strong, silent and hurt type, with the intention of making vulnerable, lonely women feel sorry for him? With me it was sex; with Aggie was there something more sinister? Did he hope to get her to sign over the cottage to him, prior to her death?

Anger wells up, together with tears and I can only hope that if Ryan notices anything he thinks it's because of the film. All love stories should end well, but even in a film it only serves to remind me that this isn't always the case.

When we say goodnight at the door to the guest bedroom, Ryan holds me so tightly that I think he's never going to let go. I know what he's thinking and I hate myself for what I've done. The one thing he's asked of me is the one thing I can't give him and that hurts so much. His kiss is urgent, although we both know we aren't ready to take that next step – especially after this evening.

Lying in bed, alone, I let the tears come, hoping that in some way it will cleanse me of the guilt and the anger. I'm so lucky that Ryan is here to save me from myself and from making any future decisions that could pull my world apart. How can I still be so naive at times, after everything life has taught me?

LEWIS

CHAPTER 32

Having just managed to get Joanna to leave, I check my watch and see that it's ten o'clock already. I was hoping to be on the road early, given that I wasn't able to get away yesterday as I'd originally planned. For some reason, I convinced myself the traffic would be lighter this morning. I have no idea why I'm still dragging my feet, though. If I'd left first thing I could have avoided her this morning. Joanna's constant interruptions have been annoying and I have no idea how Terence puts up with it. This time she brought round a mini Christmas cake in case I was hungry on the trip home.

I've done everything I can with the materials Madeleine ordered. The flooring was probably the easiest I've ever laid and the click-lock system worked well. The kitchen cabinets took a bit of juggling as one wall ran out by two inches and I had to cannibalise one of the cupboards to make it fit. But it's done and I know she'll be pleased.

"It looks good, Aggie, doesn't it?" My voice echoes around the conservatory, strangely hollow now because of the new floor and the sparse furnishings.

In my mind I'm transported back to the last time I saw Aggie, sitting in her chair and looking out over the valley.

"You aren't yourself this morning. Do you want me to ring the doctor?" She'd looked so pale and tired; it was hard to hide my concern.

"No, I couldn't sleep last night, that's all. Come and sit for a while, never mind worrying about that dripping tap." She was always the same whenever I called in, she didn't seem to notice that the cottage was badly in need of attention. All she ever wanted to do was to sit and talk.

"There are things to say, Lewis. Things I want you to know."

"It's not necessary, Aggie. I'm fine and I'm here for you, no matter what you need, you only have to say."

She'd reached out and laid her hand over mine. For an old lady her hands were delicate still, and soft. The pressure was light, but she'd lingered, as if it was a special moment for her.

"It's good to have you here, it's a blessing. You have a kind heart, Lewis, and that touches me more than you can know. It's also a relief because I have high hopes for you, you know."

She looked at me knowingly, as if she had a secret she had no intention of sharing and yet the effect would be profound.

"Well, I can only hope I won't let you down." I said it half-jokingly, but beneath my words there was an undercurrent of sadness. I was too set in my ways to change the man I had become and I wasn't sure that Aggie could ever really understand that.

"Don't you worry. When you need a nudge in the right direction I'm going to be there. You don't think I have any intention of leaving you, do you?"

She looked so frail that day and something inside me welled up. I had to swallow hard to remove the huge lump that was sticking in my throat. It never occurred to me that it would be the last time ...

I hear the door click, realising I didn't lock it after seeing Joanna out and when I spin around, Ryan is standing there. His jaw is set and he's in the mood for a fight. I let out a deep breath and close my eyes for a couple of seconds. I don't want to let go of the image of Aggie and bring myself back into the moment, but she's gone and I have to accept that.

He's staring at me, barely holding back his anger.

Clearly, Maddie told him.

My hesitation puts me on the back foot and he's in my face before I can even evaluate the situation. Know your enemy; know their weak point – but this man isn't defending his territory, he's defending his woman. A woman he believes has been wronged. I deserve whatever I get.

I stand immobile as he angrily grabs the edges of my jacket, pulling me into his face with a strength that comes from raging anger.

"You piece of scum. You think that doing this," he spits out the words as he casts his eyes around the room, "will make up for what you did? You just couldn't help yourself, could you? Lonely woman, vulnerable and at an all-time low point in her life. I bet you couldn't believe your luck. This isn't some worldly woman who was looking for one night of fun. This is Maddie – gentle, caring, with a heart so big she can't bear to think of anyone hurting. You seized your moment and played the sympathy card, knowing full-well that was the only way she would ever have dropped her guard. You think that nothing can touch you, that you can live without due regard to the people you come into contact with. But you'll live to regret what you've done, mark my words. I'm the one she's going to be spending her life with and I'll make sure she's never vulnerable – ever again."

Reluctantly, he allows his hands to slacken off their grip, realising that he's on the edge. His eyes are wild and he turns away from me, running a hand through his hair in desperation. He wants to hit me, but that's not the sort of man he is and we both know that. He's an intellectual and not the sort to demean himself by getting into a fist-fight.

Whatever I say now is redundant. 'Sorry' will inflame the situation – an explanation will sound lame because there is no excuse. I know the difference between a woman who can handle casual sex and a woman who is the commitment type. I can't dispute a single word, so I say nothing.

"You need to leave, *now*. Maddie thinks you left yesterday and I'm bringing her back this afternoon. I expect you to be long-gone. If you try to get in touch with her, then I'll seek you out and next time I won't hold back."

I have to admire the man. I could fell him with one sweep of my leg and have him lying on the floor in an arm lock. I feel uncomfortable about the mistake I made, which wasn't planned, as he seems to believe it to have been. She's the sort of woman you feel safe with and maybe I wanted to savour that feeling for a while. That doesn't excuse the fact that I should have known better. I've hurt her because I've left her with a memory that's both confusing and, now Ryan knows, will always hang between them. I wouldn't rob her of the happiness she deserves and I can only hope he's the bigger man and will see it for what it was.

He may have a lot going for him, but from where I'm standing I can see one big flaw. Madeleine isn't a trophy; she's about more than looking good on someone's arm. He'll do and say all the right things because he's hit a mid-life crisis. Unless I'm very mistaken, he's panicking that if he doesn't get a ring on someone's finger pretty darned quick, it will be too late. I've seen it before. I only hope that this will turn out well – for them both.

"Next time you take a woman to bed, stop and check out your conscience first. The reason Maddie is with me is precisely because I'm not the sort of man to take unfair advantage of her. She deserves more than that. The difference between you and me is that I know it and you don't." He spits the words out with all the bitterness he's feeling, turning only to add, "Time you left. You've done enough damage already."

MADDIE

CHAPTER 33

Next morning Ryan disappears for a couple of hours while I pack up my things. He has to drop something important in to Nathan and on the way he offers to pick up some fresh supplies for me to take home.

The journey back is uneventful. The work on the culvert is well under way and the flood water is, thankfully, under control. Only a sparse stream flows down the hill, confined to the gutter and that is now diverted by a wall of sandbags before it hits the dip in the road.

It isn't a surprise to find Ash Cottage empty. What is a complete surprise is the unexpected transformation. The walnut flooring has been laid throughout the entire ground floor. Venturing into the kitchen, it has been turned from bare, plastered walls into something out of a magazine. This isn't the same cottage any more.

Ryan's reaction is laced with anger and I'm not sure why. "Is everything as you expected it to be?"

"Yes, and more. I thought Lewis was only laying the flooring in the kitchen area." It's hard to believe all of this has been achieved in seven days.

We walk back through into the sitting room. It's still full of boxes, which are now neatly stacked in one corner and include several new, unopened ones. Probably birthday and Christmas presents from the boys. The walnut floor looks simply beautiful and the temporary kitchen is now gone. The freshly painted white walls everywhere are a testament to Lewis' hard work. The landing, too, is pristine and throwing open the door to the master bedroom reveals a walnut floor without a speck of dust or debris on it. Lewis was right; the finished walls look so good that a minor imperfection here and there stops it from looking too bland and uniform. Rustic, he'd said.

My head is buzzing with questions. Why? Why had he worked non-stop, going way beyond our agreed list of tasks to make the cottage feel, at last, habitable? Ryan continues to follow me as I walk around from room to room. The dilapidated state of the second bedroom, the shower room, and the downstairs bathroom are now in sharp contrast and a reminder of the original state. It feels like a home in the making.

"This is going to cost you a lot of money, Maddie. I hope you agreed a price up front. You can't criticise the man's work, only his somewhat dubious persona."

Was I wrong about Lewis Hart? Did he do this more for Aggie than for me, his customer? Or was he content to plough on, knowing full well that before too long it would probably be up for sale again?

Confusion begins to overwhelm me and as we head back out to the kitchen again a sideways glance into the dining room reminds me that Ryan cannot stay. There's only one bed and it's *the* bed. I couldn't bear the thought of lying next to him, knowing what I'd done.

"We need to move your bed upstairs," he touches my arm lightly, realising I'm deep in thought.

"Yes, good idea, although perhaps I should wait until the second bedroom is ready and put it in there. I think I might go for a white frame, and not cream, for the main bedroom."

I'm thinking on my feet, not wanting Ryan to touch anything in that room. I will dispose of the sheets and the bedding and along with them the memories.

"I'm still not sure you should stay here all alone, Maddie. Admittedly it has warmed up a fair bit today and now the damp has been treated, and the rain has stopped – things are drying out nicely. But you will need to have those fan heaters on, though, to continue to put heat back into this place, or you will have a problem with condensation and mould."

He follows me through into the kitchen again, and Lewis has executed my plan to the letter. I run my fingers along the walnut worktops and over the shaker-style cream panel on the fridge door. He's good at what he does and a man who pays attention to detail like this can't be all bad, can he?

That's when I notice the envelope tucked away behind the kettle. It has 'Miss Brooks' hand-written on the front. With nervous fingers I prise it open, conscious that Ryan is watching me intently.

Inside there are two sheets of paper. The first is a short note from Lewis.

"What does it say?" Ryan is too polite to look over my shoulder, but his forehead reflects a hint of a frown and his demeanour is one of suspicion.

"Only that the keys are in the post box and the engineer came to sort out the fault on the telephone line. The phone is now working." As I turn to the second page my eyebrows shoot up.

"I knew it! You should have made sure you had a written agreement in place with prices for each of the jobs."

Ryan looks so angry, but I have to keep re-reading the words, which are just a list of jobs done, as my eyes can't believe the bottom-line total.

"No, quite the reverse. We didn't agree on an actual amount, but this is what I expected to pay for just stripping out and replacing the kitchen. He hasn't charged for laying the flooring in the rest of the cottage, or the work he did upstairs ..." The man has also left without a single word, not even a 'good-bye'. What was I expecting? A little sign-off saying, 'It was nice sleeping with you?'

Ryan raises an eyebrow. "I suspect another invoice will arrive in the post, shortly. You know what the going rate is, Maddie, so don't let him take advantage of you. It was his choice to work over the holiday period."

None of this makes any sense. With Ryan here, all agitated and angry beneath the surface, I'm trying to act as if I'm mildly surprised, but pleased. I am pleased, of course, but what I really want is to understand what's going on. Is this about guilt? Maybe Lewis has a conscience after all and he must surely realise by now that Ryan and I are together. Why else would I walk out of my home and leave a contractor to his own devices? Perhaps he was worried that I'd make a fuss, say something that would tarnish his reputation. After all, everyone knows everyone's business here and this is where he hopes to make his home.

Ryan is fussing, wanting to bring in the groceries from the car and sort the fan heaters before he leaves. He's back to work tomorrow and I know he's stressing about that. His mind will already be in work-mode.

When we eventually hug goodbye, it's a solemn moment.

"I'm going to really miss you, Maddie. You've become like a fixture and fitting, the house won't be the same without you. At least you'll be back to work in two more weeks, well, I mean online, of course."

He's really anxious and I can see he's in two minds about whether to leave or insist he stays.

"I'll be fine, and now I have the phone line working I'll get the internet connection up and running. If you need me before then, just shout. It will only take about a day or two to paint the second bedroom and then I can sort the interior. I'm going to miss you, too. But that's a good thing, isn't it?"

His hug is gentle, but at the same time it almost lifts me off the ground.

"This is going to be our year, Maddie; the year of no looking back and moving forward together." The words are a mere whisper as his lips brush against my cheek and he buries his face in my hair. It's a tender moment and a part of me doesn't want him to go. Maybe I never was the sort of person who could survive on their own and now I'm too old to change my ways. I need to be needed, but I also want to be wanted.

At that precise moment the decision is taken, I'm going to sell Ash Cottage as soon as the renovation is complete.

"Thanks, Ryan, for everything. At last I'm beginning to feel whole again, instead of a person who has been torn into little pieces. Now go, that's an order and let me know if there are any problems on your first day back."

CHAPTER 34

It was the longest night of my life. Tossing and turning, even between the crisp new sheets I'd taken out of the wrappers without having the motivation to iron them. Everything on the bed was new, memories seemingly erased. But how do you erase the memories inside your head and the questions that come through, unbidden, in a steady stream?

The other problem I have is Lewis' invoice. Clearly, he didn't just work a standard seven-hour day, so I need to reflect that in the cheque I'm going to send off. I decide it's only fair to divide the total by the number of days he worked on the kitchen alone. That gives me his standard daily rate. Multiplying this by the total number of days he was here, and adding twenty per cent on top seems the right thing to do. I know he could have chosen to ramp up the bill because of the holidays and I don't want to take advantage of his situation. There are too many unanswered questions floating around in my head for me to simply accept that he's a good man who enjoys breathing life back into a wreck. Without knowing his precise motive, he could just as easily be something akin to a conman. My heart sinks, to think that people can stoop so low.

I write out the cheque and address the envelope, noting that at least he's now a couple of hundred miles away and out of my life for good. Before I can seal it, there's a tap on the door and I look up to see Joanna, from next door.

She peers over my shoulder, seemingly unsurprised at the dramatic change.

"Is Lewis here?"

"No, he's finished his work. I only arrived back late yesterday, so I'm not sure when exactly he left. Is there a problem?" No pleasantries I notice and it looks as if she's recovered from the 'flu, then.

Joanna's eyes flick over me, taking in my paint-covered jeans and baggy sweater. There's disdain in her look and it's a puzzle why Terence is attracted to someone whose personality is so very different. He's so laid-back and friendly by nature. Was it a case of opposites attract?

"Yes, there is, but if Lewis isn't here then I'll have to find someone else to come out and fix it."

"I didn't realise he was doing work for you, too." It's a throwaway comment, but her eyes flash.

"He's a handyman; he does work for a lot of people in the Forest. I hope you didn't take advantage of his good nature, Madeleine. It was difficult enough that he was working here without any facilities. It was the least I could do to ensure he had a hot meal every day."

Is that really what she thinks? I wonder if Terence feels the same way. It's going to give entirely the wrong impression when I put the cottage back on the market; they'll no doubt think I used Lewis' connection with Ash Cottage to get the work done quickly and make a nice little profit from his hard work. What a mess!

"Thank you for that, Joanna. To be honest, I'd intended working through the holidays, myself. My boss meant well, he, um ..."

"Yes, well, I can't stand here chatting. I need to ring a plumber. Did Lewis say when he was coming back?"

Clearly she knows he's gone back home, but I have to shake my head as I have no idea what his plans might be.

"It's upset him, you know. Aggie wanted him to have this place and everyone knew that." She literally throws the words over her shoulder as she walks away from me.

I'm so angry, I'm shaking. That was so mean; Joanna has no idea about my situation – unless Lewis told her. The thought of that makes my blood run cold. It might account for the venom in her voice if she thinks I'm the sort of woman to use every tactic to get what I want.

I slump back down into the folding chair and stare out at the view. What a difference just a couple of weeks have made. As I scan around, this is no longer a strange, slightly alien, environment. Even without proper furniture and the trappings that make a house a home, it's distinctly cosy. My eyes rest on Aggie's box, pushed back beneath the coffee table, and I reach for it. I remember stuffing a lot of documents into the side pocket of the holdall when I left that day and I realise now that I simply forgot they were there. Grabbing a coffee, I figure now is as good a time as any to finish going through them.

I begin with the ones from the holdall, as I'd already leafed through what was in the box. Mostly it's a big wedge of papers that seem to be the original deeds, now redundant in this electronic age. One huge sheet of parchment folded into eight carries a large red seal. There are notarised papers indicating that a part of the garden was purchased from the owner of the barn back in the early fifties. Everything is old – nothing newer than that document – so I assume the issue with the strip of land to the rear is always going to be a puzzle. It looks as if someone was careful to keep every single document relating to the cottage – and there are even more recent invoices for the re-wiring and the central heating.

As I shuffle the loose pile into some semblance of order and lift the lid off the box to place them back inside, I notice the documents are all sitting squarely within the box. Someone has been through them in my absence. If Lewis hopes to end up with Ash Cottage, does that strip of land at the back concern him that much? It would devalue the cottage if someone suddenly stepped forward and decided to build a garage on it or something. I laugh, disdainfully, at Joanna's words; if anyone is taking advantage, it's Lewis Hart.

CHAPTER 35

As winter finally gives way to spring, the garden begins to come alive. I wander around discovering little areas full of shoots as the earth starts to warm and the first bulbs break out. Inside the cottage, the two men from Chappell and Hicks are putting the finishing touches to the downstairs bathroom. To celebrate, and thank Ryan for his help in organising the remodelling of the bathrooms, he's coming over to dinner tonight.

Standing here, looking up at Ash Cottage in the spring sunshine, all I can hear are the birds twittering as they flit between the trees. There's a marked chill in the air still, but it's clean and sweet as I fill my lungs. With the sun on my face it feels good to be alive and surrounded by nature rather than modern living keeping nature at bay. Does that sound odd? That's the difference between city living and life in the country, I suppose.

Hugging my woolly jacket closer to me, it's hard to believe that not so very long ago this *was* my dream. This was my idea of heaven and where I saw myself living a quiet and gentler life. I wanted to get away from the city and the frenetic pace of life. All the stop-start queues of traffic, short tempers and pressures associated with that pace of life. It was easy to let things go past you; we call it keeping out of other people's business. Since living in the Forest I've come to appreciate something very unique. It's true that village life revolves around gossip, but the pace of life is

235

gentler and people have time to *make time*. Yes, there is gossip for gossip's sake, but there's also a lot of genuine caring and kindness. There's a real sense of community, when what I was expecting to feel was almost a sense of isolation. From the postman to the lady who lives at the bottom of the hill, they take the time to enquire after you and listen to what you have to say. Several of the locals invited me for Christmas lunch, knowing my situation and I felt guilty, politely declining. My excuse was that I needed to be here to work, but while that was true, another reason was that it takes a while to adjust to a new set of values. I suppose I wasn't ready for people to get to know me, the new Maddie Brooks, cut off from her old, familiar life and trying so hard to find herself. I wanted to hide myself away. How quickly life can change and now the cottage is about to go on the market. It is with much sadness, though, and I know I will have to steel myself to say goodbye. Every day I question whether I'm ready to move on, to take that next step with Ryan. I suppose I won't know that for sure until I'm turning the key in the lock for the last time, but that's a few months away, thank goodness.

"Well, your dream came true. You have that slipper bath with a view of the heavens. They've done a great job and it looks amazing, darling." Ryan slides his arm around my waist and draws me close for a celebratory hug. "This is a big moment for us."

"It is something rather special, isn't it? And thank you for calling in a favour with Chappell and Hicks."

He spins me around gently, so that we are facing each other and peers down into my eyes. He's a man who likes to have control of every single aspect of his life and he's happy that a plan is beginning to come together.

"They've done a few jobs for us over the past couple of years and I was going to use them for the big eco-house project anyway, as it's almost on the doorstep. It was nothing. Besides, getting it done quickly was important to me. The sooner you sell Ash

Cottage, the sooner you move in with me." He kisses my forehead, choosing to linger for a moment.

I should feel just as happy, but now everything here looks as I imagined it on that very first visit, it's hard to believe I'm going to hand it over to someone else.

"I need to rescue the pasta before it sticks to the bottom of the pan," I say, wriggling out of his arms. "Go into the conservatory and make yourself comfortable; there's wine on the table waiting to be poured if you can do the honours."

As I layer the home-made sauce over the spaghetti and grate some parmesan on top, I look through what would have been the old exterior side window. It's now an open view straight through into the conservatory. The eight-foot-long dining table in white is offset against the dark walnut floor, and with the dark-brown Lloyd Loom chairs it looks stunning. The candles send shards of light out to reflect on the wall of glass windows and a wave of satisfaction washes over me. It's done and it's beautiful, as I knew it would be. Maybe it isn't as magazine-perfect as Ryan's house, but it's a happy place with good vibes. At first I felt like a stranger here, someone who had stepped in uninvited and it regarded me as an intruder. Everything that could go wrong did, and I wondered if it was a sign that I'd made a mistake. Any doubts I had have long since disappeared because, for whatever reason, renovating Ash Cottage was something that was a part of my fate. It's been a journey of discovery about so many things.

"It smells good," Ryan inclines his head to catch my attention. I can count on one hand the number of times he's been here. Maybe tonight is the night he, too, will fall under the spell of Ash Cottage.

"Nearly done."

I finish loading the tray and carry it through. The ambience is very romantic and cosy. Outside, the pale gleam of the garden lights set an intriguing boundary in the darkness. From inside, all you get is a sense of openness and nature, as the sky darkens and the stars begin to appear. There is no light pollution here and looking up through the glazed roof of the conservatory it feels as if there is only *us* and this moment in time.

As I take my seat opposite Ryan, we raise our glasses to toast the occasion.

"To the end of this part of the journey."

We chink glasses and I wonder if now is the right moment to test the water.

"It's been an interesting one. But it's turned into a lovely little place to relax in and enjoy some downtime, don't you think?"

Ryan has a mouthful of pasta, so I wait patiently for his reply, absentmindedly rearranging the food on the plate in front of me.

"Perfect. It looks great. When is Sarah coming over to take the photos for the brochure?"

My hint hasn't even registered. I know he's going to be disappointed with my answer.

"I haven't contacted her yet. I wondered if, maybe, selling it now is the wrong thing to do."

He places his knife and fork down on the plate and leans back in his chair to look at me with a slight air of disappointment.

"I thought we'd agreed you would press ahead quickly? I know it's a great little cottage now it's finished and I understand the lure of wanting to spend some time here to enjoy the finished product. But time is precious, Maddie, and we have plans to make."

He misunderstood me.

"Um ... I wasn't talking about timing. I wondered if I should just keep it as an investment. We could use it as an occasional holiday home; a place to come and get away from everything for a few days."

He shakes his head and an involuntary sigh escapes from his lips. Ryan reaches for his wine glass and takes a long sip before settling back in his chair again.

"How often would we do that? You have to be practical, Maddie. If you don't want to let it go, then maybe think about renting it out, but do you want the hassle of being a landlady? I think you are better off banking the money, maybe even letting your sons have some of their inheritance to reinvest sooner rather than later."

He leans forward to pick up his knife and fork, taking another bite of the pasta.

I feel as if I'm being ungrateful. Ryan is going to take care of me and here I am, making a fuss over a little cottage that will, no doubt, turn out to have been a wise investment.

"So you couldn't see us coming here and using this as a … retreat?" I continue, pushing the pasta around my plate. I'm trying my best to appear relaxed, when my stomach is actually tied up in knots over this.

"Our life together can be whatever we choose to make it, Maddie." He places the cutlery back down once more and leans forward, intently. His eyes search mine and his expression is one of concern, but beneath that is a sense of excitement. "I know that you have misgivings about moving in with me because you feel it's my house and not our home. I understand that, and it's a natural reaction. But it won't be for long. Maybe now is the time to air a few ideas I've been kicking around."

I put down my own fork and sit back, wondering what he's going to say next. I think I've known for a little while now that he's been planning something.

"I've had the house and business valued. I have quite a healthy pension fund and if I decide to retire next year, when I'm fifty, it will still give me a very respectable monthly return. I know this is going to be a bit of a step for you and I want you to think about it for a few days before you let me know what you think. But what if we bought that dream holiday home and made it a permanent base? What if we found some sprawling, rustic house in a sunnier clime, where every day would feel like an adventure? Your sons could come and stay whenever they wanted and together we'd turn it into *our* place. Life's too short to get stuck in a groove and not stand back to see all of the options. It's something I guess I've been heading towards for a long time now, but having you by my

239

side makes me want to grab the opportunity now. I'm excited about this, Maddie, and it's do-able. I reckon it would take a year to organise everything and that's perfect because ... wow, I didn't think I'd be saying this tonight, but when the time is right, I'm going to ask you to marry me."

I open my mouth, not sure quite what to say, but he stops me.

"No, please, don't say anything now. This wasn't how I wanted to broach this, but I need you to understand that I know you will be letting go of something that has become meaningful to you. I'm prepared to give up everything that my life has centred on so far, to prove how much you mean to me. I'm only asking you to do the same, so that we can start our life together with a fresh, completely blank, page. I'm excited for *us*, Maddie, and I hope you are, too."

He pushes back his chair and rises, never taking his eyes off me for even so much as a second, as he walks around the table. I stand and he wraps his arms lovingly around me with an intensity that reflects his passion and excitement.

It wasn't quite the night of celebration I'd expected. I didn't manage to change Ryan's mind, but he managed to change mine. The next morning I ring Sarah to arrange for her to bring the paperwork over and take the photos.

CHAPTER 36

"Hi, Sarah, come in," I hold open the door wide, as she steps inside carrying a bulky briefcase.

"Gosh, what a difference! I can hardly believe it."

"I know. It's beautiful, isn't it?"

Taking her coat, I indicate for her to grab a seat at the table. When I return, the contract and some brochures are spread out on the table and she's scribbling in a note pad.

"Would you like a tea, or a coffee?"

"No, I'm good, thank you. We need to talk about price and I have some comparable properties to show you. Things that have sold recently and I hope you'll be pleasantly surprised, as I'm sure it will reflect a handsome profit."

She smiles encouragingly as I take my seat.

"I didn't do this for profit and it is tough to sell it, but I'm getting married."

Her eyes open wide and she breaks out into a beaming smile. "Oh, fabulous news! Congratulations, Maddie. I did wonder why you were moving on so soon. Especially when I look back on your first viewing and how you instantly fell in love with it, as tired as it looked then. Still, it's onwards to more exciting things in your case."

If I'd stayed in the Forest I know we would have become good friends. She's a lady who grabs life and it's clear she's doing a job she loves. She's in a happy place in her life. It's no coincidence that lots of women of our age often seem to have mellowed, learning the knack of acceptance and understanding that there are some things you can control and some you can't. So you seek out the things that bring you happiness and suddenly it's not all about more money, more material possessions and having high expectations. It's about savouring the moment and living each day as it comes.

"I think this is the sort of price we should be targeting, although you would normally expect a buyer to haggle, especially when they are buying a fully renovated property. I'd say you'd achieve within five thousand pounds of the asking price."

Sarah slides three brochures across the table and they are all small, Forest cottages.

"However," there's a hint of concern creeping into her voice. "You do have the issue of that strip of land behind the cottage. I know it didn't concern you personally, but the worst-case scenario is that someone does own it and they decide to use it. If someone parked an ugly, old caravan up there, or a lorry, it would be a blot on the landscape for you when you were sitting on your top terrace. Okay, you would be facing the view most of the time, but to look up and see vehicles at that level would be like looking up into a car park."

"I guess I was rather cavalier about that, wasn't I?" I admit, remembering that I had totally ignored my solicitor's advice not to leave the matter unresolved. But the clock had been ticking then.

"All you need is a buyer who falls in love with the cottage and the views, who will feel the way you did on that first day. It's unlikely anyone would suddenly appear and begin using the strip; it might even be common land – who knows? I don't think it will affect the purchase price as such, but it will put some buyers off. Solicitors have no choice but to make it very clear to their clients there is a risk involved."

Although I'm sad about selling the cottage, I feel a little deflated. How could anyone be negative about that one little thing, when simply turning your head gives you a view that takes your breath away every single time?

"There is good news, though. I already have a full asking price offer on the table. Cash purchaser, quick sale."

"But we haven't even agreed a price."

"The purchaser is prepared to pay whatever price you decide Ash Cottage should be marketed at."

Sarah's smile is genuine and I can see she's expecting me to be pleasantly surprised by her news. I feign a smile, none too successfully.

"It's Lewis Hart, isn't it?"

"It is."

"Does he want to view? He hasn't seen the cottage since the work was completed."

Sarah is beginning to sense my reservation and now I feel awkward.

"No, there are no caveats to his offer, whatsoever. In fact, he notified us in writing over a month ago, saying that if we were ever instructed to market Ash Cottage, he wanted his offer to be put forward before it was even advertised. When I talked to him yesterday, he said the strip of land is not an issue for him and he's confident the renovation will have been completed to the highest standard. As this is such a quick turnaround, my boss has agreed to lower our fee. I'll make sure everything goes through smoothly, and quickly. You need to focus on that wedding." Her smile is one of satisfaction; she thinks this is the perfect solution.

I'm in shock. I expected Lewis to make an offer at some point, but not the full asking price. I thought his motive was money, but there's no further profit to be made now the work is finished. He could see the value affected, as Sarah pointed out, if someone started using the strip of waste land. Why would he risk that? Unless ... did he rifle through Aggie's box and find something I missed? Did he knowingly steal a document, thinking that maybe it would mean I'd have no option other than to sell the cottage to him? He left me in no doubt whatsoever that this is where he wanted to live.

"I'm not sure I want to sell it to Lewis."

Sarah jaw drops.

"Why? He's a cash purchaser and he's unlikely to back out. We can increase the valuation slightly and see whether he baulks at that. Most sellers can only dream of this sort of scenario. People tend to come to the Forest looking for their own renovation project, so it could take a while to find another purchaser. Besides, I'm not sure where you would stand legally, refusing a carte blanche offer from a party so early in the process and ultimately bypassing that to sell it for the same amount to someone else. I'm not sure whether he could sue you for discrimination, or something, down the line as it's never happened before." Her frown is genuine and I know she must think I'm mad. I can see she's puzzled, but doesn't like to ask why I'm so disturbed by Lewis' offer.

"What if we jump it up to a silly price, just until he finds something else?"

"Maddie, what's going on here? Lewis is a nice guy. If you increase the price you simply won't get the interest, so there would be no point in marketing the place at all. Lewis didn't over-charge you, did he? From what I've heard, he's popular because he not only does a good job, but he's fair. He never has to look for work; it's all by word-of-mouth recommendation. I'm sorry if things went wrong here."

I obviously can't tell Sarah the whole story and my conscience won't let me discredit someone when I don't have any proof.

"Nothing went wrong. I guess when you said 'a quick sale' I panicked there for a moment. I thought I'd have a few months to adjust to saying goodbye. I was hoping to be here for the start of the summer, you know, just to see it in one more season ..."

"Ah, Maddie. I can see this is hard for you, but can I say something, just between the two of us?"

I nod, trying to keep at bay the turmoil churning in my stomach.

Lewis Hart used me in the worst possible way.

"That first time we met I felt you were a woman on the edge. You sounded strong, but there was an underlying sadness and fragility. I was hesitant to phone in your offer that day, because I feared you were looking at it with rose-tinted glasses. Obviously you'd been through a tough time and you saw this as a new beginning."

"I was aware that I sort of poured out a lot of unnecessary information, I am sorry about that." I sounded rather pathetic that day, trying to convince myself I knew what I was doing. The truth was that I was stumbling around trying to find something to cling to that would give me a sense of purpose.

"Don't apologise, it was fine. You'd be surprised what people tell you when they are viewing a house. It's an emotional process, believe it or not! That's why I love my job. The point is, you are in a very different place now in your life and it shows outwardly. Look, don't rush your decision. Maybe wait a couple of weeks before signing on the dotted line and moving forward. I'll leave the contract with you and just let me know when, and if, you want to proceed."

I can see that Sarah is putting two and two together and coming up with her own assumption of what this is all about. She thinks I have formed an attachment to the cottage and it's hard to let go. She's right, of course, but this is more about the sting in the tail. Lewis isn't quite the nice, quiet, unassuming man everyone thinks and I've seen his true colours. But he's left with me a memory I'm ashamed of and somehow I have to get past that.

"No, it's fine. Tell Lewis Hart his offer has been accepted if he really is prepared to pay the going rate. I'll probably be moving back to the city sooner, rather than later, so a quick sale will be fine."

I can see the sense of relief passing over Sarah's face and I don't think it's to do with returning to the office with a signed contract in her pocket. This is woman-to-woman empathy.

"Change is never easy. I lost my husband a couple of years ago. After a few months of living life in a very mechanical way to simply get through each day, I had to face up to a future that was scary and unknown. I moved home, changed jobs and decided that I couldn't keep looking back with anguish. I make myself try new things, meet new people and now I wake up looking forward to each day and what it will bring. I've learnt not to dwell on the process of change, but to focus on the positive side of the opportunities it brings with it. Who knows, I might even be lucky enough to find someone new to share my life with. But if I don't, that's fine too."

Her words are touching and I blink, not wanting to shed a tear. I notice her fiddling with her wedding band, absentmindedly twisting it around on her finger. The lesson here is that life goes on and crying over what might have been doesn't achieve anything. It's what you do that matters.

"My mind's made up and Ryan will be thrilled."

With eyes brimming with tears, we shake hands and the deal is done.

When I ring Ryan to tell him the news, his response is positive, but his tone is surly when I mention the offer is from Lewis. I counter that by telling him I've decided to move out ahead of the sale going through. I need a couple of weeks to sort my things and then we can start making plans.

"That's great news, Maddie. I'll start things rolling at this end and we can begin thinking about where we see ourselves settling down. Have you spoken to Matt and Nick?"

"I'm about to do that now. Having a purchaser so early on in the process means I'm going to have to bring them up to speed on what we've been discussing in general. I'd hate them to think that we'd been making firm plans and left them out of it. We have time though, don't we? This isn't all going to happen overnight?"

His tone softens.

"We have plenty of time. You don't have to worry about anything – just get your head around moving back to city life. One step at a time, Maddie. Love you, darling."

As the phone clicks, I sit back in the chair before I attempt to dial Matt's number. I don't think either Matt, or Nick, will be too surprised by the news, although the fact that within a year or so I'll be living abroad will, no doubt, take a little while to sink in. But they're grown and have their own lives. Once I'm out of here and living with Ryan, I will have time to go and visit them to catch up properly. That grandchild will be here before I know it and Nick, too, is going to be proud to show me around his new flat. Life is good and the future is exciting. I have to let go of old wounds, even those that are still fairly new.

LEWIS

CHAPTER 37

Sarah rang to say my offer has been accepted and it's a huge relief. I couldn't have lived with myself if I'd messed up a second time and Aggie's cottage had gone to yet another stranger. *Stranger* – it's funny, but Madeleine Brooks as a purchaser didn't turn out to be such an awful disaster, after all. Aggie would have loved her ideas and what she's done to the place, so the dream has been realised and soon it will become my home for the rest of my days.

What I hadn't anticipated is how that woman has managed to get under my skin so completely that her image is always inside my head. I seem to spend my time dodging advances from so many lonely women these days – some single, some married. So why is it that the one I can't have is the one I want so badly?

I'm not callous enough to try to compete with this Ryan guy. He's well off, good-looking and suave. Everything I'm not. Why would a lovely lady like Madeleine Brooks even consider someone like me? Rough around the edges, a big chip on my shoulder and emotionally screwed. And yet, that night we were together it wasn't lust, it was passion and there's a huge difference. But she's meant to be with someone like him, so everything he said was true. If I could undo that night, I would, for her sake – not for his. I guessed he'd move quickly and whisk her away to safety. She'll slot into his perfect life so easily, because there isn't one thing about her that isn't real, caring and full of heart. Women like Madeleine don't fall in love with sad cases like me. I feel awful not telling her the truth, but I knew that if I did it would pull on her sympathies. She'd probably have offered to sell me Ash Cottage there and then. The truth is, Aggie was my biological mother, but it's a secret I intend to take to the grave with me.

I feared there would be a paper among Aggie's personal effects that alluded to the adoption. It was there all right, but I felt it would have been betraying a client's trust to take the document, even though it has nothing to do with the cottage. Instead, I hid it, tucked it away inside one of the larger documents. When I get the deeds and the documents in the box, hopefully it will still be there and I'll burn it. The secret will, once and for all, be safe.

I was very young when my adoptive father died, almost too young to have any memories of him. However, my mother had lots of photos and they became my memories as the years went by. All I really knew was that my mother changed as time went on. It turns out that she never really wanted children at all, but it was her husband who convinced her to apply for adoption. Instead of being a comfort to her, I became a thorn in her side. She wanted to shut herself away in a little world where she could live with her memories, but having me around meant living in the moment. I was never neglected in any way physically, but mentally I felt unloved. The day he died she'd locked up her heart and I represented a burden with which she'd been left. She had rules that didn't always make any sense to me and when I hit my teens rebellion set in. It was at that time she sat me down and told me the truth. Shortly after that I left to join the army. I had a lot of respect for her, for the job she'd taken on and for seeing it through. But I never felt like her son, I was her charge and she was the person taking care of me.

It wasn't until much later in life that I decided to try to find my biological mother. Yumiko had convinced me that it was something I should do when I was ready, but it took a long time to get to that point in my life. It was only when I realised my adoptive mother probably didn't have too many years left that it occurred to me it might already be too late to find my biological mother. There was no one to ask about where to begin looking, so I approached a company who were experts in the field. I answered a long questionnaire about where my adoptive parents lived, what I knew about them and their backgrounds. It only took them a couple of weeks to identify the agency who had placed me.

They tracked Aggie down quite easily once they had her name. She'd never married, and the main family home had remained unchanged since the eighteen-hundreds. Aggie had left for college; always a gifted student, it had been her dream. When we met up for the first time she told me the whole story. It was love at first sight and the inevitable happened. My father's name was George Warner, and Aggie told me they were besotted with each other. From the day they first met they were inseparable and her trips home became less and less frequent. Her family thought she was simply applying herself to her studies; the truth would have been unimaginable to them.

My real father died late one evening when his motorbike was hit by a lorry. Patches of black ice caused several fatal accidents that night. At university during the day, he was working evenings and weekends to get some money together. His family rallied around her, as she was inconsolable and in no condition to be left alone. By then her own father was ill and Aggie knew she couldn't tear her family apart by revealing her situation.

So George's parents stood by Aggie until after the birth and I was given up for adoption. On paper my adoptive parents were good candidates. I know I was lucky, but things would have been very different if my adoptive father had lived. When he died, hope and love died too – but as a child you don't understand that the person you call mother has had her heart broken beyond repair. I simply thought of her as being a rather cold woman who didn't love me because I didn't deserve to be loved.

As an adult, of course, you understand the bigger picture. But the damage had been done and I still can't handle emotional stuff. My life has been about discipline and control. It's the only way I know how to function. When Aggie told me she had never stopped loving her lost son, it unleashed feelings I couldn't handle. She thanked me for giving her the one gift for which she'd prayed every single night of her life, and that was the joy of knowing I'd grown up to be a good man. I was humbled and she made me feel proud. That was a first for me, but it opened up feelings that were alien and hard to comprehend.

She wanted to sign the cottage over to me, so that after her death it would be mine. I couldn't let her do that because people would start asking questions. This intelligent, gentle old lady had been a victim of time and circumstance; one generation later and it would have been a completely different story. The guilt and pain she'd had to endure for all those years had weighed heavily upon her. I wondered if she had clung on to life in the desperate hope that her prayers would be answered. It was a miracle she'd lasted so long and we were both grateful as the weeks, then months went by – affording us borrowed time.

I called in on her a couple of times each week, and even though there wasn't an awful lot I could do, what she appreciated most were our chats. With no reason to have secrets from each other, and with a very different sort of relationship to the norm, there was no judgement on either side. I talked frankly about my life and Aggie listened, telling me that if I wanted to find someone to love, I had to learn to love myself a little, first.

"Why do I need to find someone? Anyway, who'd love me?" I'd laughed the day she'd said that.

"You're a catch, Lewis, and I'm not just saying that because you are my son and I'm proud of you. Remember that deep within you are the genes of your father and myself. There's nothing bad in you, Lewis, you've just had to bury your sensitivities through no fault of your own. You were the innocent one in all of this. Your career was an honourable one, but required you to divorce your emotions from your actions. It's a job not everyone can do and one which most people prefer not to think too much about. War and death go hand in hand. You're tough, Lewis, but what you need now is someone who will see the inner part of you and strip away those layers of armour. You don't need that in your life any more, my son. It's time to let it all go and become your own man."

I'd rubbed my shaven head, giving her a big grin.

"Only a mother would say that," I'd joked.

I clearly remember how she'd leaned forward to place her hand on my shoulder and stare deeply into my eyes.

"You are your father's son and that's all I ever wanted. He was a gentle man and, above all else, a gentleman. He was also as strong as iron in his determination."

Soldiers don't cry on the battlefield, their tears are within and silent. I couldn't cry that day either, but I did cry after she died.

If I'd found a woman like Madeleine, then maybe my life could have been different, but that's unlikely. I genuinely believe I'm meant to be alone. But what is important to me is that Aggie's family home remains in the family until my dying day, because that's my mark of respect to her. After that, a new family will take over and Aggie will accept that with grace. She was a woman who had no concept of bitterness, or anger, over the happy and loving life she could have had. A different sort of person put into her situation might have felt both of those emotions and ended up pushing people away. Instead, she was a kind and loving woman, adored by friends and distant family.

I vowed then that I would always try to make her proud of me. Helping Madeleine Brooks renovate Ash Cottage was my gesture towards that. Unfortunately, something else happened and instead of doing a good deed, I did something really stupid and selfish. It will weigh heavily on my conscience forever. I told myself I was doing it for all the right reasons, helping Madeleine Brooks regain her self-esteem because she's an amazing woman. The reality was that I fell in love, without being able to understand that was at the root of the problem.

MADDIE

CHAPTER 38

The packing is not going well and so far there are only three boxes stacked in the corner of the sitting room. Contracts will be exchanged later this week, with a completion date just a couple of weeks later. I'm moving in with Ryan this weekend and a removal company will be here early next week to put everything into a temporary storage facility. I thought I was organised, but Ryan puts me to shame.

The problem is that I'm so very tired. I haven't had a good night's sleep since I accepted the offer on the cottage. I will be glad to leave, but I just can't seem to get stuck into what needs to be done. Ryan is too busy at work to help out and, besides, it's not such a huge task for one person.

The cold feeling I had when I first moved in last December is back, despite the fact that outside the temperature is very pleasant now as the spring sunshine warms the earth. There are times I've even checked that the central heating is actually working, but since the motor was replaced it hasn't let me down once.

Weird things have been happening, or maybe the tiredness has made me careless, putting things down and then forgetting where they are. Stupid little things that make me cross with myself, like Aggie's heart-shaped pebble, for instance. I still kept it in the downstairs bathroom after having the work done. Why would I move it? But obviously I did, because yesterday I found it sitting on the coffee table. I can't ever recall feeling so all over the place before, that I became this confused. Should I be worried? Is this some sort of short-term memory problem?

Last night was the worst yet. I was in a deep sleep and awoke, feeling that someone was shaking me. As soon as my eyes flicked open it stopped and I realised that it was simply a dream. I sat up, loathe to fall back into something that felt weirdly unsettling, although I couldn't recall very much of the detail. Sitting there listening to the silence, I didn't feel comfortable. Is this how it's supposed to be when you are hurtling towards moving day? Is this how you mentally divorce yourself from a place you've come to love and think of as home? In my married life we'd only ever had the two houses when the boys were young. Leaving our first house was hard, but we'd needed the extra space. I was, I think, happy to let go. I can't recall feeling anything as disturbing as this before.

The air is so chilly that my arms feel cold to the touch and I lie down, snuggling the duvet around me.

Sleep comes in fits and starts. I'm working in the garden and helping someone to cut down one of the old apple trees. It's hard work and the sun is so hot it must be summer, but I'm laughing a lot as the pile of debris grows into a mound. I'm standing there, looking at the view that is no longer obscured by the gnarled old boughs before I sink into a peacefully deep sleep.

This morning my head is fuzzy and a dull pain keeps creeping across my forehead, wanting to settle over one eye. The sound of tapping on the conservatory door makes me groan slightly, as I'm in no mood for company.

It's Terence's face I see beaming back as me.

"Good morning, Terence, how are you?"

This man always has a smile on his face and it's impossible not to be cheered by that.

"Great — and you?"

Even raising a smile hurts and he notices the wince, despite the fact I'm trying to hide it.

"Oooh, suffering a bit there, I see."

"I think this headache wants to turn into a migraine. I've not been sleeping very well lately – too much churning around inside here," I tap my forehead and he grimaces sympathetically.

"Well, sometimes it's a warning to slow down a little. Maybe I'll come back another time. You should take a couple of painkillers and lie down for a while."

"I might take the tablets, but I have to focus on packing today. Time is running out. What can I do for you?"

He seems a little hesitant and I wonder if he's on an errand and Joanna's sent him round.

"Well, Joanna was wondering ... with the sale going through and all that, did you ever discover who owns the strip of land at the back? She's concerned that someone will fence it off and we'll lose our back entrance. I've told her not to worry; it's been like that for so many years it's unlikely to change now."

"Come inside, Terence."

He steps in, wiping his feet at least a dozen times on the mat and I'm sure Joanna would have made him take off his shoes.

"It didn't bother me too much when I moved in, as you know. I was given a box of old documents that they found when they cleared out the cottage, but I've been through them and didn't spot anything relating to the boundary at the back. However, I think Lewis Hart might know a little more."

The moment I utter those words, I regret it. Terence's eyebrows shoot up, as now his interest is peaked.

"He does?"

"Sorry, brain fuzz today. What I meant to say was, *perhaps* he knows a little more about it. After all, he seemed to spend a lot of time visiting Aggie, from what I gather."

Terence grimaces, sympathetically, then smiles.

"He called in a couple of times a week, right up to her death. I've never mentioned this to anyone before, especially Joanna

258

– poor Lewis, she just likes to watch him working – all that solid muscle. She's harmless, of course, but she can be a pain. Anyway, Aggie once told me she was going to leave Ash Cottage to Lewis. I would never have repeated that, because you know what people would have thought. It would have ruined Lewis' reputation. Whatever his intentions, she couldn't have managed during those final months without his help. I know you won't repeat it. It's a shame nothing has turned up about the boundary, though, if only to appease Joanna."

He raises his eyebrows once more, but this time in exasperation.

"Thanks for sharing that, Terence, and my lips are sealed. I'm moving out this weekend, by the way. Back to city living."

"As long as you are happy, that's all that matters. I wish you well, Maddie, and I'm sorry to lose you as a neighbour. If ever a place tested someone and their commitment, Ash Cottage did that to the extreme. Old Aggie always admired people who had resolve, those who didn't give in easily. Seems the old girl had a bit of a time letting go herself."

He fixes me with a look. There's a question behind that stare, but I have one of my own.

"Have you seen her?" I can't stop myself asking the one question to which I don't really want an answer.

"Once, in the garden. You?"

"Once, last night."

"One of the mysteries of life is death."

On that cryptic note, Terence turns the handle on the door and without as much as a backwards glance, he makes his way out and up the winding path.

My head is spinning with pain, anxiety and thoughts I can't even pull together in any particular order.

"What do you want from me?" I mutter, as I make my way to the kitchen to grab some painkillers and a glass of water. "Do you hate what I've done, is that it? So you wanted Lewis to have Ash Cottage and I'm about to make that happen. Doesn't that make you happy?"

I start to sob; the pain in my forehead is now shooting down and stabbing into my left eye. A wave of nausea engulfs me and I retch into the kitchen sink. This is a full-blown attack and it's too late now to take anything. My body slowly slides down to the floor and I huddle in a heap, my head pressed up against the cool surface of the kitchen unit. The pain comes in waves, accompanied by the nausea, and it's like a drum beat. Each time it's a pounding that reverberates through every single part of me and the pain is excruciating. Random thoughts ping into my head and are lost before I can even focus on them.

I close my eyes, no longer able to bear the light and curl up into a ball, tucking my head down onto my knees. The only clear thought I have is a feeling of tremendous unhappiness that I can't seem to shake off and I'm beyond confused.

CHAPTER 39

"What the hell are you playing at?"

As soon as I heard the sharp hammering on the door I knew it was Lewis Hart. It's a visit I've been expecting. I can hear every single word quite clearly, even through the double-glazed panel. Turning the key in the lock I swing it open wide and walk back into the conservatory.

"The cottage is no longer up for sale. I've changed my mind. It happens, sorry." I cradle my arms around my body, creating a barrier against the anger he is unable to control.

"Sorry? It happens? You're messing with people's lives and all you can say is sorry?" He raises his hand, stabbing one finger in my direction, accusingly.

"My plans have changed due to unforeseen circumstances."

A movement at the doorway makes me look over Lewis' shoulder. It's Terence. He steps inside, gingerly, glancing from Lewis to me and back again.

"Is everything all right here, Maddie?" His voice is tentative. He's not sure what's happening and that makes two of us.

I glance at Lewis, wondering if everything is all right or whether I should be worried for my safety.

A few moments elapse and the silence is strained.

"I shouldn't have come, I apologise, but I was gutted to hear the news that you've pulled out of the sale."

Terence's jaw drops and he immediately turns to face me. I nod, giving him a little smile of reassurance. "I'm fine, Terence, thank you for checking. Mr Hart is understandably upset and deserves an explanation. I'm about to make some coffee, would you like one?"

Terence shakes his head. "If you're sure you're okay, I'll leave you to it," he nods at Lewis, fixing him with a stare, "Lewis."

Lewis steps forward, "Sorry Terence, I was bang out of order." He puts out his hand and Terence responds, shaking his hand firmly.

"I'm not the person you should be apologising to ..." he replies soberly and exits, shutting the door behind him.

"Sorry," Lewis says, spinning around to look at me.

"Is that all you can say?" He sees fit to apologise properly to my neighbour, but, it seems, not to me.

"For a nice lady you sure don't pull your punches! Was this a wind-up from the start because you knew how much this cottage means to me? I suppose you're going to hang onto it now and rent it out. Get a nice little income and not give a damn that it will be filled with a stream of people who will form no attachment to it whatsoever. That's cruel, lady."

His words stop me in my tracks, but I don't want to answer to him or offer an explanation. I turn and walk into the kitchen, flick on the kettle and grab two mugs.

I half-wonder if he'll take the sight of my back as a cue to leave. I can feel him standing in the doorway, watching my every move as I noisily bang down the mugs and vigorously stir the coffee. I want him to know how angry I am that he has the cheek to take the moral high ground. He hasn't even had the decency to be straight with me. I expected him to be disappointed, of course, and maybe demand that I foot any abortive costs, but this is still my property until the contract has been signed. When I spin around he's standing less than an inch away from me, so close I can feel his body heat and before I know it his mouth is all over mine. He's pressing me up against the kitchen units as if he wants to devour me and my body begins to respond. As it does, he recoils in horror.

"Oh, my God, I'm sorry! I mean ... I don't prey on women. I'm not that sort of guy ... I didn't come here to exact revenge. I don't know why I came here. It's just I'm absolutely gutted ..."

We both take a second to compose ourselves and then I turn, pick up the mugs and hand him one. We walk through into the conservatory and sit in silence, looking out onto the panoramic vista that today is bathed in warm, spring sunshine.

"You lied." I don't turn to look at him, I just let my words settle and keep looking ahead.

"Some things just can't be shared. I don't know what you think you know, but I've come to ask you one thing. I helped you out when you were stuck, I mean, really stuck. I'll admit that a part of me was hoping you'd change your mind about living here because you'd miss the buzz of the city. But I never meant for things to become ... personal. If I could undo what happened, I would, but it seems I'm unable to control myself when I'm around you. I'm glad things are going well and you are moving on, but please, don't rent out Ash Cottage or sell it to someone else just to lash out at me. Our paths will never cross again, I promise you, but I can't lose this place for a second time. I just can't."

The desperation in his voice is heart-breaking.

"I'm not doing this to get back at you for lying to me, or for taking advantage of the situation. Ash Cottage is going to continue to be my home."

Lewis is staring at me, but I keep my head focused on the trees and the white doves circling and swooping as they flit between their dovecote and a shed roof.

"That's it, then."

"I know your secret."

"How?"

"You didn't think I'd guess there was something going on here? That I wouldn't go back and revisit Aggie's box with her life history, lying there in pieces like a jig-saw puzzle? I found your birth certificate, hidden in the folds of the plans for the conservatory. I know it wasn't there originally, because I remember pulling them out, so I knew you'd been through everything. But why didn't you just take it, when you didn't hesitate to take the document relating to the strip of land at the back?"

"I'm many things, Madeleine, but I'm not a thief. I took nothing at all. Look, it was a mistake coming here. It's just really hard to let go of Aggie's cottage. I have to stop doing that ..."

"Doing what?"

"Talking about it as if it's still hers; or that there's any chance it will ever be my home. It's bricks and mortar, she loved it while she lived here and now it's time for everyone to move on."

He pushes back his chair to stand, looking down at me with acceptance.

"No one in the Forest knows Aggie's secret; I'd appreciate it if you could find it in your heart to let it remain buried. As for the other thing ... you're an amazing woman, Madeleine Brooks, and Ryan is a lucky man."

I stand, facing up to him to let him know that I am an amazing woman and I'm not going to fall apart because *suddenly* I know exactly what I'm doing. And what I want.

"And you are an amazing man, Lewis Hart. Aggie knows that, and now I do, too. This is my home for the rest of my life and Ryan has had a lucky escape. I think he's getting over his mid-life crisis and will soon be jetting off to the sun for a life of partying and thrill-seeking. I, on the other hand, will be here – just a lonely, single woman with no one to help her to get this jungle of a garden into shape. That's rather a shame, don't you think?"

He hasn't moved a muscle. His face is set, as if he doesn't know what's happening and he doesn't understand what I've said.

"Goodness, Lewis. For an intelligent man you can be rather dense at times. This is the point at which you get to speak. Where are all your words, now? Do you have anything to say to me at all? *Anything*?"

"About what?"

"I know that Aggie was your mother and I know that her intention was to give you Ash Cottage. Yes, it's important, but I'm straight on all of that. I want to hear what you have to say. Is there anything *you* want to tell me, or were you just using me that night I threw caution to the wind?"

"You want me to explain myself?"

"Yes. I want words."

He looks at me and then turns his head away, gathering his thoughts. Then he begins pacing back and forwards in front of me.

"Okay. I can do this."

It's not clear whether he's giving himself a pep talk, or the words are for my benefit and he's asking me to wait a moment. I have all the time in the world and I'm really enjoying seeing him squirm. He does one more cross in front on me and stops, running his hands down over his thighs and along the side seams of his jeans; the ones that are covered in paint, cement and every builder's material known to man.

"I like you." He stands there, looking at me expectantly.

"That's a start, continue."

He does a double-take. Suddenly one brow lifts and he screws up his eyes as if he's smarting from some sort of head pain.

"A lot."

He appears to relax.

"I want meaningful words. Not just the first thing that comes into your head."

"Really?"

"*Really.*"

He paces around in a circle this time. One rotation and once more he's standing in front of me, his face a shade of grey and there are beads of sweat on his forehead.

"At first I thought you were the most annoying woman I'd ever met. But now I know differently."

I open my eyes wide with surprise, steeling myself not to laugh, but to look appalled.

"And that's supposed to what ... make me feel grateful? To be some sort of backhanded compliment? You were on the right track: you just used the wrong 'L' word."

He frowns, then stands up straight and this time he looks me directly in the eyes.

"Miss Madeleine Brooks I'm in love with you. There, now will you please let me off the hook?"

"For goodness' sake, just kiss me! I've had more meaningful conversations with Terence's cat."

When I finally pull away, I look up into his eyes, "All I want is someone who really needs me as much as I need them. You can handle that, right?"

"Yes, ma'am." His words are spoken with army-like precision and a firm sense of commitment. However, there's something hidden behind those wonderful eyes of his.

"What?"

"I think I loved you from the moment I first saw you. I also knew you'd be trouble, and I was right."

I want all of the love and passion you have buried deep inside of you, Lewis. But you're not ready to hear that right now.

"Well, don't go forgetting that after you move in. I have every intention of keeping you very busy indeed, Mr Hart. I think you are going to need a new decal for that white van of yours – *Maddie's Man Who Can*."

ACKNOWLEDGEMENTS

With grateful thanks to my wonderful editor, Charlotte Ledger, for constantly looking over my shoulder, keeping me on track, and believing in my characters. Of course, every novel is the result of a much wider-team effort, so a 'high-five' and grateful thanks to everyone involved at HarperImpulse.

And a big hug to my very own 'Man Who Can', Lawrence. While this is a work of fiction, some of the events linked to the move and the deliveries etc affected by the awful floods, were based on actual incidents we experienced in 2013. I stress that all of the characters are fictitious, but the cottage is very real. We are very happy living in our dream cottage, on the edge of the Forest of Dean, as renovation work continues.